Biographer's Note

Charlotte Laurent's book *The Fire and the Phoenix* was published in the early eighties. This was a 'self-help' manual, together with her account of her real life experience of marital betrayal, loss of faith and ensuing personal degradation that she experienced during the 1970's. Her book became an inspiration for people in similar circumstances when faced with the mounting divorce rate and the problems arising from that decade.

Since her death in 2001, further autobiographical writings for her unfinished book 'O is for Orphan' have come to light and have been donated by her daughter to a charity close to Charlotte's heart. I was asked to piece together these early chapters, and include some documents from her original manuscript for *The Fire and the Phoenix*. This current book concludes with the extraordinary revelations concerning the long search for her mother's family and her joy in finding true happiness later in her life.

I have maintained her original title *'O' is for Orphan and Optimist* for this work and some names and dates have been changed during this process.

Drew Harrington
Editor of *Mission for the Missing*

'O' IS FOR ORPHAN
AND
OPTIMIST

DREW HARRINGTON

Matador
9 Priory Business Park
Wistow Road
Kibworth
Leicester LE8 0RX, UK
Tel: (+44) 116 279 2299
Email: books@troubador.co.uk
Web: www.troubador.co.uk/matador

ISBN 978 1784622 572

British Library Cataloguing in Publication Data.
A catalogue record for this book is available from the British Library.

Typeset in 11pt Aldine by Troubador Publishing Ltd, Leicester, UK
Printed and bound in the UK by TJ International, Padstow, Cornwall

Matador is an imprint of Troubador Publishing Ltd

CONTENTS

'O' IS FOR ORPHAN AND OPTIMIST

Every baby born comes with everything and nothing. They come with bags already packed with untamed genes but their tiny hands are empty and their eyes tightly shut against revelations that may be hailed or shunned in the years to come. They are ignorant of their welcome, whether longed for or despised. They may be born into family feuds, may inherit titles, good looks or have deformities. At the age of four I was blissfully ignorant of my circumstances or those of my parents. I was to remain so for the time being.

Charlotte Laurent from *The Fire and the Phoenix*

Charlotte wrote vividly of her early childhood and teenage years, beginning with a family occasion in the 1940s. The first two chapters of this book are set down mainly in her own words when she first began to write her autobiography at the end of the 1990s as recorded in her notes and diaries.

CHAPTER ONE

IN THE BEGINNING

An unknown lady stared quizzically at me from our shabby sofa as I came into the room. I stared back.

'This is your grandmother,' said my guardian cheerfully. 'Your grandma and a grandpa have driven a long way to see you!' She smiled brightly. I stared again. Grandma was lying down which seemed rather odd and although it was early September, she was covered with our plaid rug. She looked pale and austere like the pictures of Queen Mary I'd seen in a book. She wore black at her throat, which contrasted with the whiteness of her hair. Her lips were a thin red line and her eyes a piercing blue. For some reason I felt a foreboding beyond my years.

'She's a big girl for four.' My grandfather spoke for the first time. He looked kindly at me, his moustache a revelation at such close quarters. 'We've brought you a present.' He extended a big parcel in my direction wrapped in brown paper. My large blue eyes grew even larger. No one had ever given me a present of such size and importance. Was it Christmas or my birthday? I thought not. I knew too well when they came around, quite close together.

'Open it!' commanded Grandma from her throne.

My guardian helped me and soon a large box was uncovered.

'Oh!' she exclaimed. 'A doll's tea set!'

'A Mickey Mouse tea-set,' I said, holding my breath. It was china and depicted the well-loved characters on the six cups and saucers, milk jug and teapot. The little cups were funnel shaped with triangular handles.

'We'd better put them away now,' said my guardian, 'before they get broken.' What they didn't say was that something far more precious had already been broken a few weeks earlier. The tea set had been a mere placation. My father was dead and I had become an orphan.

Charlotte described Henrietta Mary Prior, or Netta to her friends, as her guardian and no relation at all and as far removed from her grandparents' way of life as it was possible to be. For one thing she was a devout and practising Christian whose work had taken her to the slums of the East End of London where she had held the position of matron and midwife at a London maternity hospital. She was trained to be a Salvation Army officer and worked tirelessly for others bringing medical aid and spiritual comfort to those around her before poor health and angina intervened. At the time of Charlotte's arrival, she was in charge of Bourne Lodge, a home for fallen women in Hackney.

One Christmas Eve a couple had arrived at Bourne Lodge in the cold and snow. They were homeless and carried a tiny baby ten days old. Matron was quick to notice the fine clothes and expensive shawl that the baby wore. The father, a penniless portrait artist, left, but the mother stayed on with her baby until one day, driven by mental anguish and what we would call today, post-natal depression, tried to kill her child. She was sent away. Only four and a half pounds at birth and ill with whooping cough at three months, Charlotte survived. Two years later, by arrangement with her father's parents, Miss Prior became her legal guardian.

Northumbrian by birth and the eldest of three, all practising Salvationists, Netta retired early and left Bourne Lodge, taking Charlotte with her to Ingatestone, a village in Essex. Charlotte was her gift from God and would fill her life with joy, or that was to be the plan. Netta's sister Izzy, joined them periodically when not working in Head Office in London and their brother Gilbert, would visit on rare occasions when not abroad with the S.A. where he ran a catering service for the troops. The two-bedroomed bungalow inherited from their father was called 'Dovecote' and stood in Bridge Lane. This was to be Charlotte's home where she blossomed in the fresh country air.

Miss Prior, or Netta, was the district nurse and midwife to the village and she would regale me, as I got a little older, with the outcome of her calls. I had not yet started school.

'I've just laid out Mrs Ellington,' she confided late one night, as she got ready for bed in our shared room. 'She looked so peaceful.'

'Is she in heaven with my daddy?' I asked sleepily.

'Oh yes.' She spoke with conviction. Netta stood in the half-light and removed her full corset, unhooking it with immense satisfaction before scratching at the reddened skin beneath. Her breasts hung limp and empty. She was fifty years old but worn out with service. I watched her with love and tenderness. She was my mother figure. She could do no wrong and I couldn't be without her. Comforted, I went back to sleep.

Charlotte admitted to being a wild child, self-willed and high-spirited. Her beautiful father, whom she remembered only twice when he made the long trip to Ingatestone, had gone forever. A creased photo of them both shows her riding on his shoulders, thick blond hair blowing in the wind and a big smile on her face. Turbulence grew in her. She had not been told of the cause of his death. She had been a war baby but was it to do with the war? She had been too young to be told, and what had happened to her mother? Charlotte wrote that they never mentioned her name. This omission was to haunt her for many years. Her memories of life in Ingatestone during the war are clearly recorded as set down here and later her time spent at Brentwood High School and The Royal Wanstead.

'This old war's a nuisance. Bicycles are very expensive.' My guardian had looked sorrowfully at my downcast expression.

'Why are they?'

'Because metal is needed to help fight the Germans.'

'You mean bombs and guns?' I'd heard about this from the boys in the lane. 'Why does God let people bomb people? Was my daddy hurt with a bomb?'

'No darling, it wasn't a bomb.' She said no more.

'Doll's prams are made of metal!' I had protested. A pram was the last thing I had wanted for Christmas but it made a good cart.

Wartime life in Essex was mercifully bearable. I slept in an Emerson shelter in our room, protected by it's iron roof, and lulled by the wireless, 'White Cliffs of Dover' and 'You are my My Sunshine' sounding out from the next next-door room. Rationing of food was the norm but we never went hungry and Christmas was filled with rare delights sent by her many friends. Netta would 'put down' eggs in a preserving liquid when she could or use egg powder in a packet. I would help clean currants for baking and crush salt that came in blocks. She would eke out her pension and make savings where possible. Sugar was scarce, the bowl covered with beaded muslin, but I knew where she kept the opened tin of condensed milk.

'Charlotte, what are you doing?' Netta would call from the bedroom. 'Just getting a drink of water.,' I would say as I hurriedly climbed down from the chair, sucking at the spoon. I would be mindful not to take too much for fear of discovery.

Christmas was a wonderful time. I would sleep in the put-u-up with Netta by the fire whilst visiting friends or Gilbert and his family would come to stay, their son Graham being six years my senior but good fun. Homemade treats and simple gifts would be eagerly awaited and opened on Christmas Day. Sister Damson, a spinster friend from the London Maternity Hospital and annual visitor, would draw up her huge bosom with indignation and tell me 'You're much too big for you boots!' which would leave me totally confused but undaunted. The Salvation Army band would come from Chelmsford and play carols down our lane on Christmas Eve and then all pile into the bungalow for homemade elderberry wine, mince pies and a cup of Bev coffee.

'Hallo Lottie,' they would greet me. 'Got your stocking ready?' I loved their shiny instruments: the big euphoniums, smaller horns and cornets and sliding trombones, together with the cold fresh smell of the bandsmen's coats as they stamped their feet on the mat, but it made me long for a father in my life.

There were few bombs dropped though I remember one night when one exploded fairly close to the lane. The doorbell woke me up.

'Come in, come in you poor souls!' Netta's voice sounded from the hall. 'Come into the sitting room, I'll get some things together.'

The casualties came to our home, bleeding from cuts due to shattered glass. My guardian treated them in turn, picking the glass from their heads and limbs. I watched from a crack in the door but I was more curious than afraid. Auntie Netta, as I now called her, was a tower of strength and faith, for all her small stature. I felt quite safe and remembered the prayers she taught me: 'Gentle Jesus meek and mild, look upon a little child, pity my simplicity, suffer me to come to thee'. After this, I'd go happily to sleep.

Our garden was long and packed in abundance with every kind of fruit tree and bush. I grew strong and healthy. I had learnt much from the children in the lane, playing games in the ditch, riding on the crossbars of their bikes and taking dares on the railway line that made my guardian pale, barring me from that end of the lane. Although I attended Sunday school I was not turning out to be the cute little girl she had hoped for. Sunday school was in Mountnessing. I attended there with the other children from the lane walking the two miles on our own. It was held in the Elim Church Hall but I enjoyed the swings up by the old windmill much more.

I was nearly five and ready for 'big school'. Would that be the answer?

'Shall we spend our bus fare on a penny bun?' I suggested to Jean as we swung on the metal frame of the bus shelter waiting for the bus.

'How will we get home?'

'We'll walk!'

Brentwood High School was a bus ride from Ingatestone. We would be put on the bus each morning where we were entrusted to an older girl already on the bus but who soon lost interest in us after the first week. Left to our own devices, Jean and I bought our buns from the bakers by the bus stop and, munching happily, set out to walk the eight miles home. We were located several miles later by her distraught and irate dad who scooped us up in his farm truck. This, together with other pranks, caused some concern. Although the headmistress had honoured me for my ability to repeat the Lord's Prayer off by heart, I had argued with my teacher that '"O" stood for orphan not "ostrich".' Worse things were to happen.

'Charlotte! Stand up!' I stood up behind my desk. 'Susan says you have taken her crayons from her desk. Is this true?'

'I just wanted to look at them,' I confessed.

'But that's stealing Charlotte,' sighed my teacher. I was good at drawing and colouring, inherited no doubt from my father, but my crayons were crude and made of wax. These slim beauties were made of wood with fine coloured points. I had never seen such treasures. Besides, I didn't hide them so to me it wasn't stealing. They were too good to use but the headmistress thought differently and saw it as an act of deprivation. A year later, change was brought about by the school when I was seven years old. Brentwood High School authorities no longer wanted a junior or primary section and I was asked to leave.

'Now I want you to be very brave,' began my guardian. 'Your grandparents have decided that you must go away to boarding school.'

'Oh!' I wasn't too sure what that meant but it caught my imagination. I was growing fast and ready for adventure. I longed to be like the other children in the lane but it was not to be. There would be no brothers or sisters, just my guardian and Auntie Izzy who were old-fashioned spinsters and elderly compared with the mothers of my peers.

'Will there be other children like me?'

'Yes. Lots. It used to be called an orphanage but now it's a school for children like you. You'll make lots of new friends.'

The stealing episode had pointed up the fact that for all her love and devotion I was becoming a handful, though more through high spirits and too much energy than vice, and needed to be with children from a similar orphaned background.

'You'll be home for the holidays,' she assured me. 'But you'll stay with your grandparents some of the time.'

This filled me with trepidation but I would worry about that later.

The Royal Wanstead School in Snaresbrook was originally an infant orphan asylum founded in 1841 by Andrew Reed, a congregational minister with influential friends in society. He saw a need to protect fatherless children from a middle-class background with the help of charitable funding, the very poor being cared for in the workhouse. He acquired Crown land on the edge of Epping Forest and Prince Albert laid the cornerstone. Queen Victoria became a patron and was the first in a line of monarchs of what became the Royal Infant Orphanage. After the Second World War it became a school for children with one or no parents, the entrance age being raised to seven.

It was a large grey-stone building built in the Victorian style with many chimneys and turrets and stood beside a big lake. The school badge depicted a swan and her three cygnets embroidered in gold thread. Two thirds were taken over by the senior boys' quarters and chapel, the mixed juniors being on the far side of the building. It was still run by charity but fees were accepted where possible.

'Oh what a noise!' I had put my hands over my ears as I stood on the threshold of the dayroom, staring in complete amazement. About seventy children were having the time of their lives or so it seemed. The noise was deafening and the activity boundless but I felt no fear. I never looked back at my poor grieving guardian who had kissed me tenderly goodbye and held me close but pitched in with unnerving confidence. I could not wait to be part of it and joy of joys I had seen several small bikes in the playground and three large rocking horses now looked at me from a corner of the room. I was enthralled.

I adored the headmaster Mr Hawkins who was a gentle giant, but could dispense discipline at a stroke. I loved the boys and played their games of making dens in the woods and 'kiss chase' but my real friend was called John Bond.

'Will you be my sweetheart?' John had asked, offering me the small truck he had been pushing along the path as proof of his commitment. I took it solemnly and held out my other hand.

'I'll be your sweetheart,' I confirmed, 'till death us do part.'

I felt a loss for this dear boy, who taught me chess and how to shoot with a bow and arrow, when he failed to return one term. I was told later that he had met with an accident. I was heartbroken and became withdrawn, wanting to go home there and then.

There was no half-term at school as this was considered unsettling as most of the pupils lived a distance from Snaresbrook, but holidays were more than welcome. The children would wait for collection in the lobby with their small cases packed, hopping up and down with anticipation.

'I don't want to go!' I was in the train and on my way to my grandparents. 'I'll run away!' I threatened. 'I don't want to go!' My guardian hugged me close.

'It's only for a little while and then you'll be home with me.'

It appeared that with her encouragement my grandparents, both now approaching sixty years of age, had adopted me and I was legally bound to spend half my holidays in Hampstead Garden Suburb with them and the other half in Ingatestone.

'There's a lovely garden and you'll have a room all to yourself.'

Holding her hand and dragging my feet, we walked up the quiet leafy roads of the suburb from the bus stop in Market Place to their house in Heathway. I was eight years old and full of fear at being left by my guardian to face this ordeal: far more frightening than the first day at school. My memory of them was still fresh in my mind after their visit four years ago. The house was large, built to my grandfather's design and modelled on the houses of Georgia in America where he had visited on business. It was white with a red tiled roof, Georgian windows and dark green paintwork. There was a balcony at the back and a loggia with wicker chairs and a well-tended garden.

'Now be a good girl.' Netta had embraced me and taken her leave to make the long journey home alone. I wanted to cry but they were watching me intently with unsmiling faces.

My first impression was one of space and grandeur. Beautiful shiny furniture, long curtains, pretty rugs, pictures and Chinese souvenirs from Shang-hai. To me it was like a palace but it wasn't home. I wanted to be back in the cramped bungalow with the shabby settee and my bed in the shared room with Netta, warm and safe. I wanted to hear her voice with its comforting Northumbrian lilt. I was in the smallest of five bedrooms that had once held my father. His easel stood in the corner and his paint box on a table. I lay in his bed and cried, lost and homesick but comforted by the few personal possessions that had once belonged to him. No one came and I went to sleep to the sound of silence.

Over the years I was to become a chameleon, adaptable to change: boarding school, Hampstead and Ingatestone, each demanding a different set of values and behaviour. I would grow a new skin each time to arm myself against adversity or criticism. Who was I? My grandmother tolerated me but with little affection. I had taken the place of her beloved son. If only I'd been a boy. I bonded with my grandpa who began to warm towards me. He would wind up his gramophone with the big horn and I would listen spellbound to 'The Road to the Isles' and 'When You and I Were Young Maggie.' The latter making me sad, the longing in the singer's voice for what he had lost sounding a chord somewhere inside me.

They were both happy to leave me alone and eventually, over time, I was to appreciate my newfound freedom and to meet the aunts and cousins who would come into my life.

At the end of the summer term at the Royal Wanstead in the late forties I finally said goodbye to the man who had been my father figure for nearly four years. My time at this school had been one of structure and stability. I was sad to leave. There would be no boys where I was going and my only legacy had been to introduce shorts for girls at playtime, my dresses constantly needing to be repaired. Mr Hawkins smiled at me. 'You'll do alright,' he said, patting me on the back. 'You came top of your class this year, intelligence that is, not maths! You'll like Hyde Hall.'

'You're a lucky girl,' Izzy had said, looking up from a prospectus. 'It says here that your new school is a large old house set in forty acres of grounds. Are you looking forward to going?'

'I don't know.'

I didn't want change. I wanted routine. I had got used to life at school in Snaresbrook. It had been my home for nearly four years. What would the senior school hold for me? Part of me was refusing to grow up. I felt safe in my childhood surroundings and had learnt to cope. Was I ready for new challenges?

'Will there be a swimming pool?' I had just learnt to swim at the Whipps Cross baths.

'I don't think so but there are tennis courts and a gamesfield.'

CHAPTER TWO

HYDE HALL

Hyde Hall was set in the beautiful Hertfordshire countryside on the edge of the small town of Sawbridgeworth. Built of sandstone in the style of an Elizabethan courtyard house in 1565, it was remodelled in 1803. The extensive grounds included: rose, sunken and kitchen gardens, orchard, wood and gamesfield with pavilion. Three impressive "Roman" busts stood among the shrubbery and stone urns sported flowers in the summer. It had once been the home of the prestigious Jocelyn family and the Earl of Roden. Now 140 years later it was part of the Royal Wanstead patronage.

'Be sure and write each week,' Netta had implored me, waving a gloved hand from the platform of Liverpool Street Station where I met with other girls bound for Sawbridgeworth and Hyde Hall to begin the autumn term. I lugged my suitcase from the nearby station to the school gates. There was no one to meet us as we toiled up the long meandering wooded drive, the older girls striding away easily. Inside, the rooms were vast and I was overawed by their grandeur, although it would be some time before I would appreciate Adam fireplaces, ornamental cornices, panelling and carvings.

'Put these on!' Matron threw me a pair of house shoes from a large heap on the floor.

'They hurt a bit,' I offered timidly.

'They'll do.' Her blue-grey eyes bored into mine. 'You don't want your feet to spread all over England!'

Netta had equipped me with a dressing gown made from an old mock fur coat. This caused much derisory laughter from older girls who saw me standing outside our dormitory one evening. I had been talking after lights out and put outside in disgrace. I was the butt of many jokes. I didn't swear, wore glasses, had no possessions to speak of and had large feet. I was the youngest in the school, still only ten until December and the most naïve.

Finally after a year or so, Charlotte was able to settle down. Some of her old friends had accompanied her from Snaresbrook and her confidence returned. She found herself looking forward to each new term and the lovely house and grounds, and to the dormitory in the old squash court, the red lines still visible on the walls that would inspire her to play the game in later life. She conformed to the routine: church on Sundays, all walking in a long crocodile, the tuck shop on Saturdays after awful darning with Matron, long walks along the river Stort led by older girls and the occasional tea and cake in Sawbridgeworth provided by some benevolent visiting relative of a friend. Their diet was plain and Matron ran a tight ship, no extras but post-war rations and no treats. Pocket money was sixpence a week, eagerly spent in the tuck shop or on a new tin of Gibbs SR toothpaste in a shiny round coloured tin.

Her schoolwork improved with English and art at the top of her list. She was still the class clown and tomboy who would climb every possible tree and walk tightrope fashion along low boughs before falling into the stinging nettles below.

'Charlotte Laurent! What ARE you doing?'

'I'm sorry Miss Havers, I was demonstrating how to meet royalty by walking backwards and I tripped.'

'Have you got any idea how long that took to create, every bit of plasticine made to scale and you fell into it clowning about!' Havers' eyes were popping and she was quivering with indignation as she hauled me out from the centre of the Globe Theatre, her pride and joy that took weeks to build and inspired by a desire to please the head, Miss Edwards. Fortunately the model could be repaired unlike my reputation.

I loved games and played hockey and tennis but was useless at athletics and netball. I still managed the occasional prank but once again changes were on the way.

'Happy Easter!' I was home for the holidays and Netta was joyously celebrating the Christian message. Pretty primroses and decorated eggs adorned the table. Soon we would be off to Chelmsford on the bus to the Salvation Army meeting and the rousing message of the band: 'Christ the Lord is risen today!' On this occasion, for some reason during the service, I felt different. I had attended services since early childhood, quietened with pencil and paper during the address, but something the Major talked about on that day opened my heart. I wanted to become a Christian and adopt Netta's way of life. It seemed to me to be so inspiring in her love for others. I walked down to the front and knelt at the altar. Would this action become an anchor when life was to throw everything at me? Would I still be at the altar when I was betrayed and when I was with my back to the wall and fighting on the wrong side for the wrong reasons? I would have to wait and see but at twelve years old I was blissfully ignorant of what lay in store for me. At that time my faith was simple and God took the form of a friend to talk to during difficult times.

It was later that same year that my guardian said, 'There's something we need to talk about.' She was choosing her words carefully. I was enjoying an ice cream as we ambled along the pier at Southend. 'You're twelve now and things begin to change.'

'What things?' I was wary. Not another school surely.

'Bodily changes.' Netta began to explain the marvels and mysteries of womanly menstruation in her knowledgeable way but omitted any reference to sex, a taboo subject and one I was not clear about at all.

'I'm sorry, dear, have I put you off your ice cream? Let's talk about something else. Izzy and I are thinking of moving to London...' But the sweetness of the day had gone.

Sure enough, later that year I began to change. I became sullen and angry, not wanting to leave my old familiar self behind but where was I going?

'Charlotte!' The head's voice stopped me in my tracks. 'Come to the assembly hall. I want you in my next play.'

The school was renowned for "putting on" something at the end of the summer term. I had watched with interest *Hiawatha* and *Tobias and the Angel* during the first two years of my attendance but Miss Edwards was aiming high.

'This year we will be performing in the town hall to the good people of Sawbridgeworth. I want you to play the part of Ensign Blades.'

I was tall and had a strong voice and I was to be an officer in J.M. Barrie's *Quality Street*. This was followed a year later by Jack Purdie in *Dear Brutus* and Dunios in Shaw's *St Joan*. This last play was to provide a pure feast of painting as Jennie and I squared up the huge backcloths on the floor of an old Nissen hut in the woods, vacated by the R.A.F. after the war, and brought to life, with poster paint, the Loire and Reams Cathedral, all schoolwork forgotten for the time being. The arrival of the costume hampers from Fox's in London was to be hugely anticipated.

'Laurent, you're wanted, head's study.' I groaned as the prefect glowered at me. *What now,* I wondered and tried to think of a misdemeanour.

'Come and sit down.' Miss Edwards softened her tone. 'I'm sorry to tell you that your grandfather has died. Miss Prior wants you to attend the funeral.' I was fourteen years old.

'You'll manage,' said Netta as we got off the bus in Market Place. 'Go on they'll be waiting for you.'

'Can't you come too?'

'Not to the house. I'm not family but I'll be at the crematorium. I had a lot of respect for your grandpa. He did the right thing by you.'

She gave me a gentle push and I walked up the road to Heathway.

As I went I reflected on what I knew of my grandfather and his three daughters. The thought of meeting all three aunts and their husbands at once was more daunting than the funeral itself. They were so different from my guardian and much more of the real world, where money and position mattered, rather than that of the next. Netta had taught me to think and care for others before oneself. The aunts were critical and unforgiving and grudging in their warmth or love – but were the family genes already multiplying? Would I grow into them and absorb nature's great intention or were adopted values stronger? Was blood really thicker than water?

Charlotte's grandfather, Francis William Laurent, was born in Saffron Walden and one of eleven children. His ancestry could be traced to the Huguenots in France in the 17th century, who were Protestant lacemakers. He left the family farm for London when he was fourteen years old. He became an office tea boy during the day and studied at night school in the evenings. He joined the staff of a tobacco company in London and rose to chief buyer for tobacco in America and China during the thirties, but retired soon after the outbreak of war. He married Rose Burgess in Clerkenwell in 1905 and they lived in Virginia Water and Hampstead Garden Suburb. They had four children: Rosamund the eldest, Myra and Marcel who were twins, and Rita who was the youngest.

By the time I was nine I had met all three aunts and their respective husbands. Brian, who ran a successful number of butcher's shops during the war, was married to Rosamund. He was "in trade" to use my grandmother's expression which intimated "second rate" and in a "reserved" occupation. For all that, he was most generous to me and I loved riding in his sleek black Riley that he drove when he first collected me. 'Help yourself to some books!' he had said, sweeping an expansive arm in the direction of the children's books in WH Smith.

'Any one you like!' I was dumbfounded. No one had ever made such an offer to me before. Rosamund was kind and funny and enjoyed the high life.

Myra was a doctor and the complete opposite of her twin brother. She was serious and studious and applied herself to her profession. She was married to a doctor from Wales called Evan Evans. They practiced in Saltdene where I would go for holidays and where I met my cousins Linda and her younger sister Anette. Linda was three years my junior. 'What's boarding school like?' she would ask. 'Do you have midnight feasts?' I enjoyed their company but I never felt that I came up to Myra's expectations and that my enforced holidays were irksome. I was blamed for all misdemeanours and considered rough and ill mannered and told not to say 'smashing' at every opportunity.

Rita, the youngest and most attractive of my aunts, lived in Finchley with David Franklin, her bank manager husband. He was ten years her senior and had served in the R.A.F. during the war. To their disappointment they were to remain childless throughout their lives but they were to play a big part in mine and influence me greatly in the years to come, by refining my tomboyishness and giving me support – but there would also be conflict.

Marcel, my father, was the oddball of the four children. He didn't conform or fit into their organised world. He was a portrait painter who had attended the Royal College of Art and who had taken a studio in the King's Road subsidised by my grandfather. He wore open-toed sandals and frequented the pawn shop, to be redeemed at a later stage by his long suffering parent. At the outbreak of war he was conscripted into the Royal Engineers and stationed in Dover. He had good looks with blue eyes and a very thick head of dark hair. His sisters failed to "recognise" his way of life and kept him at a distance. I knew little of my grandmother who remained remote and unapproachable for some years but who I would win over eventually and come to love.

As I neared the house in Heathway I could see that I was neither expected nor wanted but they were gracious enough and took me with them in one of the big black cars to Golders Green. The crematorium was full of people and the scent of hyacinths. Francis William had been greatly revered on the Suburb. Heads turned to look at me with curiosity, unable to place a teenage member of the family. Those in the know would ponder, 'Is she the child of Marcel, their wayward artist son?' The aunts in black, his sisters closed around me, shielding themselves from conjecture. The service began and many tributes were paid before the coffin, bearing his body, slowly disappeared from view, ending a chapter in my life.

'When did my parents get married?' It was an innocent question as we travelled back on the tube to Liverpool Street Station. We had been talking about the funeral and the other members of the family.

'Well.' Netta hesitated. 'They weren't married.' I was shocked into silence. 'It was wartime and they went to a bogus priest who took their money but the marriage was not legally recognised. Your mother said it didn't matter because marriages were made in heaven.'

'You mean I'm illegitimate?' The words stuck in my throat. Here I was, brought up to believe in the strict moral code of the forties and fifties, and that of my guardian that at least I was a respectable citizen. Flower power and free love were a decade away. I stared ahead unable to take it in.

'It's alright,' Netta reassured me. 'You were a love child. They both loved you. Your poor mother, Vanessa, wasn't strong. You were so tiny because she didn't get enough to eat. She wasn't strong,' she repeated, shaking her head. I felt a responsibility for my mother's plight. Vanessa. It was the first time I had heard her name.

'You know,' she went on, 'the Virgin Mary wasn't married to Joseph when Jesus was conceived.' I felt mollified but the enormity of my situation sat heavily upon me.

'What happened to her? What was she like?'

'She could sing and play the piano like an angel your father told me once. I did hear her play at Bourne Lodge. She was tall with long black hair, strange when you were so very blonde. I'm sorry sweetheart but I don't know what became of her.'

'What about my father? You never told me about him. Did he die in the war?' I was giving Netta a hard time but I wanted to know.

'Your father was stationed in Dover with the army. It was a hot August bank holiday. He loved climbing and would spend his spare time on the cliffs when off duty. That day...' she faltered.

'Yes. That day?' I prompted, expecting the worst.

'That day he threw the rope over a projection of the cliff and started to climb – I'm sorry darling, but a piece of the cliff broke off. He fell... into the sea. The lifeboat...'

'Marvellous,' I said sarcastically. 'So he wasn't even a war hero. He was just an irresponsible clown like me.'

'Don't say that. He was full of life and hated the war. He was always a climber and a swimmer, but his neck was injured. Your hair slide was found in his uniform pocket when it was sent home. Next year I'll take you to see his grave in St Margaret's Bay on top of the cliffs where the sea birds call...' But I wasn't listening, it had all been too much to take in.

Back at school the old resentment returned. Why me? What had I done to deserve this shame and unfairness? I had always nurtured a secret longing that Marcel would reappear one day, a war hero, missing presumed dead but alive and well and ready to embrace his teenage daughter. What happened to my mother? Vanessa. Did she commit suicide or die of a disease? Did she take on a new life for herself, forgetting all about me, or did she end her days in prison or an institution? How would I find out? A bastard! I was a bastard. 'Be you bastard of Orleans?' Shaw's words were to haunt me a year later when, taking the part of Dunios, I was asked by the maid, Joan, and my reply, 'You see the bent sinister.' I became moody and difficult and lost my exuberance. I was still coming to terms with the speed of my developing body and would slouch in order to hide my bust. After the funeral Rita had sent me a black lace bra that must have belonged to her but was the talk of the dormitory. I was the envy of all but to me it was just a piece of necessary equipment that I would rather not have needed. My body was growing faster than my emotions could cope with.

'Charlotte, I'm going to make you a prefect.' Miss Edwards twirled her glasses. 'Perhaps it will instil in you some responsibility. You are becoming feckless and high handed. I'm sorry about your unfortunate parentage but you're not alone and its time to move on.' Miss Edwards replaced her glasses on her nose and gazed at me. 'You have potential. Stop wasting it.' Feeling somewhat pacified, my spirits lifted but I was a useless prefect and sent down as one the following term.

During the last two years at school Charlotte finally got her act together. She won her colours for hockey and tennis, gained prizes for her poems in the school magazine and in the last year became both prefect and house captain and thoroughly enjoyed producing and directing the end-of-term house entertainment for both school and staff.

On speech day I read a passage from the Apocrypha, 'Let us now praise famous men.' The assembly hall was packed but my knees no longer knocked as they had done three years earlier when I was first asked to read in prayers.

David and Rita drove up in David's open-top, two-seater Austin Special that he had constructed in his spare time and Rosamund and Brian arrived in their Riley. I loved being in the Austin but it never seemed quite "finished". David was still tinkering and perfecting her whenever he could. They all congratulated me on my achievements at school and for once I felt wanted and accepted and had something to offer but I was sad that my guardian couldn't be there. She had always been proud of my smallest triumphs and had encouraged me all my life. Things were looking up but was I ready for the big outside world? I had been cushioned and sheltered and a little spoilt by her although not in the material sense.

'Can I have your address?' Several senior boys were leaving Wanstead and had come to join us for our 'Leaving Dance'. It was good to see them again looking so handsome and grown up! Ballroom dancing lessons with Mr Scott to the music of Victor Sylvester had not paid off. I had not taken them seriously and as usual I had clowned around in his classes, partly because he made me take the part of the man, which didn't help. Besides, I thought it rather soppy. Mr Scott was frowned upon by Miss Edwards, but tolerated; likewise Mr Harrison who taught art and recommended me for the Slade School of Art in London. Both male teachers lived away from school and were not considered a threat but a grudging necessity. I would one day find my natural talent for modern dancing but for now I hobbled around the floor with the boys who were brave enough to ask me.

'Charlie, can I have your address?' Another request but this time by a special friend from those far off days, Roger Atkinson, and I was only too happy to oblige, but which address? I was leaving school with no fixed abode or plan for the future. What had THEY in store for me?

Two letters had arrived for Charlotte the previous term and were to have an influence on the years ahead.

14 Valentines Avenue
Ilford
Essex

Darling Charlotte
 You will be surprised to see the new address but we have finally moved from Ingatestone. As you know it has been a

difficult time for us but with the Lord's help we have arrived and are in the 'throes of unpacking. I'm sorry you weren't here to go through your things and hope you won't mind but we have had to let them go.

You'll love Valentines Park at the end of our small garden. There is a lake with boats and tennis courts. We are nearer the corps now and can walk which makes all the difference. They have made us very welcome and the band and songsters are a joy, even better than Chelmsford.

There is talk of Graham getting married next year. I hope we can get you into uniform for the wedding. That would be wonderful wouldn't it? I know you were fond of Graham but you'll like Jill.

They have both received "'the call'" and are going to training college to be S.A. officers. We are all so pleased. Well, there's a lot to do so I'll finish now. Izzy sends her love. Don't forget the new address when you write.

Yours affectionately
Auntie Netta xx

The other letter was from Rita.

30 Rose Hill
Hampstead
N.W.11

Dear Charlotte

I am writing to tell you that the house in Heathway has now been sold and we have found a house for your grandmother at the top of the road near us. It has been decided that when you leave school you will move in with her and keep her company. She is managing well but tires easily. To begin with you will stay with me and David until the final arrangements have been made with the new house.

The allotment is doing well, lots of raspberries and courgettes.

Hope you are keeping well. Good luck with your exams. Regards Rita.

My school days were finally over. I walked down the drive for the last time with little more in my suitcase than when I had first arrived. My dress sense was non-existent. The thought of wearing Salvation Army uniform to Graham's wedding was a worry. Who would it have belonged to? It wouldn't be new. I rather hoped I would not receive "the call" as I would find the uniform hard to cope with. I made one or two rather poor efforts at skirt making in needlework class and these would have to do. I had sports shirts and shorts so these, together with my school gingham dresses, were the extent of my wardrobe.

I was leaving my comfort zone. During the last year in Hyde Hall I had become a self-reliant individual and reasonably competent, but it was cold outside. I suffered from anxiety and under confidence when confronted with people I didn't know or the unexpected. What was I going to do next? I was a dreamer but one by one my dreams began to fade. To be fair, most of them were totally impractical: to swim the channel, fly a plane or drive a car in the Monte Carlo Rally like Sheila van Damm. I had also taken a fancy to the R.A.F. officer who came to our school to talk about a career in the Air Force. This had sounded an exciting option.

'You're not going to art school,' declared Rita emphatically. 'One artist in the family was more than enough.' My dream of attending the Slade School suggested by my art teacher was a non-starter.

'You could read English,' said Miss Edwards. 'You have a natural aptitude and your marks qualify, but who will pay your fees?'

Fees were not a problem with my family if I had the temerity to ask and being a writer or "journalist" had been on my list but I thought it was time to be independent and start earning my own living as soon as possible.

'You'd make a lovely nurse,' said my guardian. 'Nursing is the most rewarding profession. I loved my nursing and you'd be paid while you trained. I think Drama is nice for a hobby but most precarious and unsuitable for you with your upbringing.' Her same views were held for fashion models and pop musicians. She heartily disapproved of Buddy Holly and Frankie Lane whose songs I would sing at the top of my voice. I was doomed.

'Shall we settle on nursing then? Are you happy with that?' I nodded dumbly unable to think of anything better. Rita had been a masseur at Guy's Hospital, now she was a dental nurse in Market Place. She seemed to be efficient at everything but smoked a lot and enjoyed a "drink". This bothered Netta quite a bit when she knew I would be living with her and David. It had saddened her to let me go but she had no say in the matter. 'I'll pray for you,' she promised. 'Remember all I've taught you and keep away from harmful influences.' She had given everything in her power to bring me up in the best way she knew, but they would be reaping the benefits. Once again I donned my chameleon skin and took on a new guise, it was my way of coping with yet another set of conflicting ideas and standards. What would the future hold? I hardly dared to contemplate. Who was I? Where was I going? Netta loved me but she was far away. It was time to grow up.

CHAPTER THREE

THE BIG WIDE WORLD

Charlotte settled down to the new changes in her life with Rita and David, eventually moving in with her grandmother, Rose, some months later. She became a cadet nurse at the Edgware General Hospital and would cycle the ten miles each day. The cadets were too young to start training or take positions on general wards but would experience other aspects of hospital life, one day a week being spent at the nearby technical college, learning about anatomy and other subjects. Charlotte was dispatched to the maternity unit where she spent happy hours in the nursery with the newly born babies. This was a completely new field but she soon learned to care for them, which was to be an advantage to her at a later stage in her life.

A month after leaving school and before she moved in with Rose, she received a letter on blue Basildon Bond paper.

12 Victoria Road
Willesden Green
London
August 3rd

Dear Charley
I hope you don't mind me writing to you.

I was wondering if you could meet me in London? I was thinking of the zoo in Regent's Park, on the 15th? Please write and let me know. It would be good to see you again. I hope you are well.

Yours
Roger (Atkinson)

Rita had smiled at her, seeing her pleasure. 'Is it from Elizabeth?'

'No, it's from Roger Atkinson.'

'Oh, a boy!' Rita had looked pleased as though meeting a boy signified adulthood. 'You'd better give me his name and address if you're going to meet him in London.'

Diary entry August 16th:
Roger and I strolled around the zoo talking of Wanstead. I felt strangely shy in his company but happy to be with him. Leaning on a rail, he had turned to look at me. 'You have such beautiful eyes, such long lashes,' he had said, gazing at me. He too was blue eyed and fair haired but taller with wide athletic shoulders. We were no longer children in the junior playground. 'May I kiss you?' It was my first kiss, gentle and brief like a touch of silk. He held my hand. 'I've been wanting to do that.' Then he bent his head and kissed me again, firmer this time. I felt a warmth steal over me as our lips met and I knew then that this was what I had been yearning for, to be desired and held close by another human being. We stood, locked together, before he broke away. 'I've joined the Merchant Navy. My ship sails next month and it may be some time before we meet again, but I'll write.' He had stroked my hair and

looked at me sorrowfully, this newly found warmth of ours already cooling and tempered by loss. Would we meet again as planned? Our lives may diverge like the sea between us. We are young but one of life's miracles has already been tried and tested.

Her first dance was equally exciting to Charlotte who was still very naive for her age. She had joined the local tennis club and the summer dance was an annual fixture.

Diary entry August 28th:
To start with I was feeling very nervous. It was my first dance but my confidence returned as I came downstairs and David said, 'You look terrific. I take it you've changed your mind about coming out with Rita and me tonight. Have a good time. I'll wager you'll be married at nineteen!' I know he's only teasing. I was wearing my new turquoise dress with white polka dots. Mary was wearing red. It was a sultry evening, warm and close. I met a man called Peter. 'How old are you?' he asked as I tried to keep in time with the dance tune. He was tall, dark and good-looking. 'Seventeen. And you?' 'I'm an old man of twenty four.' Peter had laughed. He and his friends saw me home later. He told me they were only visiting at the dance but he had probably already discerned my inexperience with men. How would I gain this experience when I'm so shy and gauche?

Life took on a routine that Charlotte began to enjoy. She had made new friends, gained some confidence as she was moved to new duties in the hospital, lost weight, and looked forward to spending her own money on few but selective clothes from the boutique in Golders Green. Her pay was low, but living with Rose was free. She wore uniform at the hospital but enjoyed dressing up on college days.

One day, after cycling back from the hospital she was surprised to find that Rose was not at home. Putting her bike away she walked down to Rita's. 'Rose has had a stroke. She's upstairs in bed.' Rita informed her.

After several weeks, Rose became too difficult to nurse and was admitted to a nursing home where she died peacefully. Charlotte was able to see her days before she died. She wrote to a friend:

> *I did not attend Rose's funeral as Rita thought it would be hard for me. I had learnt to love my grandmother and to care for her at our home together. She would give me encouragement and had come to accept me as Marcel's daughter. What will happen now?*

Although Charlotte was enjoying her new life, Hampstead was a long way from Ilford. She had greatly missed her guardian and all that Netta represented. There had only been one visit as travel was difficult and expensive. She began to question her values and priorities. There had been no Sunday worship since her arrival and this left a gap, although to start with this had hardly mattered with other things crowding in to take her time. It had been somewhat enjoyable to be released from such strictures as formal worship after so many years, 'like swimming without a costume'. Instead, on Sundays, she would idle her time away, making little effort to improve herself or take up her painting or writing. David was keen on sport, which they would watch on the black and white television and Rita divided her time between the dental surgery where she worked in Market Place and her tennis club in Finchley, where she was a county player and at thirty-seven still a formidable opponent. She had already classed Charlotte's tennis as mediocre. Charlotte was now nearly eighteen and felt the need to give a structure to her life. A decision needed to be made. Would she continue her nursing in Edgware, living with David and Rita, or start her real training elsewhere? Deep down she had already made her choice. She would return to the fold. Netta had missed her and somehow she felt it to be her duty. It had other benefits too. She had met some boys at the youth club last time she visited and one in particular had caught her attention. Would he be there again?

Charlotte packed her case, this time with a finer assortment of clothes than before but few possessions: paints, some books and her treasured fountain pen. She wore no make-up on her high cheekbones, spent little time or money on her hair, which had always been very blonde and straight, and kept early nights. Apart from the occasional trip to the cinema, her outings were seldom, and a good book was good company. A place had been held for her in King Edward's Hospital where she would start her training in September, if her interview proved successful. Charlotte bid a fond farewell to her aunt and uncle who had supported her for the last eighteen months and returned to her spiritual home.

Netta met her at the station and they took the bus along the Cranbrook Road. Charlotte lugged her case up the long street to Valentines Avenue, through the front door and up to the bedroom that she would share with Netta. Things had changed. There was an air of sparseness and staleness mixed with liniment. The contents of their two-bedroomed bungalow in Ingatestone had sprawled into eight rooms of Victorian terrace house. There were new cheap items of furniture that were already showing signs of wear and the carpets were dowdy along with the curtains that had been made to fit. The house, one of many identical buildings in the road, had sash windows and high ceilings with no central heating. Coal had to be brought upstairs to the large sitting room. There was no phone or fridge. For Charlotte it was like taking a huge step backwards. The bay window in the sitting room looked out onto the road, likewise the window of the double bedroom. She would miss her little room in Rose Hill. The back bedroom housed an inmate of considerable age. Netta had taken to nursing elderly bedridden private patients to supplement her pension. Mrs Carter raised her head from her pillow as Charlotte was introduced. There was a tiny converted kitchen, and small bathroom to complete the flat.

Izzy lived in the rooms downstairs and also housed a lodger, Connie, who was her one-time colleague in the London S.A. headquarters. Their flat was cheerless and lacked homely touches. Izzy had taken to joining Netta upstairs where they would watch a variety show on a new small television which Charlotte found mildly shocking: the aunts being so straight laced and the sight of dancing girls and men with no dress sense, telling lewd jokes, seemed inappropriate to their narrow vision. Everywhere was grey compared with the suburb. No leafy roads or fine houses with pretty front gardens.

Charlotte felt lonely and disorientated. The aunts had changed too. They were even older than she remembered and seemed diminished by the move to London. What had she given up: independence, freedom, a room of her own? Or had she changed? When had shabby furniture and carpets bothered her? Not in her former years or when she was growing up. It was true she would miss the phone, a fair walk to a call box, and drives in the car with David but she would gain her peace of mind. Charlotte reined in her disappointment and reminded herself why she was there. She loved Netta and all that she represented. Charlotte would make the best of it for her sake.

Setting her mind at rest, she took herself off to the park and hired a skiff. After an hour's rowing on the lake, she felt better and brightened up. She would contact a friend from schooldays who lived nearby for a game of tennis on the local courts. In the meantime she would read, write and paint until Thursday's youth club.

Diary entry July 31ˢᵗ

Today something strange happened. I was ironing for Netta when the front-door bell rang. Izzy answered and called up the stairs, 'Netta it's for you!' I heard voices downstairs and then louder as they came up and into the room. 'Charlotte this is Mrs Lytton.' Netta looked very nervous, almost wringing her hands. Mrs Lytton was a large lady, about fifty, finely dressed, well spoken and with dark curly hair. She looked at me keenly and then said 'she's just like her mother, softly spoken, gentle and with the eyes of a doe.' For some terrible reason I felt a great fear of the unknown. I shrank before this strange woman unable to comprehend the meaning of her words. I became tongue-tied, whilst Netta grew paler than ever. Finally Mrs Lytton pressed an envelope into my hand then left. Netta came back into the room and sank onto the settee. I gave her a drink of water as she was trembling. 'She thinks I stole you from her sister but I was shielding you from a fate worse than death.' I took her hand and reassured her. I told her I was so scared myself I didn't know what to say. I had buried those thoughts of my mother long ago, along with those of my dad. The envelope held an early eighteenth-birthday card with an address in Kingston but it might just as well have been in Kingston, Jamaica. Right now I can't take on any more emotional baggage and I'm afraid of what I might find out. One day perhaps… but not now.

After a month of re-adjustment to her new surroundings and circumstances, Charlotte wrote to Rita.

14 Valentines Avenue
Ilford
Essex

Dear Rita

Since my last letter telling you about my interview, I have now started training for real at King Edward's. This is a small hospital with eight wards, A&E and Outpatients. I have been allocated a tiny room in the nurse's home but will spend some time in Valentines Avenue on time off. My uniform is blue and white striped with a white pleated cap and black cape. I was feeling really excited on my first day but this did not last long. I was appointed to women's medical but mainly geriatric with surgical side wards. I wanted to run a mile. I was told to go and help behind some screens where I was confronted by an old woman with a dreadful bedsore, being bed-bathed, heaped around with soiled linen. I think the sight and smell of that moment will live with me forever. It was so degrading. I suppose I'll get used to it. Spend much time trying to prevent these awful sores with massage.

On a happier note I have made friends with a French girl. She is older than me, twenty-two, but also paints and likes classical guitar. Her name is Michelle and she admires the impressionists and comes from Vence in the south. Lectures are going well and I'm keeping ahead because of the time at Harrow tech.

Thanks for lending me your bike. I collected it from the

station and rode it along the Cranbrook Road. I think I'll get some new modern handlebars if you don't mind and use it to visit the aunts during shifts.

I was sorry that David has sold the Austin Special. Have you still got Grandpa's Austin 16?

Hope you are both well, will write soon.

Love Charlotte

In the months to come, work on the wards and lectures in the hall continued and became routine. Charlotte's day would begin at 7am reporting for duty at 8am. She would work through until 8pm with a two-hour break during the morning or afternoon: these would include lunch, and one early evening a week, finishing at 6pm without a break in the day. She would cycle to see the aunts on her afternoon shifts and find them dozing in the sitting room, Izzy joining her sister for company. She would give them her news and stay for tea and a fig roll biscuit, before setting off back to the hospital. Days and half days were worked into the schedule but weekends were rare, about once a month. She lacked stamina over a long period as it could be ten days before a day and a half could be taken together and her feet let her down badly. Dances would come and go but Charlotte was too tired to enjoy them and would spend some evenings with her feet in a bowl of water in readiness for the next day. Besides, dances were not for nice girls according to Netta, and pubs were places of temptation, even for zealous S.A. soldiers selling the 'War Cry'. Charlotte didn't mind. She had enough to keep her busy and looked forward to the social club when possible.

On Sundays, when time allowed, Charlotte attended the Army meetings. She would wear her uniform, mainly to please Netta, as she shrank from being conspicuous, the bonnet strange with her straight hair. When Connie had died earlier in the year, her uniform had been passed to Charlotte; uniforms were expensive.

Torchbearers, or the army youth club, was held once a week but she was restricted by her timetable. Several of the boys escorted her home with barely a kiss goodnight but Charlotte's interest had been aroused elsewhere. A young R.A.F. officer had appeared in the band in his uniform on the occasional Sunday meeting. In answer to her question Netta told her that he was Ralph Fielding and that his parents were both officers in the S.A. and lived in Chigwell. Ralph played in the band when home on leave. He was stationed at Buckton.

Christmas came and went and Charlotte spent time on the ward. New Year's Day and other entries are recorded in her diary.

Diary entries: January 1ˢᵗ 1957

A new year and a new ward. Hurray! My first day on men's medical and I was greeted with smiles and a 'Hello darlin', and 'here comes sunshine' from some of the older patients. The men seem most appreciative of small kindnesses and are more cheerful. I felt quite odd when I saw some of them naked, quite a shock really but still a revelation!

Amongst the diverse cases are prostate patients. These are referred to as "bladder daddies" which I thought was quite hilarious but they are a friendly lot and don't complain. Too tired for any more. Must buy new stockings and soap. Need new shoes but they'll have to wait!

January 20th

Michelle is going to the theatre tomorrow. I wish I could go too. She is going to see a Terence Rattigan play with her amorous boyfriend. The only theatre I'll be going to is theatre 2 with George Fellows. Glad his tumour is non-malignant. I still blush to think of my first op case, haemorrhoids! That wretched strapping! I was so nervous in my hurry, and nearly died when the surgeon fixed me with a cold stare over his mask, gloved hands raised, scalpel at the ready, as the patient's strapping slipped and his "bits" fell down and then, with everyone watching, I had to re-strap them up again.

Torchbearers tomorrow so off at six but no sign of Ralph so far. Cliff said he'd come out on the lake with me on my next w/e off but it's too cold at the moment. He's invited me to partner him at the Valentine social in Feb. Perhaps Ralph will be there then? Must put in for a half day so not too tired.

February 7th

Broke a thermometer on the ward today and had to go and see Matron as it was not the first time and so became a major sin. She dressed me down a bit but then told me that she was pleased with my progress and my apparent aptitude for nursing. I didn't tell her of the pain I suffered when my patients died or were in a hopeless situation. Only last week I washed the dead body of a middle-aged man. A long weal ran down his entire torso, the hurried ugly stitches closing over and hiding the unknown source of his disease. He had walked into the ward, upright and outwardly normal. For some reason I had felt angry that he had not been cured. I wonder if I'm cut out for nursing at all. Will I ever get used to it? I'm too sensitive and can't switch off. I lack physical stamina with my wretched feet, on the wards all day and sometimes too tired to eat. I'm mentally up for it and enjoy the lectures and practical exercises with the other nurses in my year. I feel like a child again, let out at playtime. I'm really doing this for Netta. She's so proud of me and there's no doubt that it's a rewarding and responsible vocation and besides, what else am I fit for? Apart from a few poems and articles published in two years there's not much to celebrate. Too tired for any more.

February 19th
Last night was super! We played silly party games but I really enjoyed everything and Ralph was there! He has the most beautiful green eyes with long dark lashes. He was wearing a sports jacket and grey trousers. He said he had noticed me too and wondered who I was. We talked about cars and he told me he drove an ancient Morris Eight called 'BEA' and would take me for a drive sometime. He left early with the girl he came with. Was Jennifer his girlfriend? Cliff walked me back to Netta's as it was too late to go back to the hospital, and left after a chaste kiss on the doorstep. My mind was on Ralph. Will I see him again? Is he really interested in me? Feel much better.

CHAPTER FOUR

WHAT THE WORLD
NEEDS NOW...

Charlotte described Ralph Fielding as being slightly below average height but good-looking with a strong jaw, fair hair, stocky but not athletic, and twenty-three years old. He was considered quite a "catch" by some of the S.A. fogies. It was some time before Charlotte saw him again; in fact she had given up all hope that he would be interested in her, but after a rousing service one Sunday in early summer, he had tucked his cornet under his arm and offered to drive her back to the nurses' home.

Charlotte enthused over the little Morris and Ralph explained BEA's various moods and technical drawbacks and his hopes for something better in the near future. 'When I'm made up to flying officer, I'll get more pay,' he explained. He told her about his life on the R.A.F. station at Buckton and his aspirations while she told him about her work on the wards. They seemed to be mutually attracted to one another and because Ralph's brother Eddie was many years older, he said he also felt like an only child and this seemed to cement their friendship.

As time went by they saw more and more of each other when their different duties allowed and to start with it was on a friendly, cordial basis as they got to know each other; he was good at technical drawing and enjoyed classical music, while Charlotte wrote poetry, painted, and loved sport. Netta invited Ralph to meals on occasions and watched, somewhat bemusedly at first, but then with a gathering alarm as the couple grew closer together. She had prior knowledge of his dubious reputation and disapproved of his father who went to football matches, not approved of in her small world of the S.A. These things she kept to herself in the hopes that it was but a fleeting romance.

Charlotte's diary entry for 26th August reeinforces her fears.

Charlotte met Ralph's parents and was surprised to find that they were as old as Netta but seemed much younger in their outlook. Ralph had been a late arrival but much cosseted after the death of an earlier sibling. Eddie, the eldest, served in the British Army but was now married and living in Surrey. Bruce and Jean were friendly and welcoming. Bruce was a talented musician and they both attended a corps in London. They were proud of their son and his achievements in graduating from being a national service airman to a pilot officer after officer training. Their house in Chigwell was comfortable and homely but S.A. property and although now retired, the Fieldings still paid rent.

As Charlotte's next exams grew nearer she was busy studying with little spare time for recreation but was looking forward to her fortnight break in October. Michelle had invited her to go with her to the South of France. Charlotte was ecstatic and even the thought of being separated from Ralph could not deter her from accepting.

Letter to Rita:

Nurses' Home
King Edward's Hospital

Dear Rita,
I'm writing to tell you the good news that I have passed my prelim with flying colours and came top in both theory and practical. I have received two prizes, both medical books, at the prize giving do. This next lot will probably be harder.

More good news is that our journey to France is booked and we cross the Channel next week, then train all the way to Nice. We can't afford a couchette and will travel third class some of the way but who cares! I'm so excited! I have bought my first pair of slacks, navy corduroy and am narrowing the legs as they're a bit floppy and unfashionable (Netta is most disapproving and says trousers are for men!). We are taking our paints and will pretend to be real artists like the impressionists!

Life on the ward is hectic as we're short-staffed. I'm taking more responsibility each day and becoming more competent. I can pass a Ryle tube, stomach tube and flatus tube. What an exciting life I lead! Did I tell you that I think I'm in love? More next time, must get on duty. Love to David and yourself.

Charlotte.

P.S. Will send postcard from Vence

Charlotte and Michelle set off for France on a bright, blustery day; a photo shows Charlotte standing on the deck of the ferryboat wearing her new tapered slacks and duffle coat. They took the train from Calais to Paris and then on to Nice, travelling through the night on hard uncomfortable seats in a third-class carriage; crammed together with other passengers, but nothing could daunt their spirits. As they journeyed further south, the carriage gradually emptied until at last they were able to stretch out and sleep.

> *Postcard to Ralph*   *20th October*
> *Arrived safely 9am. Awoke to a pink dawn suffusing the red rocky coastline of the Cote D'Azur. Already I'm painting a picture in my head!*
> *Pension sparse. Will write soon. Send letters to Poste Restante Love Charlotte.*

Charlotte was enthralled. She had never been further than Eastbourne in her own country and to her it was another world, the world of the impressionists, the artists she admired, her only guide to what to expect. She enthused over the "light" the turquoise sea and the beauty of the houses stacked like children's toys up on the top of the walled towns. She loved the French way of life, the markets and the churches. Charlotte pondered her French ancestry and felt at home.

They had taken a taxi from Nice, a Citroen 2CV that Charlotte thought looked to be made of grey corrugated iron and rather unsafe as it rattled along the road to Vence. Their room was several floors up and looked out over the village square with its ancient fountain. Charlotte loved to open the huge shutters in the morning and gaze down at the people going about their business under a cobalt sky. Across the square was the poste restante, where Ralph's letters arrived almost daily, printed in his neat handwriting, telling her he loved and missed her, but Charlotte was too engrossed to miss him at all.

Michelle introduced her to two young men who lived and worked in Vence and were known to her. After work they would take the girls in the Renault down to the Cap D'Antibes where they would stroll down to the marina after a frugal meal in the Ville, where Charlotte would refuse wine but enjoy the espresso coffee. Michelle was free and uninhibited with Jean Paul, but Charlotte made it clear to Alain, in her poor French that her loyalties and affections lay elsewhere, back home in England, and that she was not easy game.

They spent time painting and sightseeing and were given a lift in a pony and trap up the mountain road to the picturesque walled town of St Paul de Vence. Here they set up their paints and began to represent the famous fountain in their different ways; Michelle with bold abstract strokes and Charlotte with a more romantic approach. Another day they climbed the Baou, in the Alps Maritime and marvelled at the view from the top, the lower slopes clothed with vineyards. One evening they were given a lift to Cagnes sur Mer by members of a film crew shooting in Nice who wined and dined them royally. Charlotte was filled with nervous apprehension and out of her comfort zone. Michelle was animated and talking non-stop. Charlotte's grasp of French was insufficient to follow the fast flow of conversation and she worried about their possible intentions but she needn't have fretted. It turned out to be a good evening and enjoyed by all but she was glad to get back to their room and read again the letter from Ralph with its curious content.

Officers Mess
Buckton
Essex

Darling Charlotte,
It was good to get your letter today. So far I have only received a postcard, but I'm glad to hear that you are having a good time.

I saw Netta on Sunday and she seems to be warning me off. She kept asking about Jennifer and then went on about your nursing and how important it was to you. She also said that you would come into money one day, intimating that I was after you for that reason. I told her I knew nothing of this and didn't consider it any of my business.

When you get back I'll teach you to drive. Would you like that? I'm really missing you dreadfully but life here is not without its problems so it keeps me busy.

I have copied out a poem, it's one of Shakespeare's sonnets. It is how I feel about you. Write soon!

All my love

Ralph X X X

Charlotte read his letter again and then looked at the sonnet. He had printed at the top of the paper 'to the dearest, sweetest and kindest person I know' and at the end of the poem he had written 'with deepest, fondest, love'. The sonnet began: 'So are you to my thoughts as food to life or as the sweet seasoned showers are to the ground.' It was written out in his best copperplate handwriting, the words filling her with love and a longing to see him again. She dismissed his worries about Netta and knew nothing of any possible inheritance but what could that have meant?

Michelle suggested the cinema in Nice for their final evening in France followed by a better meal than usual, supported by the last of their francs, the holiday costing a total of twenty pounds each. They said 'Goodbye' to the South of France, now cooler in the autumnal air, and headed for home. The train was less crowded than before and they were able to find an empty couchette.

The crossing was stormy and Michelle and many other

passengers became sick, but Charlotte held fast to the rail out on deck and vowed to keep her stomach under control with admirable determination but back home she collapsed with a high fever, brought on by a streptococcal infection contracted in France. Netta called the doctor and Charlotte took to her bed for the next two weeks.

When Charlotte returned to work she was put on night duty; still weak from her illness she found this period of darkness dispiriting and the sleepless days unsettling. Ralph was away in Suffolk and Netta was recovering from a severe gastric problem. Finally the long night shift was over and she was back on days, this time on the private ward. This had its compensations. It was smaller than the main wards and the sister in charge was an older woman who took things in her stride and displayed an air of equanimity. She took Charlotte under her wing and helped her recover her lost esteem.

Diary entries for 12th and 17th February
Am feeling much better and can't wait for the weekend. Ralph says he has some important news. Have swapped duties with Joan Clayton so that I can have the whole day off. I hope Netta will be feeling better too. Feel guilty I have not been around much but took her some flowers yesterday tho' they didn't seem to do the trick. Her consultant thinks she needs a barium meal to discover the problem. Having observed this in other patients it looks pretty awful. It would be good if they could find some other way instead of having to make them swallow all that chalk. Will have to wait and see. Meanwhile, roll on Saturday and this important news!

February 17ᵗʰ

So far this has been the most significant day of my life. I hardly know where to begin; my thoughts and feelings are all over the place! Ralph has asked me to marry him! We were driving back from Chigwell and I found myself saying 'Yes!' 'No! 'I don't know!' He told me that he was being posted to Germany in early October and that he would be made up to the rank of flying officer.

I told him I ought to finish my training but he just shrugged and said maybe he wouldn't be around in two years after a spell abroad. He said to think about it but in the meantime we could become engaged. What am I to do? I don't want to lose him because I love him so and to start a new life with him is tempting beyond belief.

Can't sleep. I'll be like a zombie in the morning. Mrs Fielding! Sounds good to me!

Innocent of the ways of most people, Charlotte firmly believed that if anyone was a Christian and even more so if they were a Salvationist, they would all hold the same ethics, standards and values as Netta. For these reasons Charlotte thought that she could do no better than marry Ralph. The fact that she had so little experience of the world of men did not deter her and her lack of a father only heightened her desire to hold on to her relationship. Here was her chance to become part of a unit, to have someone of her very own, to love and be loved. But on the other hand, what about finishing her training? It was true that in many aspects she was physically unfit and found the long hours and increasing responsibility tiring but she was beginning to enjoy the benefits and rewards of being of service and relieving the pain and discomfort of others. She was a good nurse, despite her sensitive disposition, and well thought of by staff and colleagues alike. This added to her dilemma but a decision had to be made. She deplored but accepted her newly found sexual drive that she felt must also add weight to her argument. Ralph would be leaving for Germany by October and she had six long months to make up her mind before the proposed wedding. She would have to discuss it with Netta.

February 28th

Today was a dreadful day. I finally plucked up the courage to tell Netta of Ralph's proposal. (I have accepted his offer and we intend to announce our engagement next week. Jean and Bruce are delighted. They seem to approve of me as a future daughter-in-law.) Netta and I were walking down the Cranbrook Road. She seemed a lot more like her old self, chattering on about the over-sixties group that she ran each month down at the hall. I then mentioned, in a matter of fact way, that we were going to become engaged and hoped she would say something like 'Well that's wonderful news!' She didn't say anything at all for some time, and then she spoke in a voice I barely recognised. It was hard and strained, as if inwardly struggling to maintain composure.

'I would have expected a lot more of you,' she began. 'What about your training, you're only nineteen, and what will you do with the rest of your life with nothing to fall back on?' I told her that I expected to have a husband, a home and children to look after. 'You're throwing your life away,' she said. 'I don't trust Ralph Fielding an inch. He's a philanderer and an opportunist. Look how he's treated Jennifer. He's broken her heart and he'll break yours. You're not his first love you know. What will you do then?'

'Get a divorce,' I said carelessly, needled by her onslaught and wanting to end this unbelievable conversation we were having. My words went home. Her sadness was apparent but I ignored her pain.

'But what about your children?' she pointed out. I made no answer. 'I've kept my council all these months in the hope you would come to your senses but I can see that your heart is set on this road to ruin. Once you are married I will not darken your doors or cross your threshold. I have done my best for you and this is my reward.' I was stung by her ferocity.

'How can you say all these things? His parents are Salvation Army officers. He comes from a good home. He's a Christian. Does that count for nothing? We love each other.' I finished, sounding lame in spite of my protestations.

'You do now,' came her reply, 'and what about me? Don't I matter anymore? I've lied for you about your beginnings. I've given my life to you. God gave you to me for a purpose. I must fulfil that purpose. I held you in my arms, you were so tiny, so special and I made my promise to Him. Does this mean nothing to you?' I told her that it had been her choice not to marry and that I may be fulfilling God's will by marrying and that I would always love her and be grateful to her but that she had wanted my happiness above everything and this is what I wanted.

'But at what price? I had such plans for us both...'

'What plans?' I was losing patience. 'You mean when I get my inheritance?' A pained look came over her worn creased face and I knew I had overstepped the mark and regretted my words. How could I hurt her like this? A demon seemed to take control. I was possessed, with no room for reason or dissuasion. We parted at the bus stop, our once smooth path now strewn with rocks. I felt unusually defiant and impetuous. 'I will marry Ralph,' I said to myself as I strode away, 'and everyone else can stew.'

Later that night I lay awake reflecting on our conversation. I was deeply saddened by the rift between us but unrepentant. How could Netta fail to see the good in Ralph? He was kind and considerate and would take good care of me but what was really making me take this option? Why was I so anxious to give up everything for him? I examined my own heart. Had I not prayed to God to send me someone to love? Netta had prayed for a purpose after her retirement when God had sent me. Was that how it worked or was I betraying her trust and would Ralph one day betray mine? I began to think about my mother. I had pushed her to the very back of my mind but now I wondered had she had these same feelings for my father? Had she been reckless and selfish for her own gains or had she been strong and resolute but unlucky in some way? Genes, I thought. Was it all down to genes? I fell into a troubled sleep, forgetting to say my prayers.

The next day Charlotte wrote to Rita telling her of her troubles and asking if she could bring Ralph over for an introduction. They had not met but Rita had been kept informed of the progress of their courtship. Rita replied suggesting sometime in July, when they could celebrate the final touches being made to the new kitchen which David had so lovingly and painstakingly nearly completed, after over a year, in his spare time.

May and June were warm happy months for Charlotte. She smothered her conscience with regard to her debt to Netta and began to enjoy the thought of what lay ahead. It was like being free after years of guidance. Suddenly her life was in her own hands and she was intoxicated. Perry Como's voice sounded from the open French windows of the nurses' sitting room and "Magic Moments" seemed every bit appropriate. They had chosen a ring, a solitaire diamond, and celebrated their engagement with Bruce and Jean and a musical evening.

During this period Ralph kept his promise and took her to the edge of the airfield at Buckton where he gave her driving lessons. The little Morris bucked and stalled under her inexperienced handling. 'Foot on clutch, foot on clutch,' Ralph would yell as the gears crashed in protest but Charlotte took control and finally gained his approval. She soon picked up the rudiments of driving but it would be some time before she would take BEA out into the busy traffic. Ralph had put a small portrait photo of her above the rearview mirror and she was touched by his token of love for her.

These and other days spent together, when time allowed, were special magic moments and exclusive of all other outside interferences. They got up early, one day, and drove to Folkestone, laughing on the beach, then taking the tiny train from Hythe to Dimchurch, and later, driving up to the top of the hill in Folkestone, where BEA's clutch gave way at the traffic lights and four burly men were forced to lift her bodily out of the way. Ralph, ashen faced, made arrangements for repairs and then bought tickets for their journey home by train. He would come back a week later to collect the repaired car but it made a hole in his savings.

Another time BEA took them to Norwich where it pelted

with rain. This time her wipers packed up on the way home and they were forced to drive with the windows open and their heads stuck out to see where they were going. The week before it had been the exhaust pipe, which had to be tied up with one of Charlotte's stockings.

They both had bicycles and Ralph proposed a ride to Southend along the old arterial road. They got up early one morning and left Chigwell, cycling the thirty odd miles to the seaside town. They enjoyed a picnic lunch on the shingled beach then cycled straight back again, stopping briefly for a greasy meal in a greasy transport café along the way. They arrived back tired and sore but happy with their achievement. Ralph said that he had cycled to Bournemouth from Chigwell and that it was a lot further and that he would take her there for a weekend if BEA could cope. His car was taking all his savings.

Ralph took her to Bournemouth where they stayed in a boarding house, both conscious of the need to maintain propriety, mainly as it was run by a couple in the Fellowship known to his parents. A step into the wrong room and Ralph could blow his chances. Charlotte listened to his footsteps passing her door in the night and held her breath. Would he come in? She was filled with a thrilling alarm that he might not keep his word but she breathed again when he returned and passed by without incident. She would hold fast to her vow that she would be married a virgin. She would save the moment for their wedding night.

Charlotte had given in her notice at the end of June and would leave at the end of the following month. Matron had not been at all impressed by her reason for leaving and had intimated that you could have a man without having to wash his socks and that she was losing a good nurse. Charlotte was rather shocked at Matron's view of marriage but left her office feeling relieved. She had not looked forward to her interview and handing in her notice.

Her last month of duty was on men's surgical. This was a lively ward with youngish men in various stages of post-operative care and recuperation from diverse operations. It contrasted with the strangely quiet children's ward, with so many little ones in subdued circumstances that she had encountered the month before. Perhaps Matron had had the last word when she put Charlotte in charge of night duty on the men's ward for the whole month, despite her lack of qualification for the task and a raw probationer for company. She found the added responsibility disconcerting and was glad when it was over, which helped to make her final leaving day more palatable.

CHAPTER FIVE

TRANSITION

Rita and David invited them both over to Hampstead to meet Ralph and hear of their wedding plans. The occasion was met with a mixture of polite well-wishing tinged with reticence judging by the letter Charlotte received from her aunt.

30 Rose Hill
Hampstead
N.W.11

Dear Charlotte,

Thank you for your letter. David and I were pleased to meet Ralph at last, tho' this has been our fault as much as anything that it has taken this long. He seems a responsible young man and in a good position to take care of you in spite of some reservations on our part. Miss Prior too is not encouraging us to give our consent, partly it seems because she thinks you are too young. However, you seem set on the idea and we don't want to stand in your way. We'll both look forward to your coming to stay in August as arranged when we can make a good time of it and shop in London for your dress etc. Your Uncle Brian and Aunt Rosamund have offered to pay for your reception and we'll talk about this when you come. David and I will pay for your dress etc. as our contribution.

As you say, the wedding sounds a little bizarre. I'm not surprised you will not be wearing your S.A. uniform as it sounds rather dull for the occasion and if Ralph will be in his R.A.F. uniform and you say your best man's a guardsman with bearskin, it will be some wedding! Is Ralph's father really authorised to marry you and will it really be teetotal?

David sends his love and was pleased you liked the new Formica worktops etc. Must get the meal.

Love Rita.

Charlotte left the hospital and moved back to Valentines Road but things had changed. Charlotte had changed. The sweetness of her nature was challenged daily by the accusation in Netta's eyes and for the first time Charlotte gave way to latent moods and sulks of adolescence. Never before had she slammed doors or shouted through her tears at the one she loved. It was becoming unbearable and she counted the days to her release when she would be with her aunt in Hampstead.

Finally the day arrived and Ralph drove her to Rose Hill and returned to Buckton the same evening. Charlotte was dismayed to find her aunt and uncle in a state of anxiety. They were both chain-smoking and the air was filled with fug and foreboding. Charlotte felt she was the cause of their discomfort and apologised for her intrusion once again into their ordered lives. 'We've received another letter from Miss Prior,' Rita informed her. 'She strongly urges us again not to approve the marriage. We only have your word against hers that it is in your best interests and that it is the right thing for your future happiness. Are you sure you want to marry Ralph? After all he is the first boy you've ever met, not counting a day in Regent's Park with your old school friend Roger.'

After a few days of tears and heartache, Charlotte managed

to discuss the situation rationally. Rita seemed to think that she could do better for herself from a social point of view; Ralph in her opinion was lacking in grace, held controversial views and was arrogant. He had come "up through the ranks", was not aircrew and had not been to Cranwell. Charlotte argued that these things were not important and that he had other qualities including ambition and business drive, both things she lacked and that his arrogance was a cover for shyness and that he failed aircrew training due to hay fever that he couldn't help. It was true he didn't enjoy sport for the same reason but he was a talented musician, a technical artist and enjoyed rally driving. She finished with an appealing argument that she wanted nothing more than a husband and a home of her own where love and dreams could flourish and a life that could be challenging.

Excerpt from *The Fire and the Phoenix*.
I feel all washed up and totally alone. I don't know where I'm going. When you're an orphan you seem to belong to everyone and no one. I have only myself to turn to. Even my prayers seem to be blocked. Netta has become my number one enemy. She is so convinced that she is right; that she knows human nature; that nursing in the slums of the East End has taught her everything about broken homes and abandoned children and that I'm sacrificing the lives of my unborn babes by marrying a man she believes to be wrong for me. I think it's because she doesn't want to let me go, that perhaps her hopes are for me to care for her in her old age as she has cared for others. Is it "payback time"? Am I being totally selfish? Must I give up my life for her? She still has family of her own. Perhaps she has never been in love. It can be a deadly disease, demanding all, sometimes even life itself. There's no room for compromise. I have broken away from her control and must follow my heart.

I will marry Ralph and move to a new country and a new life.
Is destiny another word for the will of God?

Eventually, with much persuasion, Charlotte won her aunt and uncle round and they gave their consent. She settled back into her own room and took up life again as she had left it two years previously. She began to unwind from weeks of stress and strain. Time here seemed more leisurely and although there were plans to be made, she allowed herself breathing space.

Diary entry for August 12th
Up early this morning and off to London. Rita and I took the bus to Golders Green and then the tube to Oxford Circus. Rita asked what sort of dress I had in mind but I had no idea. I'm unused to sophisticated shopping in the city and found the enormous departmental stores overwhelming. Rita was quite tireless and relentlessly ploughed through "bridal wear" in every one. I wasn't keen on masses of fabric or trains and settled on a modern style; a simple short-sleeved, fitted, pretty lace designed bodice coming to below the hips and then finishing with a tutu effect skirt in the new length, down to the knee. The fitted part shows off my figure well (three cheers for my weight loss!) and I don't have to worry about walking in a long dress. The netted skirt is striking and I feel like a ballerina. We then chose a short veil with an attractive crown, long white gloves and lastly white satin shoes. We finally sank down onto welcome seats and ordered lunch. After what seemed like no time at all Rita announced 'now for your going away outfit and other clothes suitable for the wife of an officer,' and away we

went again. I now have a smart navy barathea suit with navy and white buttons and navy court shoes; a beautiful lavender blue coat dress, a wool checked skirt, coral twin-set and two white blouses. My final items were a camel coat and brown flat shoes with leather tassels.

We arrived back quite exhausted but pleased with our shopping. I'm a very lucky girl and very grateful to them both for their generosity. It has made up for all the pain of the last few weeks. I can't wait for the wedding and to wear my new clothes. I seem to have spent most of my life in a uniform of some sort or other and at last my personality can blossom!

The wedding was to be held in Ilford. Charlotte would prepare back home in Valentines Avenue two weeks beforehand. Izzy had come unexpectedly to the fore, declaring herself in favour of the marriage and offering Charlotte her spare bedroom in her downstairs flat for her sole use, for which she was most grateful. Izzy's show of generosity and support had both pleased and surprised her and as a result, she felt able to make the necessary arrangements with Ralph and the help of his parents.

As promised, her uncle Brian met her to discuss his part in providing the reception. This was to be held in the Cranbrook Hall function rooms not far from the Salvation Army Hall where the ceremony would be held. The meal would be a mixed buffet affair with soft drinks, tea and coffee, the time of the wedding being set for 3pm. Although not a conventional army wedding with regard to dress, uniform being optional, there would be no alcohol available. Charlotte included a pianist to play while the guests arrived, indulging her romantic sense of occasion and a touch of class.

Bruce drew up the couples plans for the service and hymns were chosen along with the well-known passage from St John's Gospel, "Tho I speak with the tongues of men", with Jean giving nods of approval and applauding their choice. A small refined woman and a proud Scot, Jean Fielding suffered enormously with rheumatoid arthritis, was constantly cheerful nonetheless, and possessed a generous nature. She took Charlotte to her heart and blessed them both. This was a great comfort to Charlotte, who had been warmed by this response, making up for Netta's absence from all discussion, the gap between them ever widening.

The guest list had been drawn up some time beforehand and included fifty guests. Ralph's brother Eddie and family, several of Ralph's other relations, Charlotte's aunts, uncles and cousins, and friends on both sides. The couple had disagreed over the invitation of one particular family and Charlotte was surprised to find it in herself to be somewhat unreasonably adamant. Jennifer Bates had a very young brother who Ralph thought would be suitable for a pageboy but Charlotte made it quite clear that she was not prepared to share her wedding day with his ex-girlfriend or members of her family as it would put a blot on the day. Ralph complied but was at a loss to know why it would be a problem. Charlotte perceived something new in herself. Jealousy. She didn't like it very much and wondered where it had come from but she had got her way.

Presents arrived and were stacked on the table in Charlotte's bedroom. The Sunday before the wedding Izzy had rustled up some savoury snacks and Charlotte invited her few local friends to join her for a girl's evening. She confided to one friend later 'I dreamt the other night that a strange woman came into my room and tore my dress into shreds like Mrs Rochester in Jane Eyre. I couldn't see for the smoke but heard a voice whispering "I'm your mother" over and over again, then I woke up with tears running down my face and a sense of loss as to who she really was.'

On the morning of the wedding she found herself full of nerves and anticipation for the day ahead. After breakfasting with Izzy she spent all morning in her room trying to remain calm, and avoiding a confrontation with Netta. She packed carefully for the honeymoon that lay ahead. Rita arrived soon after lunch and helped her dress. David would be giving her away and was waiting outside with the wedding car. Netta and Izzy had set off earlier together on foot, both wearing uniform and leaning upon one another. Charlotte had watched them from the window and a lump had come into her throat. Suddenly an overwhelming love for her guardian had come over her and she was wracked with guilt; that it should have come to this, not a word passing between them, but then it was gone, banished, as her resolve closed the door and took control.

On the way to the hall David told her she looked stunning and that he was proud to be giving her away. Charlotte smiled and thanked him, her spirits raised. She looked down at the simple posy she held in her gloved hand and then up at him. Her face was radiant, without even a trace of makeup and as she stepped down from the car, she lowered her veil, and taking his arm, walked confidently up the aisle.

Ralph and Bob stood side by side, Bob nearly a foot taller and resplendent in his scarlet guard's tunic, and Ralph smart and handsome in his blue officer's uniform. Charlotte took her place beside him and he squeezed her hand. Bruce came down from the platform with welcoming arms and announced the first hymn, "Love Divine All Loves Excelling", the bandsmen rose to the occasion and led the crowd of guests and members of the congregation into joyful song. Bruce took "tolerance" as his message to the couple for the years to come, and finally after the exchange of vows, pronounced them man and wife.

After many photographs of the couple posing on the steps of the hall and getting into the car, they were whisked away the short distance to the reception hall. Netta and Izzy had joined in the group family photograph, but whilst Izzy smiled into the camera, Netta hung back like a spectre at the feast.

Inside the Cranbrook rooms the pianist dutifully played romantic pieces as the guests arrived. All Charlotte's family were present including her cousins Linda and Anette. Bob made a rousing speech exalting his friend and congratulating him on his choice of bride. David replied and was most complimentary about his niece, praising her attributes and wishing them both well. Brian, Rosamund, Myra and Evan all looked on smiling at the happy couple and Charlotte was pleased to see that Linda, now quite grown up, was holding the posy that she had thrown into the crowd. 'You'll be next Linda,' she had smiled. They all wished them well and a new and exciting life in Germany. Ralph's relatives made themselves known to Charlotte and showed pleasure at meeting their new family member. They said that living abroad was a great way to travel and experience new cultures.

Bruce and Jean kissed them both as the couple finally took their leave of their guests and made their way to BEA, now trailing ribbons and tin cans. Laughingly they pulled away from the kerb, waving to the crowd as BEA shuddered into life and headed into a gathering storm. Charlotte had looked round for Netta but she was nowhere to be seen.

The honeymoon seemed to Charlotte, according to her autobiographical notes, to be an anti-climax. This was accentuated by the wind and rain that followed them down from Ilford, the drabness of the boarding house, and the lack of hot food due to the lateness of their arrival. Twice in the night Ralph had got up to secure their bedroom door that had blown open with every gale-force blast. This seemed to him to be an apocalyptic message from some avenging angel. He finally settled the matter on the third occasion by dragging a chest of drawers across to make it fast. Nothing came up to Charlotte's heightened expectations and their long-awaited consummation was flawed by her own over-anticipation and Ralph's ineptitude due to tiredness and the need for a good meal. All this was compounded the following morning when the couple came down to breakfast keen and hungry only to find that they were an hour early due to the clocks being put back an hour the night before to signal the oncoming winter.

The boarding house was shabby and poorly furnished but the rates were modest and the Parkers, staunch Baptists, were warm and friendly hosts. However, although the rain continued and the sitting area was dark and cheerless, the meals were good and a welcome diversion. Most of the other guests, mainly retired, seemed as though they were part of the furniture and sat behind their newspapers.

Postcard to Rita.

Lots of walking in the rain. My new shoes are quite spoilt.
Went to Lulworth Cove on Wednesday and peered at it
through the mist. I'm sure it looks very beautiful in the
sunshine! Off to Bournemouth tomorrow for some shops and
shelter?! Love Charlotte.

Their sexual forays were strictly reserved for the night but Charlotte would have been happy to spend more time "in bed" and less time walking in the wind and rain. Ralph reasoned that now they were married there was no urgency and that the Parkers would take a dim view of impropriety in the afternoon. Eventually as the days passed Charlotte became less stressed and recovered her strength. The week up to the wedding and the day itself had taken their toll but now she was fit and ready to go home. They packed up their bags and headed back to Chigwell where Bruce and Jean eagerly awaited them.

The highlight of the following week was the collection of Ralph's new car. His airforce promotion had come through and on the strength of an increase in pay, he had put down a deposit on a Renault, the rest to be paid on hire purchase. David had spoken to him of the merits of this very small car and the undoubted economy it would provide. It was a pale green in colour and Charlotte thought it quite delightful and was intrigued by the reversed position of the engine and the toy "dinkyness" of its general appearance. They would soon be off to the Midlands where Ralph would be lecturing in the universities there, before leaving England and setting off for Germany and his posting to Geilenkirchen in two weeks' time.

They had both been sad to part with BEA but the new car was fast and throaty by comparison as they headed north, arriving in Nottingham on a Sunday evening. It appeared that Bruce had used his influence with the Salvation Army network to find hosts who were willing to board the couple in their homes throughout their stay in various towns and cities.

The following morning Ralph took off in the Renault and Charlotte resigned herself to a day of solitude in a strange house with strange older people and polite conversation. This was the pattern for the next five days in different towns. None of the "lodgings" were convenient for the shops and Charlotte felt disinclined to venture out, particularly as she had no money of her own or knowledge of the local district.

The last place before returning home was Bristol and on the Saturday morning they were able to take in the sights and the new Clifton suspension bridge. Their hosts had been a kind friendly couple who owned a pianola, which the husband played with great gusto on the night of their arrival.

They made their way home in the afternoon and back to Bruce and Jean. In a week's time they would be off again, this time for three years. Ralph had made an appointment for her to see the M.O. for her jabs. Tony was a friend of his and he assured her there would be no problem.

Charlotte went straight to Valentines Avenue on their return and was relieved to find Netta at home and in a better state of mind. She had been staying with her friend Annie and Annie's sister in Southend. Netta said she would like to move again to be nearer them now that Charlotte had no longer any need of her. Charlotte was saddened once again that she had brought about this change but assured her guardian that she would always keep in touch and come back and visit them on her 21st birthday. She spent the night in Izzy's room, then, collecting up the wedding gifts, said 'Goodbye' to the two sisters and waited for Ralph to arrive with the car.

CHAPTER SIX

A NEW LIFE AND
A NEW COUNTRY

Bruce and Jean busied about helping the newlyweds to pack up their belongings ready for the long trip by boat and car to the Dutch border town of Heerlein. Once again Bruce had pulled strings and found a willing Dutch Salvationist widow to look after them until their married quarters on the camp became available. This would save the couple money, as living with Frou Bootsma and paying her rent would be a cheaper option for them and extra money for her. The R.A.F. camp was eighteen kilometres across the border in the small German town of Geilenkirchen and Ralph would travel there daily. After fond farewells and promises to write home, they squeezed into the car and set off for Ramsgate.

The weather was reasonable for late October and the ferry crossing to Ostend uneventful. They had started early and reached the Belgium port by late morning. Driving off the ferry they were full of glee and expectation. A real adventure awaited them and they intended to enjoy every minute. To Charlotte a new page was being written, as yet unblemished. They took their route through Belgium, driving over two hundred miles towards their destination.

Diary entry November

It is the first time I have written in my diary since our wedding. So much has happened but I must begin at the beginning. I am sitting on my bed (we have single beds) in the middle of the afternoon in our little room in Heerlen. Ralph is away at the camp and Frou Bootsma is beating carpets outside in the small garden. Heine, her disabled son, who is about forty years of age, is in his workshop.

Neither can speak a word of English apart from 'yes' and 'no'. We have been here a week now. We arrived after an incredibly long journey from Ostend (cobbled roads in parts) and have settled down as well as we can. They are teaching me Dutch or rather Flemish (Heerlen borders both Belgium and Germany) by holding up objects and making guttural sounds to accompany them.

Frou Bootsma is an unattractive woman with bovine features but with that inner beauty that shines through like a Rembrandt painting. She is a very good and devout soul who can't do enough for us. They have not forgotten the war and what the Brits did for them. We eat with the family (Heine and her one unmarried daughter who works in the local bakery). I find breakfast a difficult meal because it consists of cold meats, various cheeses and strange breads. Lunch is usually meatballs in a clear yellowish soup, but quite tasty. Best of all are the large fruit tarts made with delicious pastry and served with a kind of custard. They are poor by our standards at home and tea and coffee are both expensive here. Ralph hopes to get to the NAAFI to help them out with some goodies. Evening meals are usually chicken, veal or more meatballs!

Diary entry December

Great fun today! Frou Bootsma wants to take me to see some local sights and has instructed me (in Dutch) how to balance on the back of her bicycle (op de fetes!) with my legs thrust forward but without holding on! It's all in the balance! We did a few practice runs and then I got the hang of it, she really can pedal!

One of the saddest things she showed me was an expanse of white crosses stretching down a hillside, marking the deaths of so many fallen in the war. I told Ralph and we are going again together. He says it will be months before we get our married quarters as the camp is full! I'll be well conversant in Dutch by then!

Saturday

Frou B is taking us to an army service tomorrow at the local corps. We are some kind of guests of honour and expected to speak or sing! Ralph won't mind but I'll be too nervous! We'll have to have an interpreter! Fortunately the presiding officers (two women) can speak English. The small band will be playing some well-known hymn tunes. I have picked up some of the language quite quickly (nothing else to do!) and can follow quite a bit as I have spent many hours accompanying Frou on her various rounds of women's meetings. (It would be rude to fall asleep!) Next week is my birthday. I'll be twenty! They are going to have a party on the 6th. In Holland St Nicholas is celebrated in a big way and very much looked forward to by the children.

Soon after Charlotte's birthday, Frou Bootsma informed them that another more convenient lodging had become available with a friend of hers in the smaller nearby town of Brunssum. Frou Vanmeer was also a widow, in her early sixties, and prepared to let out two upstairs rooms to the couple in her larger house. This would give them more freedom and independence as they would be provided with cooking facilities in their sitting area and the other room would be their bedroom, this was large and roomy with a wash hand basin. The bathroom arrangements were minimal and the lavatory was downstairs.

Frou Vanmeer had two daughters and a son. Greta was married and lived in Amsterdam but Martha lived at home and had vacated her room upstairs to make way for the new lodgers. She moved into a smaller room on the ground floor and resented the change. Peter was still at college and away in term time, but had been banished to the attic room when at home for occasional weekends and holidays, in order to free up his smaller room for the couple. Frou Vanmeer was a very large woman with a bun on top of her head and dressed all in black. She could speak some English and was pleased to have the couple and the extra gilders that would now be coming her way. She was a shrewd, intelligent and capable person who took pride in her house and her cherry flans.

Charlotte and Ralph moved in just before Christmas but both were suffering from colds and flu. By now some of the former novelty of living abroad had begun to wear off and living in cramped quarters had kept lovemaking to a minimum. This had put a strain on the newlyweds. The thought of moving into a better situation and spending Christmas on their own was still not the ideal solution. Charlotte wanted to move into married quarters on the camp where she could make new friends but there were still none available. She was missing Netta and Izzy and her friends from the hospital. Christmas had always been such a joyful time in the past. They stayed in their small room on Christmas Day and ate chops out of a tin, warmed up in a pan on the one hotplate. Neither felt motivated to explore their new surroundings but sat huddled together on the small settee with their books and a new game of Scrabble. There was no wireless or television so Scrabble became competitive. They had the added challenge of playing with a Dutch set of letters and became adept at using the extra J's and Z's.

Extract from diary entry
The worst thing we have to deal with is the shower. This is housed on our floor in a room no bigger than a large cupboard. Underneath the primitive appliance is a large tin bath but the real problem lies in the heating of the water. This is achieved by bending down very low at floor level and putting a lighted taper to a small hole in a gas radiator. This will then explode into life when the gas is turned on and a frightening roar ensues. Ralph and I retreat to recover from the shock for several minutes until we hear the hot water gushing into the bath with a noise like hailstones on a glass roof. We have named it 'Stephenson's Rocket!' You can just about sit in the bath for a longer soak if you don't mind your knees hitting your chin. We can't get used to the "rocket" and regard the whole business as a necessary evil!

After the short holiday Ralph went back to camp each day and Charlotte emerged from her torpor. Taking down the few cards that had reached their new address, she had time to reflect. She felt lonely and useless. After years of hard but rewarding work at the hospital she was now redundant. The cards and letters from home were unsettling. They had only been away for less than three months but it seemed much longer. There was still no news of married accommodation on the camp and until then she would have to embrace Brunssum and the Vanmeers.

Brunssum was a small mining town on the borders of Germany and nearer to the camp in Geilenkirchen for Ralph. Charlotte could walk into the main street from the house and explore the many shops. The best place was the library and Charlotte was surprised and delighted to find a whole section devoted to English novels and reference books and returned home with L.P. Hartley's novel *The Go-Between*.

On Saturdays they would go into the larger towns and marvel at the huge department stores with their array of interesting goods and fine china. Buying Christmas presents for friends and family back home the previous month had been a delight. They discovered museums, art galleries and cathedrals and Roman ruins in historical Maastricht and Valkenburg. Eindhoven was home to the electrical company of Phillips and more industrial. Here they met and became friendly with Thomo and Bap and baby Margo who attended the Salvation Army there. Thomo worked at Phillips and spoke good English, giving them helpful information that made their life easier.

The slag heaps in Brunssum at the edge of the town had been cleverly disguised with grass and turned into parkland complete with chair lifts and playgrounds. There were no restaurants but the town boasted a teashop where they were tempted with fruit tarts and apple cake. Life during the winter months took on a routine that Charlotte eventually came to accept: reading, writing, sleeping and learning Dutch.

Letters from Netta were few and far between, still maintaining the emotional distance between them. Charlotte was at a loss to know how to help matters but prayed that things would get better. In the meantime she would continue to write and keep her up-to-date with their news.

Letter to Rita

Kapel Strasse 88
Brunssum
March 21st

Dear Rita
Thank you for your welcome letter. It was good to hear from you and catch up on your news. Life here is not too bad. I'm a bit stuck without transport and the language is a barrier so lots of time for reading. No, I can't paint or write because I don't feel able to concentrate on these things at the moment while in this situation and I need new paints etc. Frou V keeps her eye on me. She invites me to her sitting room for tea and cherry flan. She lets me cook and do the washing in her kitchen when she has finished and has given me her recipe for her lovely shortbread flan case.

The cherries come from her garden.

Now that the weather is better we have travelled further and made it to the coast at Scheveningen. It is a long way north beyond Rotterdam and near the Haig. We left early in the morning and got back late at night. It was lovely to walk along the seafront but there's nothing much to do there. Martha and Peter are going to take me for a scooter ride at Easter. They have become friendlier towards me. Peter is home from college and Martha is working at the bank. It seems she is jealous of me because I am married. She doesn't have a boyfriend and is much older than I am. We are going to visit her married sister who lives in Amsterdam and visit the Keukenhof, lots of flowers and bulbs. Another bit of news is that we are going to have visitors

*from Southend next month on their way to the bulb fields so
things are looking up.*

*No sign of camp life yet! A bit ironic as Ralph is in charge
of the admin!*

All for now. Love to David and hope his cold is better soon.

Love Charlotte.

One warm April day Martha kept her promise to take Charlotte
out into the countryside. They packed a picnic and Charlotte
was invited to sit behind Peter on his scooter as Martha's friend
Helene came along too. They went some kilometres into the
country, with Charlotte both thrilled and scared at the same
time by the speed and the new experience of riding pillion and
holding onto a comparative stranger. They picnicked and
gathered grasses and wild flowers where they stopped. The sun
was warm and Charlotte felt the long months of lonely winter
melt away into the blue sky above, filling her heart with hope
for the future.

Two further events were to brighten Charlotte's life in the
following months, outlined in her diary entries.

Extracts from Diary entries: May 1st
Frau V has been very keen to take us to the
Keukenhof near Amsterdam. She is arranging for us
to stay with her married daughter and family. She says
that we will have to be up early, by 6am on the
following day, to get there before all the coaches as it
is a very popular attraction, especially at the weekend.
It will also be a chance for her to see her daughter and
grandchildren as it is not easy for her to get to
Amsterdam by public transport. I hope she can fit
into our rather small car!

May 4th

We arrived safely (with Frau V in the front seat) and were warmly welcomed by Greta and Jan. They had three children, one of whom was deaf and dumb, a little girl of seven or eight years old. I was horrified to see Greta smack her daughter at table because she was not conforming like the others. She began to cry. My disapproval registered and I was told that if Heidi was not trained in table manners, no one would want her and she would never be invited anywhere. I was suitably chastised but it clouded my judgement of her mother but who was I to judge? It must be hard for both of them. Surely it's bad enough being deaf and dumb without being physically abused?

May 5th

We said our goodbyes and thanked them as we set off after an early breakfast for the Keukenhof. I was still worrying about Heidi and what sort of life lay ahead of her but the breathtaking sights of the erupting colourful blooms of the Keukenhof swept all other thoughts away. The early morning was dew-laden and shafts of sunlight pierced the trees and lit the woodland path that led through a sea of blue forget-me-nots and red tulips. The pale green of the spring-dressed trees mitigated the garish colours as each new path displayed a different planting. The soft green foliage was punctuated with snowy blossoms of Japanese cherry and the bright colours of Azalea and rhododendron. All a stunning painting that could not be replicated on canvas. Frou V said that the garden traced its roots back to a 15th-century herb garden of Jacoba of Bavaria. There were ornamental ponds and cascades and many kilometres of pathways. It was truly amazing and I was most grateful to her for showing us this Dutch delight. On the way back we passed field upon field of tulips, all shades and colours as far as the eye could see. We found an eating place on the way home and treated our kind landlady to dinner. I can't wait to tell Annie all about it when she arrives next week.

According to Charlotte's autobiographical notes, Annie Barnsley had played an important part in her life from the very beginning. Annie had nursed her as a baby at Bourne Lodge under Netta's matronly watchful eye, and it was Annie who had comforted her and given her extra feeds after discovering the threat to her young life by her sick mother.

Charlotte had always felt close to Annie although she was to move with Netta to Ingatestone, but she had kept in touch and her visits during those years were greatly anticipated. Annie was younger than Netta and her love for Charlotte was less intense and unconditional. Netta still held on to Victorian values and ideals, whereas Annie was more liberated, fun and down to earth. Charlotte would stay with her at her Southend home for holidays and learn to swim in the muddy waters of the Thames estuary.

Now in her late fifties and due to retire from the Salvation Army head office in London where she had worked for many years since the close of Bourne Lodge, Annie was on holiday with her friend May. They too were coming to see the bulb fields and Charlotte was overjoyed at the prospect of their visit.

It has been a wonderful day. I do wish they could have stayed longer. I have so missed seeing Annie. The last time was at our wedding and it was difficult to talk with so many people. Today we had so much to catch up on!

We went into town for tea and an array of pastries and fruit flans. My Dutch was misinterpreted and instead of three slices they brought the whole tart cut into three! We laughed like anything but we managed to eat it! Annie told me that Netta and Izzy were house-hunting in the Southend area as Netta wants to be nearer Annie and Southend has a good Army Citadel. Annie is going to retire soon and they will see more of each other. She suggested that I come over for my twenty-first birthday in December. I could fly from Brussels to Rochford, a little airport on the edge of Southend. I said I thought it a great idea and would discuss it with Ralph when he came home that evening. After a walk round the park in Brunssum they left for their hotel. I told them how much we had enjoyed the Keukenhof and bulb fields and hoped they would too.

Then Ralph came home with a crew cut and some great news. 'Next year,' he said, 'they can stay with us in Cologne where we'll have lots of room!' It seems that we have our marching orders! Cologne sounds very grand!

CHAPTER SEVEN

KÖLN: GERMANY'S FINEST CITY

R.A.F. Geilenkirchen was a base for fighter pilots but the accommodation on the camp was insufficient for the number of personnel so the British Forces requisitioned an area fifty kilometres away in a suburb of Cologne. After the war the German control commission built an estate of houses in this suburb called the "Volkespark" with a view to turning them into flats for local people after the departure of the British. The houses were large and unattractive and available to British officers, civilians, Ministry of Defence officials and others. On the estate was a NAFFI shop, Astra Cinema, surgery, primary school and bookshop. The R.A.F. contingent generally formed a close-knit community, the men bound for Geilenkirchen boarding a military bus to take them to the base each day. It was a bumpy journey some of the time and took two hours before the autobahn was built years later.

Ralph and Charlotte moved into Number Three Grossrotter Weg on the 30th May. They ran from room to room exclaiming at both light and space. The rooms were furnished with utility furniture, the austerity of which failed to dampen their spirits. There were four large bedrooms, one with a balcony over the garage, two bathrooms, a large sitting room, dining room, kitchen and study. To their amazement a door in the hall led down into a cellar that ran the whole length and width of the house. There were six rooms in all, one of which housed the most enormous solid fuel boiler they had ever seen. They christened it "Mephystoffles".

Diary entries: 7th June
I'm so happy! Things are so much better now that we can be a real married couple in our own space. Last night we had great fun chasing each other naked all round the house before he caught me on the floor of the landing. It's so wonderful to be free of restraints and to make love where and when we please. Ralph has bought a huge German telefunken wireless from the NAFFI. I have so missed a radio! It has buttons to press and a beautiful polished walnut surround. We can have music turned up really loudly and can't wait for family favourites on Sunday and the funny thing is our neighbour is a BFPO forces presenter.

We have acquired two cats from the previous occupants. One is a tabby called Leo and the other smaller black one is Patty. They eye us suspiciously from different corners of the house but I think we'll soon make friends and they'll be company when Ralph's away. We have quite a big garden here but not much colour.

21st June
We have been here three weeks now and so much has happened. Ralph has bought a new car, a Renault Dauphine, white with a blue roof. He says they're cheaper over here as you don't have to pay tax. I was sorry to see our little car go and it seems no time since we bought it although it was second-hand. The new

one seems such an extravagance and will be on HP for ages.

I'm a little in awe of my batwoman. She comes once a week and I find myself cleaning the house before she arrives. She is a young German girl called Gunta who neither smiles nor speaks. I usually give her the ironing. This she does in the study. "Otto" as we have named him, goes up and down the outside cellar steps to feed "Mephistopheles" with an enormous shovel. The "fiery furnace" is nearly as tall as I am! It will be wonderful in the winter as it gets very cold here we are told. We have bought a table-tennis set and enjoy playing on the enormous dining table. Leo and Patty go mad chasing the high bouncing balls.

I'm not looking forward to the officers' summer ball next month. I don't know what to wear and I'll be so nervous. It was bad enough meeting the CO's wife at her welcome coffee morning on the camp. I nearly died when she asked me how long we had been married. She said 'Oh a new bride' and all the other wives laughed. I was by far the youngest there. Tomorrow Monica and I are going to the hairdressers in town. I hope I can make them understand what I want them to do! German is a whole new word game!

Charlotte had made friends with her neighbours in the next cul-de-sac. Their gardens backed on to one another. Monica Wiltshire's husband was in the supplies and equipment office and the Rileys were in education. Mrs Riley offered to help Charlotte with her washing as she had her own twin-tub washing machine but was alarmed at the amount of soap powder Charlotte used and watched in horror as an avalanche of foam filled her kitchen.

Charlotte had a lot to learn. Most of the wives were older than her and kindly people. Ralph invited a couple from his unit to dinner and she cooked her first roast chicken, proudly presenting it to her guests breast side down. There was much amusement but Charlotte took it in good part. They told her that a colonial wife they knew cooked one with the giblets still inside which provoked more good humour.

Monica, a rotund woman in her forties, was very down to earth and had been there for two years and showed her the ropes. They went into town on the tram, shopped locally for fresh produce and went to the hairdressers together. Charlotte was invited to many coffee mornings to meet all the wives and she herself found the courage to bake scones and cakes for her own coffee mornings. Ralph announced that they must have a "moving in" party and although ignorant of alcohol apart from cider, brought home wine and spirits from the NAFFI. They both felt quite brazen as they were teetotallers and had no idea of measures. As a result the party went with a swing with everyone having a very good time as Ralph was more than generous with the drink.

All too soon the ball beckoned and Charlotte wrote to Rita for advice.

30 Rose Hill
Hampstead
NW11

Dear Charlotte,
It was good to hear that you are enjoying life in Cologne and a new car too! You sound much happier and yes we would love to come and visit but this may be next year as we have a holiday already booked in Brittany next month.
About your dress for the ball, I suggest that you wear your

wedding dress but dye it, along with your gloves and satin shoes, a pretty pastel colour. Your dress is very pretty and not too long and it's a shame not to wear it again. Do write and tell me how it goes. I suppose Ralph will be in mess dress. It all sounds very elegant.

Linda is coming to stay next week. She is seventeen now and wanting to make trips to London before going to train in Oxford as a therapist. She asks after you. Annette is thirteen and you will be twenty-one in December. Have you any plans? In my next letter I'll tell you about your inheritance and I'll need your bank details.

David is busy at the bank but we have complimentary tickets for the Leicester Square Odeon tonight. There are some advantages to managing the bank next door. Last week he met Lana Turner. It was supposed to be the highlight of his day and he had his hair cut specially. She is one of his clients but he was most disappointed when she opened the door herself wearing curlers and a housecoat! Not the glamorous film star he was expecting! I have lots of matches at the moment and hope to win the county trophy with my doubles partner. Lots of beans coming on the allotment. Do you get good fruit and veg? Must get changed.

Love from us both, Rita

Charlotte's letters to Netta were difficult to write. The underlying message of despair and accusation always seemed to be lurking beneath the banalities of everyday occurrences in the news from Ilford. Yes, they were still looking for houses in Southend now that Charlotte no longer needed her and yes she would be welcome to spend her birthday with them if all went well with the move. There was no mention of Ralph in her letters or interest in their new surroundings. Comforted by the prospect of making things right in December, Charlotte set her face to the ball.

Diary entry 25th July

I learnt something about Ralph last night that left me feeling worthless. He knew how nervous I was about meeting new people or camp protocol. Many of our Volkespark friends would not be there. I know I'm useless at these occasions and hope to improve but they all seemed rather grand and resplendent in their mess uniforms and ball gowns. I wasn't able to dye my dress and it stuck out like a sore thumb. The CO and his wife were at the door of the marquee greeting everyone and I didn't know whether to shake hands or curtsy. I begged Ralph not to leave me until I felt more confident and to introduce me to people he knew on the camp but he went off at the first opportunity without doing so. The young pilots swarmed round me and laughed when I asked for cola. They laughed some more when, in my confusion, I took some nuts, still wearing my long gloves. The older wives stood together and watched, their eyes on my dress. I just wanted to disappear. I hardly saw Ralph the whole evening. It seemed to go on forever. All he said when we got back was, 'You'll get used to it.'

It should have been a wonderful occasion. There was a good band playing and plenty of food and dancing but I didn't seem to be part of it. It was like watching it all through a prison grill. I was bound by my own inhibitions and ignorance. Perhaps one day I'll break out and then I'll find out who I really am. Who was my mother? What genes are yet to be unleashed? Was she shy and timid and full of self-doubt like me? Or was she a femme fatale? How will I ever know?

According to Charlotte's writings the months went by and there was plenty to see and do. She wrote of Germany's rebuilding of her war-torn towns and cities by sheer hard work and determination. The famous gothic structure of the Kölner Dom, or Cologne Cathedral, was untouched by the bombs and so big that Charlotte found it dark and gloomy in spite of the impressive 14th-century stained-glass window, the massive oak stalls built in 1308 (the largest made in Germany), and the altar. This one corner alone was bright with candles.

There were many Romanesque churches, historic buildings, galleries and museums to explore and write about but Charlotte's favourite place was the Kaufhof, a huge departmental store in the Hoe Strasse. Here she would browse happily, spending little money but savouring tea and *schokolade kuchen* along with Fraus in hats in the beautiful ornate restaurant. Occasionally there would be a fashion show and the first time Charlotte was present, she was quite embarrassed to find that she had walked through the middle of one on her way to a table without realising what was going on.

At weekends Ralph would drive them to various places: Bonn, where they visited Beethoven's birthplace, and all the enchanting towns along the Rhine Valley. They marvelled at the meeting of the Rhine and the Mosel at Deutsches Eck, the Loreley (the rock that caused sailors to drown in the strong currents and inspired poetic writings about sirens), and the many fairytale schloss that could be seen along the top of the vine-covered hills. Charlotte wrote, 'It is such a beautiful country and hard to imagine such beauty jeopardised by war.'

In September they went with two other people from the camp on a trip to Lake Leman, driving down through the Black Forrest and on into Switzerland. Again Charlotte marvelled at the wonderful scenery, yodelled to a surprised cow on a mountainside and luxuriated in her first experience of a smart hotel by the lake. Standing up to their knees in the water was very cold but they enjoyed tickling the small fish with their hands as they swam by in shoals, brushing their legs as they went. It was a short break with the two men sharing the driving and enjoyed by everyone.

All too soon the nights drew in and the weather became colder. Otto was kept busy and the large house was permanently warm as a result of his efforts. Charlotte took to painting with her new paints from the Kaufhof, inspired by the scenes still fresh in her mind from their travels.

November came and it was time to plan her trip home. A letter from Netta a month before had told her of their move to Tintern Avenue in Southend and that they were up to their eyes in boxes. Rita had also written and reminded her of the inheritance left by her Grandmother that would soon be coming her way. Charlotte was not mercenary and the thought of any money at all alarmed her but she felt excited at the prospect of having money of her own. However, because she had always had so little in her life, she was afraid that she might not spend it wisely and was unaware how much she would inherit. Should she open her own bank account? Since she had been married, Ralph had been in charge of finances. He said that they had a joint account. Charlotte had been happy with this and content with her housekeeping allowance.

When she was young her grandparents had despaired of her lack of ability to save her holiday pocket money and told her 'You don't know the value of money.' At school, her shilling a week left nothing for savings. She recalled a shameful incident when she was twelve and invited to a friend's home for half-term. Jose showed her the contents of her money box. 'Shall we spend it?' she asked Charlotte. Charlotte made no comment. There were two half crowns and they took one each and spent them on trinkets in Woolworths. Jose's mother was outraged and made them take the things back and Charlotte was left with a curious sense of somehow being responsible for their childish prank.

Netta had saved up the pocket money over the years, given to Charlotte by kind well-wishers at Christmas and holidays, but confessed to having spent it, when Charlotte began nursing and had asked for the money. When she was nursing her net wage had been four pounds a week after deductions for board and lodging in the nurses' home. There was little left for saving and she remembered rashly buying Ralph some gold cufflinks to mark their engagement. They had cost her four pounds but she was thrilled with the pleasure they had given him. She had tried to help Netta out when she could and the rest she spent on new stockings, shoe repairs and writing paper

It never occurred to her to keep the knowledge of the money from Ralph. She had forgotten that Netta had already spoken of it to him as a strong possibility, before they were married. As far as Charlotte was concerned, what was hers was his also as that was what marriage was all about.

In December Ralph booked her train ticket to Brussels and her flight to Southend. Both Netta and Annie had confirmed her expected arrival and Annie would meet her at the airport.

Diary extracts; Tuesday
I am sitting in the Trans-European Express. This is a wonderful train that starts in Frankfurt and travels across two borders to Brussels. It is four o'clock and the little shaded lights give a warm and comforting glow together with the softness of the velour curtains at the windows. The doors between the compartments are electronic and open by themselves. It is quite a wonder. I will not have time to visit the dining car which I'm sure must be quite splendid but expensive. The train glides along and you hardly know that you

are moving! I'm already feeling nervous about the flight but will pray for courage. Ralph says that Bristol Freighters are very safe and don't retract their wheels but I'm not sure how this helps. I wish he could be with me. I'm feeling so apprehensive about everything. I don't know how Netta will receive me. She seems so distant in her letters.

Ralph had told her that he was too busy to spare the time to go with her and that it would be an added expense. Charlotte had wondered privately whether it was because he would not have been welcomed in Netta's house. He had kissed her 'Goodbye' and reassured her that he would be at Cologne Station to meet her on her return. Telephoning was not an option as neither would be within easy reach of one so they would be out of touch for four days.

Wednesday
I am in the front bedroom of the house in Tintern Avenue. It is dark, gloomy and cold. There is a paraffin stove that I must light when I have the courage to get out of bed. I couldn't sleep last night with the events of the day still scuttling across my brain. The taxi to the airport frightened the life out of me. The driver went so fast in the dark and didn't speak a word of English. The phrase 'white slave traffic' came into my head (one of Netta's warnings) and my heart was in my mouth. The plane was small and noisy. It was funny to see its gaping jaws swallowing cars as they drove inside before it took off. Annie met me on my arrival and I hugged her to death. We took the bus from Rochford to Southend where Netta and Izzy awaited us. After a hasty meal Annie left and said that she would be at the

airport on Friday as she was working all week. I was sorry to see her go.

Netta had not greeted me like a prodigal daughter. Her face was lined and worn and the light had gone out of her eyes. The move alone had taken its toll. I felt that I was being a burden and had interrupted their daily routine. Izzy had smiled warmly and seemed genuinely pleased to see me. The house was smaller and packed with their shabby furniture and threadbare carpets; Victorian jardinieres with drooping fronds in scenic painted pots lurk in every corner and there is a "commode" in my bedroom. I missed Ralph's warm body and felt guilty that I had so much in the way of comfort back in Germany. Must get up and face the bathroom. It is so easy to forget the hardships of no central heating!

Thursday

Today was my birthday! Among my cards, readdressed from Ilford, was one from Mrs Lytton, my mother's sister, but this time there was no address. I was quite mystified but didn't mention this to Netta in case it upset her. My cheque also arrived with a card from Rita and David. 1200 pounds! I'm over the moon! It was awarded in court apparently, after my grandmother died. I have decided to give Netta enough to pay for the installation of a lav downstairs as this will benefit her and Izzy greatly. She seemed almost humble in her acceptance. I'm glad she was not too proud to take the gift. I shall give Annie fifty pounds for herself as a token of my love. I was touched that Netta made me a birthday cake, although the thick blue icing was a little daunting. I think she used semolina and almond essence instead of ground almonds but I appreciated the effort. They gave me a fountain pen as they know how much I enjoy writing. I hope they like the Christmas presents I brought with me. I wonder if I will hear again from Natalie Lytton? Home tomorrow and I can't wait! They say there may be fog at the airport.

There was fog at the airport and Charlotte and Annie paced the floor of the small lounge; Charlotte in a state of great agitation as the flights were delayed by some hours and she was unable to contact Ralph. Finally after another bear hug and promises to write, they parted and Charlotte took off for Brussels. She missed her fast train and made do with the first available bound for Cologne. As a result, Ralph missed her at the station and she took another terrifyingly fast taxi ride over cobbled streets, only to find the house in darkness. She stood on the doorstep, crying with a mixture of relief at being home and frustration that she was unable to gain access. She was on the point of going to a neighbour for help when Ralph drove up and crossly demanded to know where she had been. It was not the warm, loving homecoming that Charlotte had been expecting.

Christmas arrived and another round of cocktail parties and seasonal celebrations began. Charlotte had delighted in the pretty decorated German shops, filled with traditional fare and had bought coloured lights and trinkets for their first Christmas tree. The New Year was followed by long dreary winter months punctuated by occasional bright spots: meals out in Cologne restaurants with friends, a concert or two and visits to galleries and places of interest. Slowly spring raised her head and sprouting bulbs emerged from the frozen ground. Charlotte too emerged from a depression that seemed to have engulfed her since the New Year. Her feelings of worthlessness had returned and the long days of inactivity had made her feel guilty after the sweat and tears of her hospital days. Her life seemed empty and false but all that changed when new people moved into the house opposite at Easter time. Ralph introduced them as Roy and Stella Lovett. Roy was the new dentist on the camp and a national service man. He wore his cap on the back of his head and had little time for airforce protocol. Stella, slightly older than Charlotte, was smart, lively and intelligent and they were all to become firm friends. Suddenly life for Charlotte became a lot sweeter as she had found someone she could trust and talk to. Both Stella and Roy shared their Christian faith, and as Charlotte put it, 'spoke the same language'.

Diary entry; Easter Monday
Had dinner with the Lovetts last night. We played scrabble and a noisy game called "Pit". Stella is a very good photographer and took a photo of the four of us by setting it on a "timer" and running into the picture. We all laughed like anything when the flash went off by itself. Back in England Stella develops her colour slides herself and projects them on a screen. That's really clever! Our camera is not nearly so sophisticated. Perhaps one day I'll have a dark room where I can print in black and white the way I used to back in school with Mrs McLeash. It was so exciting to see the image slowly emerge on the bromide paper and know the right moment to remove it from the developing fluid. Stella has a science degree. She is going to collect their new car from Dortmund tomorrow and Roy and Ralph will go back to camp. Must write some letters and clean the house ready for Gunta.

The weather improved and the markets became livelier with winter fare giving way to salads and fruit as the months went by. Rita and David were expected in late June and Charlotte counted the days to their arrival. All was made ready in the guest room and special menus prepared. Charlotte had become a competent *haus frau* and was no longer the novice of the year before.

Her aunt and uncle arrived in a new red Austin Mini. David said that they were the latest trendiest car in the UK. Ralph told him that he was in the process of negotiating an exchange on the Dauphine for a Ford Cortina. He explained that he would have to keep the car a year in Germany before taking it home at the end of his time or tax would be levied. Charlotte had privately thought the expense of the new car was an unnecessary extravagance as the Dauphine was just over a year old. After staying with the couple for a few days, Rita being impressed with Charlotte's home management, and the shops in Cologne, they set off for the South of France. Ralph had been due two weeks' leave and it occurred to him, after hearing of David's plans, they could follow down a week later. It would be an exciting trip in the new car and they could travel in comfort. The Cortina was white with a Narvik red flash down each side and a bench seat in the front.

After scurrying round for holiday clothes and a jerry can for extra cheap petrol, they set off a week later. It was to become a journey to remember with many interesting places on the way. Charlotte wrote of Baden Baden:

We have travelled down through the Black Forest to this charming spa in Karlsruhe. The Romans discovered the mineral springs here and there are baths called Friedrichsbad. Ralph says that the H.Q. of the French forces in Germany moved here after the war and then the Canadian Air Force was based here after they built a runway. I hope we can come back again as there is so much history here and so much to see we would need a week!

They drove to the French border town of Strasbourg and had time to visit the famous gothic cathedral with its amazing astronomical clock. Then on to Switzerland where they spent their first night, tucked up under enormous duvets that were quite a novelty and hardly needed in July. Ralph had found it hard driving through Basel with trams coming at them from, seemingly, all directions. The following day they moved on, taking the route down to Grenoble, where they stopped for a second night. Charlotte was able to practice her French and admired the bright cleanliness of this *ville* situated at the foot of the French Alps.

The final part of the journey was the best with the most hair-raising bends of all as they went over the Alps and finally down onto the Grand Corniche where the sea sparkled below and they were nearing their destination. They drove along the coast road towards St Maxime and saw a little red mini pull out in front of them. They waved furiously as Rita and David stopped at a restaurant, unaware that the couple had followed them down to France. Ralph took David's advice and booked into the same small hotel, Raphaella. Sadly for them, they had to say goodbye, as Rita and David were setting off back to England the following day.

Diary extract
Another lazy day in the sun! Ralph got burnt yesterday so he's taking care today. He likes my new blue and white striped bikini but I feel a bit self-conscious wearing so little. It accentuates my already large bust

and the French keep smiling at me. We have hired a sunlounger and umbrella and I'm sipping a lemon presse!

I am reminded of my first visit here on the Riviera with Michelle three years ago! So much has happened since then. St Maxime is a small fishing town quite a way from Vence where we stayed before but close to St Tropez. They were filming there yesterday. I just love the whole of the French Riviera and we have driven all along the coast road to Monaco. There are surprisingly few people staying here in our hotel and the beaches are not crowded. I have been swimming everyday. The Med is so warm!

I am reading *Tender Is the Night* by Scott Fitzgerald. He's such a romantic writer!

The holiday finally came to an end and the couple made their way back over the Alps into Switzerland and on into Germany. Ralph had run out of money and once they reached the German border they were forced to spend the night in the car. It had been a long stint and Charlotte had complained of travel sickness over the Alps and was still feeling groggy. Ralph had pressed on, conscious of the need to get home as soon as possible as he was due back at the camp in twenty-four hours.

Before leaving for the holiday, he had applied to stay on in the Air Force as a regular officer as his posting and present commission were both finishing in April. He had reservations as to whether he would be successful in advancing his career as he himself admitted that although he had been praised recently for his cornet solo at the funeral of a young pilot, he was probably 'not of the right social calibre' expected of a full-time officer: that he was not a 'yes' man and 'did not prop up the bar' as he put it. He had crossed swords with his

commanding officer by omitting to attend a particular function
that had not been mandatory but had caused a raised eyebrow.
However, he thought it worth a try as the money and perks
were good and he had been in the R.A.F. since he left school
as a boy entrant. What would he do otherwise?

On her return from their holiday Charlotte had presented
her slim, tanned body to the doctor who pronounced her very
fit, healthy and pregnant.

Diary entry July
I haven't told Ralph yet as he's away on cipher duty this
weekend so I'm still hugging my scary secret to myself.
I want to be sure in my own mind that I'm ready for
this life-changing event. When we decided to go ahead
and start a family I thought it would take ages or maybe
not at all like poor Rita! Suddenly though I feel I have
a purpose: that I'll no longer be at odds with my
nagging conscience, telling me I'm wasting my time in
this synthetic but pleasurable bubble of an existence. A
baby! A new life given to us to take care of to the best
of our ability. Am I capable of what's expected of me?
Am I worthy of God's great gift? Will Ralph be the
wonderful father to him that I never had and would my
mother have welcomed my news? I wish I knew the
answers, but I'll know one day. Until then I'll do what
I can.

Ralph was quite delighted and hoped for a girl as there were
none in his family. Then he showed his pleasure at her news
by taking her out for a grand meal after buying her a new dress
and shoes. 'You'll be the belle of the ball next month,' he told
Charlotte and sure enough she attended the function with a
quiet confidence and a bloom on her skin. The new Grecian

style dress showed off her tan and she was able to take part without her usual reticence.

In September Bruce and Jean wrote to them from Chigwell.

10, Schoolhouse Rd
Chigwell
Essex
September 3rd

My Dears,

Glad to hear you are both well. Mother and I will soon be on the move now that I'm retired and can no longer afford the rent on this house, so the Army are moving us to an upstairs flat in Leytonstone. It has a large sitting room, one bedroom, a small kitchen and extra room that will be my study. I am still writing music and have made enquiries of local schools that would like brass band tuition so I'll not be idle!

Mother keeps well despite her disability and is thrilled at the prospect of another grandchild, as are myself, Eddie and Pam. They send their love. Colin had his thirteenth birthday last week so we went over to Horley to see them all. Are you coming home in April? What are your plans and where will you stay if you're not kept on?

We had a great concert with the staff band at the Regent's Hall last night. The place was packed. Did Charlotte know that the Priors are going to America now that they're both commissioned? They asked after you both.

Must get to the post. Will send the new address.

Love from us both. Dad

During the latter part of the summer and the following autumn they were busy with visiting friends but no relatives came.

Annie and May arrived in late September and stayed for several days. They enjoyed the sights that Cologne had to offer, including a tour of the cathedral, a trip down the Rhine on a pleasure boat, and a ride in a cable car, which caused much excitement, over the big river to the park on the other side where flimsy chair lifts awaited them for their further enjoyment. Charlotte savoured every minute of their stay but others soon arrived to take their place.

Each month she attended her anti-natal clinics in the R.A.F. hospital in the small town of Wegberg, fifty kilometres away. The pregnant women from the Volkespark would pile into a military van that bounced over the cobbles driven by a German civilian with little thought for his cargo. The women would hold on tightly and hope that their babes would do the same.

Christmas that year was a happy one. Ralph and Charlotte were well established with their friends in the Volkespark. They spent Christmas Day with the Lovetts and Boxing Day with the Wiltshires. Cards from home had expressed joy at the prospect of a new baby in February. Netta herself had written to wish her well and had reiterated the news that Graham and Jill had indeed left to do God's work in America now that they were both commissioned officers in the Salvation Army.

Netta was very proud of her nephew and Charlotte felt she had let Netta down by not following suit. There was no card from Mrs Lytton. Charlotte resolved to look into her address when she returned to the UK.

Diary entry 1ˢᵗ January 1961
Ralph and I didn't go to the Fitzpatricks' New Year's Eve party but offered to babysit for the Johnsons instead. They have such an adorable baby, just eight months. Malcolm is a flyer and Ginny has so much style! They are both tall and dark and come from the

Channel Islands. Ginny has been such a help, taking me through all the things I'm going to need. Only another six weeks! I'm getting quite big now and bored with wearing the same two outfits, though German maternity wear is quite chic compared with what I've seen in the British magazines. I feel quite smart and proud of my bump but long for my slacks! I love watching my tum move about in the bath and hope he'll be a swimmer like me when he's old enough!

Charlotte was sure it would be a boy. She had decided long ago when still a child that, as she was denied the privileges and opportunities afforded to the male sex and was discouraged from horseplay and exciting adventurous aspirations, she would have to do the next best thing and give birth to one when she grew up, like Mary, in the Bible. Had Netta not told her, when she was older, that had she been born a boy, her grandparents might have made allowances and forgiven their son's indiscretion?

January and February were very cold months and Charlotte kept her outings to a minimum. Ralph went off early each morning in the camp bus, which was occasionally held up by snow, and arrived back late. He had received an official letter from Command informing him that he had not been successful in prolonging his service career with the Royal Air Force; that he would be leaving Germany mid-April and that his boxes were to be packed for sea transport by 1st March. He was given instructions where to report when arriving back in the UK. He was to keep his uniform and great coat in case he was called up as a reserve for a period of time. He decided to ask his brother if the crates could be sent to his address in Horley as his parents were no longer in a position to help. They contained several small items of furniture, a large rug, and some crockery and glassware that the couple had accumulated for their future home. Charlotte's baby was due mid-February but alarm bells rang a week ahead of time.

Diary entry February
I feel such a fraud. Two days ago I thought the baby was starting. I had an enormous urge to scrub the kitchen floor even tho' it was spotless. In the evening I felt several contractions and Ralph drove me to the hospital tout suite! The following evening he arrived clutching flowers and chocolates and smiling with anticipation only to be told that he was to take me home as it was a false start. We drove home in silence and the hour-long journey seemed more like two. I feel so depressed.

Things did not go well for her from then on. A week later Ralph drove her back to the hospital and this time Charlotte had more definite signs of labour. These went on for a further forty-eight hours. The doctor in charge decided that the head was engaged but not moving and that forceps would be needed to assist the delivery. Charlotte was anaesthetised at 1am and although unaware of his birth, her son arrived half an hour later weighing 9lbs.

She wrote afterwards that her first feeling towards him was one of remoteness, that this baby could belong to anyone; that she had not in fact given birth to him at all. They had not bonded. Her distress was compounded by a high fever and infection due to the length of time the baby had lain in the birth canal. Ralph visited dutifully but it was a week before he brought them both home and several more weeks before Charlotte recovered her strength. She was pale and listless but able to breastfeed and care for the baby. In the meantime, Ralph assembled their possessions to be crated and the house took on the utilitarian aspect that had first greeted them. Charlotte was too preoccupied to care and had no thoughts about the future as to where they would go or what their lives would hold. Perhaps she had a premonition as to what lay ahead in the years to come, but until then she would let Ralph make all the decisions.

Diary entry March
I have not written in my diary since Jay Lawrence was born. I feed him, bath and bed him. He makes no demands on me apart from his night feeds that leave me drained of all substance and emotion. He rarely cries. It's as though he knows I am devoid of feeling and that if he lies low and makes himself amenable, I will love him in time. I could not have a more angelic child so I feel like a monster and pray to God that this depression will leave me soon. Ralph is busy arranging things and has little time for sickness or sentiment. We will be leaving here in three weeks. Stella is coming over to take some photos of Jay tomorrow. I have not confided in her. I feel too ashamed of my weakness and just want to hide myself away.

Finally they packed up the Cortina and with Jay asleep in his carry-cot in the back, set off for England and Ralph's brother's where they would stay and recover for the next six weeks.

CHAPTER EIGHT

OH, TO BE IN ENGLAND!

The frailty of the more sensitive orphan can be heightened by familiar routines altering, or key figures in their lives no longer being around. Institutional life in the early years, however strictly imposed, creates the missing parent. On another level, the hospital demands upon the student nurse offers a more lenient approach and time spent in the armed services could be considered the most indulgent of the three but all are instrumental in giving a sense of security and discipline that brings comfort. At the same time, they seek approval and have a strong urge to strive and excel, which many of them do.

The Fire and the Phoenix

Charlotte found herself, now aged twenty-two, on the brink of going it alone. Most of her life had been spent surrounded by other people: boarding school and a nurses' home environment and life in the forces. Apart from her devout faith and daily belief that God was with her, Ralph was her sole mentor and companion. She clung to him, but the years ahead were not to be easy ones.

It was three months before the Fieldings were finally settled in their newly built bungalow. It was situated in Swavesey, a village on the perimeter of Cambridge, where Ralph was newly appointed personnel manager to an electronic firm in the town. They had spent a pleasant time with his brother on their return to England and then moved on to the suburb where Rita and David lodged them for a further six weeks – a more trying time as both Rita and David still felt that Ralph was inferior in some way and they maintained a formal politeness that was intimidating. The couple visited Ralph's parents during their stay and approved the new flat in Leytonstone, and Charlotte spent a few days with Netta and Izzy. Everyone had enthused over Jay who remained calm and content most of the time, waving his small hands and smiling broadly but once again Netta had remained distant in her attitude to both of them. Charlotte's health had improved but she was not keen to move so far away from the people she loved, now that she had Jay. She wrote of the bungalow and their new life in a letter to Rita.

Raphaella,
Longstanton Road
Swavesey
Cambs.
July 28th

Dear Rita,
As you see we have named the bungalow "Raphaella" after our lovely holiday in France. There are six new bungalows here with very long front and back gardens all full of rubble and waiting to be cleared. The cesspit is in the back garden and we have to pump it by hand every now and then to get the stuff moving! The landscape is flat and there are few shops. It all feels quite desolate compared with the Garden Suburb.
The new pram is lovely and Jay can now sit up and take notice as I push him half a mile to the doctor, who lives in a

beautiful old house at the other end of this sprawling place. Ralph's brother and family are all coming up to give us a hand with the front garden. We will need pounds of grass seed but first we must clear the ground of bricks. It is also very dry here at the moment.

I have made friends with the neighbours across the road. They have a baby boy the same age as Jay and a daughter of three. They have a phone and I'll give you their number for emergencies. We can't afford one or a washing machine but we have bought a small fridge! We have some lovely furniture in the large sitting room and a blue fitted carpet. I like going into Cambridge with Ralph as it is a beautiful town but I can't drive there because I haven't been behind a wheel for three years and I need to pass my test. Ralph has been giving me lessons but won't let me drive in town because of the traffic! How am I supposed to learn?

Time to get Jay's lunch. He eats everything! Please write soon!

Love
Charlotte.

After the novelty of furnishing their new home and acquainting themselves with their unfamiliar surroundings, they settled into a routine: Ralph going off each morning and Charlotte filling her long day with fruitless cleaning of their already spotless bungalow and taking Jay for walks. She busied herself in the evenings with sewing and knitting and listening to the wireless. Since the birth of Jay all creativity appeared to desert her, although she tried sketching him in charcoal but her efforts were poor and she gave up.

Rita and David came to visit after the Fieldings and already new grass was appearing in the front garden. Later in the year the Lovetts dropped in for a brief stay on their way to

Cambridge, giving them news of the Volkespark and coloured slides of Jay taken in April. They would be going back to Germany for another year before coming home to England for good.

Autumn gave way to winter and Christmas was spent playing with Jay and his new toys but January brought a bleakness to Charlotte which she recorded in her diary.

Diary entry 1st January 1962
I have decided to keep a diary this year although there is little to write about. It is freezing cold here and poor little Jay had blue hands this morning when I woke him but he seems happy enough. The sewage pump is frozen and there is ice inside the windowpanes. The nappies were like cardboard on the line yesterday and Ralph had a job to start the car. I hate this place. It's Godforsaken and there's little cheer. A letter from Izzy has told me that Netta is ill and may go into hospital. I'm counting on Ralph to take me to see her in the next week or two. I feel so wretched. I've done so little for her these last three years and now it's too late to make up the time lost. I need to ask for her forgiveness. She has only seen Jay once, when he was two months old. He will be a year old in February. I must take him to see her. He is such a beautiful baby. Netta gave me so much love and had such high hopes for me but surely he is enough to melt the hardest heart?

During the next few months, big changes affected the Fieldings. Ralph had been job seeking back in London and had accepted a post in North London. He then began to commute, staying with his parents during the week, whilst Charlotte was in Swavesey with the bungalow on the market.

It was during this time that Charlotte received a phone call via her neighbour.

Diary entry Monday March 14th
Netta died today. I am numb with grief and guilt. How selfish we are when we're young. I have had so much time to think about her, since coming to live here but I've been stuck, immobilised and at a great distance. I'm so glad I made things right with her in the hospital when I last saw her. I'll go to the funeral in Southend somehow. Will things ever get better?

They were playing Mat Monroe singing "Softly, as I Leave You" this morning as Ralph left for London but he's not sentimental. He didn't hug me or kiss me. He will not share my grief and I won't see him now until Friday. I've got to wait till then. I do miss him when he's away. I hugged Jay to me instead but he started crying. I think I hugged him too tightly.

Reading through her notes things did not get better for some months to come. Charlotte attended Netta's funeral and was upset to find Izzy and her brother Gilbert laughing together at one of his jokes when she arrived at the house. Gilbert apologised and explained that funerals need not always be a solemn occasion and if you believed in the soul leaving the body then Netta was now free of pain and in a better place. The Salvation Army Hall was well attended and the band played Handel's "Largo" at Charlotte's request, knowing it was her guardian's favourite piece of music. Afterwards Charlotte was so overjoyed to see Annie, who gave her a big hug and dried her tears.

April brought warmer weather and a buyer for their bungalow. They packed up and moved down to Leytonstone with all their belongings. Bruce had organised storage for their furniture in the basement of the S.A. hall where he and Jean attended and the family moved in with Bruce and Jean for the time being. It was only meant to be a stopgap but they were still there in August.

Diary entries: May 7th
Ralph and I are at each other's throats with stress and tension. Every night we have to pull down the settee after the evening programmes have finished and make it up for our bed. Ralph is tired from commuting and I'm sure I'm pregnant although I'm only one month late. We have not had time to see the doctor. Ralph says it's no time to have a baby and it has added to his problems but I think he's pleased really. Jay is so big his feet stick out through the bars of the small cot in Bruce's study. Jean is marvellous and never complains about us being here. I try and help where I can. Bruce is out most of the day and spends most of his time teaching music in local schools.

June 20th
We are still house-hunting and I'm definitely pregnant. I'm very pleased and hope for a girl but I wish we could get settled. All the houses in the Hendon area are too expensive and a flat would mean no garden for Jay. I have gone from being totally isolated and alone to not having a minute to myself and Ralph is trying to keep all the "plates spinning". Drying nappies entails leaning out of the kitchen window and hauling on a double clothesline attached to a large tree at the end of the garden. How Jean, seventy now and crippled, manages this on her own I don't know! She does the washing in the bath and uses a rubbing board. The kitchen is tiny

and barely room for two but she makes us excellent meals. We all enjoy watching the television. This is a real treat and they have a telephone, another bonus but I don't like to use it and have no one to phone except Rita.

19a Bancroft Rd,
Leytonstone,
E11
August

Dear Rita

I am very sorry to have to tell you that I have lost my baby. I couldn't tell you on the phone. There was a sudden thunderstorm the other week and I was running home with Jay in the pushchair, trying to keep him dry. I must have run too fast. I'm deeply unhappy. Nothing seems to be going right with us.

The only good news is that Jay took his first steps in the park opposite. We were having a little picnic. I thought that he'd never walk. He's eighteen months old now but he's been talking for ages.

It will be so good to get settled. We have been looking at maisonettes in Mill Hill, so not too far from you. Housing is so expensive in London.

You would have laughed at me yesterday. Mrs F has a thing about her front door porch and step. It has to be washed nearly every day. I have been doing this for her but haven't any suitable clothes so wore Ralph's jeans! Funnily enough they gave me a great sense of freedom, as though I was no longer an old woman before my time! I felt rather modern in fact. I think Mrs F was quite shocked!

Ralph says we must sell the Cortina to release some money. Maybe we won't be able to have a car but we'll see. I failed my test in Cambridge and gave the examiner a heart attack! (Not literally!)

It's wonderful that you have joined the sailing club in Borham Wood. A reservoir is better than nothing, although I know that David used to sail on the Broads when he was young. One day I'll bring Jay along. He loves boats!

I must go. He's got hold of something in the kitchen and is banging it about! Mrs F is trying to rest!

Lots of love
Charlotte.

They finally moved into a smart estate of maisonettes in August. Lime Avenue was in Mill Hill, close to the Barnet Bypass. The rooms were upstairs, accessed by their own front door and there was a narrow strip of garden. There were two bedrooms, a small kitchen, bathroom and large sitting room. Jay's grandparents bought him the biggest cot they could find and Ralph and Charlotte bought their first small television. Charlotte was relieved to have all their familiar things about them again and to be able to put down roots at last. She still longed for a telephone and had to get out the pram each time and walk with Jay to the call box a few roads away to talk to Jean or Rita. Ralph had sold the Cortina and bought an old Morris Minor with a battered roof that could be lowered in good weather. Charlotte found the local shops and a kind elderly neighbour in the upstairs maisonette next door. She could bus to Market Place at the bottom of Rita's road and this became a real joy for the still friendless Charlotte. There were no young mothers to be seen as most of the inhabitants of the estate that she knew about were mainly elderly or out to work.

They found the S.A. Hall in Hendon and Ralph joined the band, glad to play his cornet again with the other bandsmen.

The corps officers made them welcome and Charlotte was pleased to meet other mothers with small children, and join in the rousing songs of joy and praise.

Christmas that year brought an unusual amount of snow on Boxing Day and Ralph made a wooden sledge so that Charlotte would be able to haul Jay up to the shops the following day. It was impossible to push the pram. The bad weather got much worse in January and continued until early March. It was compounded by freezing fog and ice, but by then Charlotte was pregnant again. She became more optimistic as the weather improved but Ralph was less enamoured and grumbled that it would be another mouth to feed and they were still struggling.

Jean and Bruce cheered them up by suggesting a holiday in Broadstairs from where they had recently returned. They had stayed in a boarding house run by Salvationists at a modest price and offered to subsidise the break, thinking it would help them and do them good. Charlotte was overjoyed at the thought of a holiday, as they had not been away since they left Germany. Ralph hoped that the battered old Morris would be up to the journey and worried about two-year-old Jay bouncing about in the back but Charlotte was optimistic that all would be well and that they should take up the offer.

Diary Entry: July
I feel so much better for our week away. Broadstairs is an interesting place and you could see "Bleak House" from the beach. It was wonderful to be able to paddle in the sea and breathe the lovely salt air. We have all benefited and Jay loved the waves, screaming with delight as each one chased him. It was good to see Ralph digging in the sand and wearing the boyish look

I had almost forgotten. Jay and I have a good tan and everyone was looking at us in the clinic today. I feel so fit and well and I'm four months gone now (I didn't dare swim when we were away as I wanted to keep my baby safe). Jay was wearing the little striped blazer Rita bought, and trotting along beside me, independent of my proffered hand. He is so blond with his big blue eyes and he's such a happy child. Rita says I'll never have another so good as Jay. At the weekend he surprised us both by announcing that the car in front of us had 'twin exhausts'. He was right!

Charlotte opted to have her baby at home. She had been attending anti-natal classes and had been put on a diet to keep her baby smaller than her firstborn. All appeared well and Charlotte had bloomed and blossomed throughout her happy pregnancy. October arrived and the birth was imminent. Ralph was on hand and ready to inform the midwife when the time came.

It was twenty-four hours after the first contraction that their daughter was born; but immediately after the delivery, Charlotte suffered a haemorrhage and the Flying Squad were summoned with pints of blood at the ready. Later she wrote 'My baby is adorable. She was seven-and-a-half pounds, with a little dark curl on the top of her head. I remember the midwife putting her beside me to bond us before snatching her away again when I started to bleed.'

It was weeks before Charlotte gained her strength and colour. Post-natal depression had set in and Jay had not been impressed with his new situation. The "present" the new baby brought him did nothing to change his attitude. His sister was not welcome.

Rita arrived to take them out but winter came early and the

weather deteriorated. At Christmas time, Bruce and Jean visited and the Lovetts, now home from Germany and with a daughter of their own, called in and took photographs of the three children. They would be looking at houses in the Kent area in the new year, they told the Fieldings. Charlotte was pleased to see her friend, Stella, and wanted to confide in her about a discovery she had made before Christmas but decided to keep silent and maintain a happy front.

Just before Christmas, friends from her Edgware nursing days called in to see her, on holiday from their home now in New Zealand. Keen to show them photographs of Germany and their wedding, she had fetched the album, only to find that her favourite ones of Ralph were missing. When she questioned him, Ralph shrugged it off and said he was showing them to someone at work but soon after this she found torn-up pieces of a photograph at the bottom of the lavatory. Could this evidence have been a photograph of someone else that he was destroying? What else could it be? Charlotte was troubled.

Diary entry: February.
Jay was three yesterday. Bruce and Jean came to his little party. Jemma Rose is four months old now. She has lost her dark curl and new blond hair is growing fast. She looks at me with such fierce blue eyes that miss nothing but is every bit as content as Jay was at that age. I have told Rita about Ralph. I couldn't keep it to myself. She thinks it will blow over when we move. His firm is relocating to South London so we are waiting to hear. Perhaps he'll forget whoever it was he was lusting after. I hope so. It has made me very unhappy. I must have been so dull and boring but I was still recovering from the trauma of the blood

transfusion after Jemma's birth and the ensuing depression. I'm looking forward to the move if only so that we can start again.

Ralph's firm moved office the following month and he started house-hunting once again for a suitable property and was relieved to see that house prices in the south were more affordable than in Mill Hill.

CHAPTER NINE

ON THE WAY UP!

Riverside Road in Catford lived up to its name. All the houses on one side of the street were below the level of the road and a small stream ran along the bottom of the gardens. This, coupled with the approval to build a tall block of flats nearby, offered a price that the Fieldings could afford, plus the fact that Ralph had received an increase in salary. The house itself was a nineteen-thirties semi-detached, with good-sized rooms and garden. They both exulted in their good fortune and set about making it their home.

Diary entry: April
I heard the news today from Rita that Linda is getting married in June and wants Jay to be a pageboy. He answered the phone while I was upstairs this morning and told her 'Mummy's having a wee!' Is nothing sacred! I must say that having a phone has changed my life 'tho I have to ration my calls. It's so good to hear from Jean and Rita and keep in touch with them. I no longer feel alone 'tho days go by when I hardly see anyone. The wedding will be about the most exciting thing that's happened since we were in Germany and it will be wonderful to see all the family and meet Linda's Simon.

Jay has been upset by the move and seems constantly insecure. This problem has been exacerbated since the arrival of Jemma, who is still a baby and placid enough to take everything in her stride. I can't wait to dress them up for the wedding and maybe I'll buy a new dress for myself. It will come in handy for our holiday in Broadstairs next month. I'm looking forward to going there again and this time for two weeks! The boarding house is wonderful when I compare it to the caravan in Clacton when I was fifteen. It rained everyday for a fortnight and we had to squelch our way over to the shower block each time we needed the lav. Poor Netta and Annie thought that they were giving me a treat! It must have cost Netta so much of her pension to pay for the holiday. We spent most of the time playing "Wot" and "Old maid"!

They quickly adapted to their new routines and Jay happily started nursery school. Charlotte took Jemma to the park some days and savoured precious moments alone with her daughter. The wedding had gone well and Linda and Simon both looked very happy. The children were much admired and Jay was praised for his performance as pageboy, which he executed without a qualm, although his mother was shaking with nerves on his behalf. Charlotte was so pleased to meet up with her family but sad that, after the reception, they had to leave earlier than the others, just when she was enjoying it all so much. It was the nearest she came to showing off herself and her children to the "parents" she never had; to be able to say 'what do you think? Am I doing a good job?' Myra and Evan were non-committal. She cheered herself with the thought of the approaching holiday and sitting down to stew and suet pudding after a swim in the sea.

Life continued to improve for the family. Jemma took her first steps at ten months and tottered round the house after Charlotte, trailing her "blanket". They joined the Catford S.A. corps, taking part in both band and songsters whenever possible. New friends were made and new places visited including Beckenham, Bromley and Lewisham.

The following year Charlotte took up pottery evening classes in New Cross and a touch-typing course locally as she hoped to be able to start some writing again. Ralph had agreed to her taking driving lessons now that a second-hand Hillman Minx had been exchanged for the ancient Morris.

Diary entries: August 1965

I've passed my test! I was so nervous! I have had twelve lessons with a lovely man in Bromley and a nifty Triumph Herald. Rita told me to take an "Oblivon" tablet which made me feel as calm as a cucumber until about halfway through the test when it began to wear off and I could feel my nerves jangling. Fortunately I managed to keep control and passed after a few cautionary words from the examiner who said 'You did a few strange things towards the end'. It will be wonderful to have my independence and when I feel confident enough, I'll take the children to see Stella and HarryRoy now that they are settled in Pembury. The Hillman always drives like a tank after the Triumph but it doesn't matter. I'm free!

September

Jay started school today. He came back full of excitement and has made a new friend who also lives in our road. He is a very friendly child and seems more settled than he has been. Jemma is a poppet and will be two next month. She talks quite a bit and loves playing "shops". Rita and David will see a big change in them both when they come next week. We haven't seen them since Linda's wedding last year but Jean and Bruce enjoy the drive over here occasionally and come through the Blackwall Tunnel.

At Christmas time Ralph took them to see a housing estate on the edge of Bradstead in Surrey. He had heard from one of his colleagues who lived there that Southparks was a prestigious area and boasted an excellent school with high numbers of pupils gaining the eleven plus examination. There was snow on the pavements as they toured the large estate with its attractive well-built, pre-war Gower houses in differing sizes, with well-trimmed gardens and leafy avenues. Charlotte thought that it was well out of their reach financially and that she had had enough of moving but Ralph liked the idea of living there and decided to look into the housing market. He had ambitions to improve their status and provide a better environment for the children. Jay was already showing signs of asthma and would benefit from this suburb that was about five miles from town. It would mean travelling further to work but he was prepared for that. He was not in favour of Charlotte working, with the old-fashioned belief that the wife should be in the home. Charlotte was happy enough with this arrangement for the time being as Jemma was barely two years old.

They had made improvements to the house in Catford and Ralph hoped that these would be enough to help create a good price when they came to sell.

They sold three months later and were horrified to hear that only weeks after their move, Riverside Road was flooded due to exceptional rainfall and the rising stream. The new owners faced three foot of water in their newly acquired sitting room. The Fieldings read about it in the papers but there was nothing they could do about it.

The previous three months had been fraught with difficulties. Two houses on the Gower estate had eluded them just being out of their reach and Charlotte had suffered a serious bout of flu with a high temperature and had taken to her bed, with Jemma playing on the floor beside her. Ralph took Jay to school, obtained some medicine and went off to work unruffled. His parents arrived days later and restored order but it was some time before Charlotte was back on her feet. In the meantime, with their house now under offer, more property details continued to arrive.

Charlotte, once recovered, chased after them in the Hillman and one day came back from Southparks with some exciting news. A smaller semi-detached house situated in a pine-tree-fringed cul-de-sac across the main road from the school was ideal. The previous potential buyers had pulled out and the owners were now anxious for a quick sale. Pine Trees was in a beautiful setting and on her first visit Charlotte could almost taste the freshness of the air and felt a strong immediate conviction that this was where they would come to live and she proved to be right.

Southparks was situated on the outskirts of Bradstead and was once a village of interesting character with historical buildings at the foot of the Downs. The parade of shops grew and the parish extended during the nineteen-thirties to include Upper Southparks. It has now become a thriving suburb with a 19th-century church, parish hall, library and two schools.

Pine Trees was up the hill from the shops, near the church and recreation ground, and surrounded by woodland. In 1938 the houses were originally designed to all be detached and built on a connecting main road leading to the town but the nature of the land was such that it held several springs and in bad weather these would swell and gush down from the woods behind causing construction problems. To cut their losses the builders decided to alternate the detached houses with semi-detached houses and turn the proposed road into a cul-de-sac. Beyond the wood were a lake and a golf course.

When the Fieldings moved in during April, the occupants of the thirty or so houses were older and well established and the newcomers were viewed through twitching net curtains, but times were changing and other new and younger people would soon arrive with their modern outlooks and younger children.

They were both delighted with the house and ran from room to room exclaiming at the views and the size of the garden. There was a swing at the end and a large apple tree, a big lawn and a paved terrace. The garden sloped upwards, with a gate into the woods at the back.

Each evening after dinner Ralph would start feverishly freshening the tired paintwork on doors and sills. Walls needed re-papering and floors sanding and sealing. He had great plans for the kitchen that was outdated and held only a deep sink with a wooden drainer and with no other cupboards or worktops. There was a big larder and an old coke stove for the hot water that he intended to scrap as soon as he could afford to install central heating but this would not be for a year or two. In the meantime he had plenty to get on with.

Charlotte was busy with settling the children and storing their few belongings. They were going to need shelves and more cupboard space eventually. The move had tired her physically and she suffered bouts of agoraphobia and would grip the pushchair for support when walking to the shops across the recreation ground but in other ways she was happier than she had been for months.

Diary entry: May

Jay started school today at Northbrook mid-term. His little lip quivered and his chin wobbled as he left Jemma and me at the gate but he bravely ran in to join the others. I do hope we are finally settled. This constant moving every two years has drained me and upset him. I need to put down roots, feel secure and take up new interests. This is a beautiful place, fresh and clean and good for the children. I worry about Jay. He now uses an inhaler and has another change of school to add to his stress. Jemma is less affected and loves playing in the new garden. It will be good for her to go to the nursery school down the hill when she is three, where I have found the shops and the parish hall. There are tennis courts in the little park area and a swimming pool in the next town. This is cheering as I have missed both these activities and wish there were some younger neighbours to join me here. I am by far the youngest mother in the close.

Younger people did move into the close and Charlotte was able to make friendships that would last for the rest of her life. To her, all close friends became her family. She wanted so much to share with other people, to make up for the loss of loved ones and to gain confidence in the things that were difficult for her. She was quite unworldly, not unattractive, but still trusting and naïve.

Changes were to occur in other areas too over the next few years, with regard to her family. Izzy died and Charlotte was sad that she was unable to attend the funeral. She had been a sweet soul and kind to her when she was young. David had reached retirement age and he and Rita were looking at property in the Cromer area in Norfolk where David would be going back to his roots but a long way from Surrey. They already owned a holiday cottage in Saxthorpe where Charlotte had stayed with Rita, taking the children with her for a holiday there but now they wanted something larger and more permanent. Annette had married a young executive with a "no frills" wedding and Rosamund and Brian Mayhew invited the Fieldings to visit them in their house in Epsom.

Diary entry: June 14th
Have spent the day at The Links. The Mayhews have a big house backing onto the golf course. We had a barbecue in their beautiful garden and Brian operated a gas barbecue to cook steak! It was the first time they had seen the children and both Rosamund and Brian are pleased that we have moved a little nearer to them. I felt nervous of meeting them after so long and rather overawed by the size of the house and garden. Brian is a high-powered director and Rosamund is both attractive and self-assured. I have so little to talk about but Ralph made up for my inadequacies. Brian reminded me of the time I was feeling sick in his Riley when I was eight years old. Fortunately I had asked him to stop in time! He said I looked like Mrs Laurent, my grandmother. I pictured the old lady with white hair, but was somewhat mollified when he added 'she was a fine looking woman in her youth!' I asked if he had known my father but he said 'not really' but that he thought my mother had been Russian. I caught Rosamund looking at him meaningfully and he changed the subject. One day I'll find out.

At a barn dance for the cubs in the parish hall after his seventh birthday Jay was drawn into the church choir by the resident vicar, who was on the lookout for new members. Charlotte was delighted when Jay agreed but guessed it was probably the lure of extra pocket money each Sunday with twice the amount for weddings that had sparked his enthusiasm. In the meantime Jemma was attending nursery school with extra ballet classes under the watchful eye of Miss Dancer. Jemma also had musical abilities and Jean and Bruce offered to pay for her to have piano lessons. Charlotte described how they came by a piano in an extract from her diary.

Diary Extract

The Wrights next door in the detached house are moving. Mr W is a barrister but he is retiring so they are going to Haywards Heath. They have offered us a Wilton carpet and an upright piano as they have no room for either in their new house. Ralph said we could afford the carpet but not the piano. This was some weeks ago. Imagine my surprise and delight when I saw the removal men trundling the piano up our drive! Apparently the Ws were unable to sell it but could not take it with them so said we could have it! It is a Bechstein and encased in the most beautiful burr walnut veneer. I just love tinkering on it but hope that the children will learn properly. Now that we have a record deck we are able to play our classical Ace of Clubs records bought in the NAFFI in Germany. Ralph has taught me a lot about music and Jay loves listening to Stravinsky's *The Firebird* when he's upstairs in bed but I can only manage pop songs on the ivories!

The new people are Trich and John Jackson. I took them a tray of tea and said 'Hello'. They have a small boy of about two and seem very friendly.

Charlotte joined the young wives group at the church together with another new neighbour, Sue Young, who had moved in across the way. Her husband, Rod, worked at a local bank and they had one small boy and a baby on the way. They added their names to the babysitting rota provided by the group and this meant that for the first time since Jay was born, Charlotte and Ralph could go out in the evening. It was operated on a points system so no money was involved and they got to know more local families.

The improvements in her life meant that Charlotte became happy and more confident. Essentially she was a housewife and mother as Ralph was still against her going out to work, but once Jemma started school Charlotte became in need of stimulation. The house was spick and span, the children well cared for and a meal ready on the table for Ralph when he arrived home but this was not enough for her. In February 1969 a solution to her problem arrived as described in her diary extracts.

Diary extracts: March 7th
Have just finished the sixth book on my long reading list from Cranmer College. I really relished the challenge to get it done in time as it's years since I've had to condense so much. I enjoyed the Salinger and Aldous Huxley enormously. My next interview will include another written exam so fingers crossed! I'm so looking forward to working toward something worthwhile and the college hours will fit in with collecting the children from school and this is most important.

March 20th
Spent the morning writing for three hours on various

subjects including 'contemporary life for young children today' and 'what role does TV offer?' I wrote on my own at a long refectory table. I just love this beautiful old ivy-covered building with its panelled inner walls and huge stone fireplaces. I met the head, dressed in a habit and veil, after going up the smallest winding staircase to the inner sanctum! I'm sure it was a priest's hole or secret staircase or somewhere to hide the oppressed! Being a Protestant doesn't seem to affect my application to be a student teacher here. I do hope that I get in!!

March 31st
Great news! I've passed all my interviews and exams and I'll train to teach primary children English, Arithmetic and Music. I'm so excited! I have to go for a medical and then if I'm OK I'll start after Easter. They have given me a grant of £40 for books and materials. Can't wait to phone Rita and Jean with the news! I think Ralph's pleased too.

Three weeks after her final interview for Cranmer College, disaster struck. Ralph was sacked. It appeared that he was not in favour of joining the trade union where he worked and had the choice of complying or leaving. Ralph's principles won and he chose the latter although he now had a double mortgage, wife and two children but still thought it was the right thing to do. Charlotte was devastated, not only from the seriousness of Ralph's predicament but because she would now have to forgo her course. They had been planning to buy a second-hand car ready for Easter but now in the light of their difficulties this would not be wise or affordable. Ralph had handed over his company car and as a result they had no car at all. Cranmer College was not an easy place to reach by bus and Charlotte would not be back in time for the children. Even if Ralph were on hand to collect them temporarily it would present a problem once he started a new job and could not be there. Charlotte made the best of it and got on with supporting her husband.

Diary Entry: June
It's been two months since Ralph left Hewitt's. I have been typing up his CVs and job applications but nothing yet. Rita has asked Brian to step in and help out by finding work for him at Robson's, in the personnel department. Last week he was so uptight that he deliberately dropped a pile of plates, frightening me and the children, just because of some petty request or other from Jay. I suggested that we all went to Chessington on the train for the day, to forget our troubles.

Ralph took a temporary job with Brian Mayhew at Robson's before eventually accepting work a month later in West London. Whilst this was good news it would entail significant travelling, in the company car, from where they were living, but things were critical and he had no option other than to move back across the Thames. Charlotte suffered a breakdown at the end of these long worrying months and could just about manage to get the children off to school and find food for the evening meal. She had carried the family to the best of her ability, supporting Ralph in his efforts to find work and now reaction had set in. All her old fears of insecurity and worthlessness returned. She would have to find ways of helping Ralph cope with his new problems. Cranmer would have to go on hold and she would look round for part-time employment when she was well enough.

Diary entry: August
Took the children to visit Stella in Pembury in the Riley Elf. It's a great little car! Hurray for my part-time work and Ralph's new job!

The four children play so well together as they are much the same age. HarryRoy has bought a sailing boat and it's moored on the Medway and next time we will sail with them and that will be exciting! They have been such great friends to us. I wanted to ask Stella if HarryRoy was a mason as Ralph is becoming one. I think it's all rather odd and when I test him on his lines for his initiation ceremony there are words blanked out. He says these words are secret! Stella said HarryRoy wasn't a mason and she didn't know much about it. Bruce is a Worshipful Brother and he seems to have influenced Ralph and introduced him to the hierarchy! He has to wear a special apron and white gloves. It's all rather "boy's own" secret stuff. Anyway I might enjoy the Ladies festival night in London next month. It could cheer us both up!

Charlotte was to enjoy several Ladies festival nights over the next few years, meeting up with Jean and Bruce in the Tavistock banqueting rooms in Charing Cross. She enjoyed the sense of occasion but was disappointed not to be able to join in with the dancing. Jemma had been most impressed by her mother when she kissed her before leaving for London, saying, 'Mummy you look just like a princess.' Charlotte had borrowed a long white dress with sequined midriff from a friend, and was reminded of the summer balls in Germany.

Diary entry: October
Spent yesterday over in Leytonstone for Jemma's sixth birthday. She is growing into a real beauty and talented

too. Bruce and Jean are very impressed with her progress on the piano. The school have given Jay a cello to play to add to his musical interests. He told his grandparents he's going to 'sing with the men' when he gets too old to be a choirboy but he's still only eight! I just wish that he would be kinder to his sister. Will he always resent her? Wore my new tapestry flared jeans. Still feel guilty about HP and catalogues! I noticed Bruce giving them a quizzical look but I love them and I'm glad I've got long legs! Got held up in the Blackwall Tunnel coming back and arrived home very late. It was good to see Bruce and Jean looking so well. They must be coming up for seventy-five next year.

During the next two years things took a turn for the better for Charlotte as she got more involved in enjoyable activities and took on a small part time job. She had begun evening classes with Trich and they had great fun together "lunging" during fencing classes in the winter, and "shooting" at archery targets, and tennis in the summer. She also attended history of art and life drawing classes at the art college, took up her writing again and considered joining the local drama group.

In August each year, they all enjoyed a family holiday in Studland. This was brought about by the generosity of one of the more established couples at the end of the close. June had taken a shine to Charlotte, who had helped her in some way, and Ralph shared similar business interests with Alan. They offered the Fieldings their holiday cottage and the family were both delighted and grateful to accept. Other occasional holidays were spent in Southend with Annie and her sister, and with Rita and David in Cromer, although the latter continued to maintain their distance towards Ralph. Eddie was equally pleased to see his younger brother and family from time to time and Pam delighted in making a fuss of the children.

As Charlotte blossomed into a happy, active woman, Ralph appeared to become more preoccupied. It was some time before she noticed the change in him. She was aware of the difficulties he faced with travelling the distance to work each day and would make sure that he received a good welcome home. She had always believed in putting him first because, she argued, a husband is a partner for life, whereas children grow up and find partners of their own. She began to miss the fact that he no longer reached for her in their intimate times together. He was nearing forty and she comforted herself with the thought that his impotence was due to tiredness and emotional change. Charlotte had never refused his overtures in the past and began to miss their lovemaking, but was too sensitive to accuse him of neglect. She knew her appetites needed to be addressed but thought this was a fault on her part that they needed addressing. Perhaps she should go on the pill and remove all restrictions? Was he worried about another baby coming or were these financial worries? She passed all her earnings over to him and her bonuses at times were good ones. He held the purse strings. Perhaps she should work full time? There was a research laboratory in the next town; perhaps she should try there? The Head of Cranmer had declined further attempts to enrol her at the training college, due, she said, to no available places.

Charlotte decided to pray about it and in the meantime, leave him alone and hope for improvement.

In November, Charlotte read in the local paper that the Zurich Wolf Research Laboratory was looking for casual workers to work over the Christmas period. She applied and got the job. There was no guarantee that she would remain in their employment after this time, but she was glad to have the opportunity to help Ralph, if only for a month or so as her part-time job had finished.

Charlotte wrote about this in a letter to Annie.

> *16, Pine Trees*
> *Southparks*
> *Dec 14th*

Dear Annie,

> *I'm so sorry we are unable to visit as promised but I am now working full time at the lab I was telling you about. It occupies very beautiful grounds and the main offices are in the lovely old manor house of Whitworth. The various labs are spread out around the grounds and I'm busy preparing agar plates for cultures as well as being a dogsbody! It's quite some place! There is a canteen, shop, and sports club here. I've seen tennis courts and squash courts but have not had time or energy to investigate. I think you have to be on the permanent staff to enjoy these facilities. One day perhaps! I'm too busy at the moment for anything sporty!*

> *The children will be sorry not to see you but hope you have a wonderful Christmas and we'll post our presents. Ralph is talking about building a model engine and carriage for the children. I think it might be fun and give him a new interest as well as the masons!*

> *I've had a story published and am working on a book but this will have to go on hold as I'm too tired at the end of the day! It's quite hard work.*

> *Hope you are both well, take care*
> *Love Charlotte xx*

The first few months of the new year were blighted by miners' strikes and blackouts recorded in her diary. In March, she was told that she was no longer needed in the lab where she was working but that a vacancy had become available in the general office. Alternatively, if she was prepared to train and take exams, she could become a qualified technician. Charlotte jumped at this opportunity but Ralph explained that it would cost money to train and that she would be better off working in the office for the time being. This did not appeal to Charlotte as she had never worked in an office and had always vowed that she never would, but because she was "on site", thought it prudent in the short-term; besides, membership to the sports club would become available. She was nervous of what was expected of her but found the *camaraderie* in the big room relaxed and friendly and she need not have worried. She soon took things in her stride and put the idea of training on hold. When one of the scientists offered to teach her squash, her enthusiasm knew no bounds, but other female staff thought this hilarious and merely a chat up line on his behalf, but Charlotte was most serious and couldn't wait for her first game.

One day in May when Charlotte was driving back to work after going home at lunch time she had an unfortunate car accident as recorded in her diary.

Diary entry: May 18th
I'm feeling very down about yesterday's accident. The Elf was towed away to the garage with a badly dented wing, but more upsetting than this was Ralph's reaction to my phone call. It happened on the road near Whitworth, where a van decided to do a U-turn without seeing me coming. Fortunately I was not hurt but was very much in shock. When I got to the office, I phoned him to let him know and was further shocked by the chill in the voice of his secretary who answered

the phone, and more so by Ralph himself when he said 'what do you want me to do about it?' not 'how are you, are you OK?' Sometimes I really wonder if he loves me at all. I'm so depressed.

On happier days, Charlotte was enjoying life in the office and joined in the many minor celebrations that occasionally went on in the lunch times of the working environment, when she was not playing squash. She had been more than grateful to Trich, who collected the children from school and gave them tea if she was not back in time. She was proud of Jay who had won a big painting competition with "Quaker" and was also voted best end-of-term "fancy dressed" boy in the class. Charlotte wrote: 'It wasn't the fact that he had chosen to be a pirate, but that he wanted to have a "peg leg" so bent his leg up, attached my sink plunger and then crammed his bent-up leg into his trousers. I said he'd get pins and needles but he insisted, and kept it up all afternoon! Ten out of ten for perseverance!'

Although Charlotte was happy enough in herself and with her life, she still missed Ralph's attentions, and as she became more enamoured with the sports club, so Ralph appeared to become more preoccupied. She continued to do her best for him and assumed it was problems at work that he did not want to discuss with her. He seemed happy enough with the model train he was building in his spare time. She added riding to her list of pursuits that was subsidised by Zurich at the local stables. It was something she had longed to do and for which she found she possessed a natural aptitude. After talking it over with Ralph, Jemma began lessons on a Saturday morning at the same place and enjoyed the challenge. Jemma had delighted them by excelling at swimming and achieving many certificates as well as for her piano playing.

In September Ralph was busy getting ready for the Ladies Festival night that he and Charlotte would host. He had become a Worshipful Brother and was now to take on Worshipful Master of the Lodge for the following year. He would be expected to make a speech and lead off the dancing which was not his forte. Charlotte looked forward to the occasion with mixed feelings. On the one hand she could anticipate a beautiful new dress offered to her by Rosamund and on the other, quavered at the thought of making the response to the toast on behalf of the ladies.

Diary entry: October.

To the Ladies,
Ye of the fairer sex, whose husbands' nights,
So oft are spent in sampling the delights
Of arts Masonic and their attendant pleasures,
May now for once, adopt retaliative measures
This is Your Night—the time for your enjoyment,
The Brethren, for once, as an employment
Using their charms—reserved on Lodge night
For their Brother's—
To entertain their wives—also the wives of others.

(written on menu!)

I was really surprised at myself last night! I thought I'd be a bag of nerves, but it was a bit like our wedding day; I even found myself thoroughly enjoying welcoming all those people and shaking hands with them. It felt quite unbelievable to be sitting at the top table and being the wife of the new Worshipful Master and president! Ralph looked marvellous in his hired DJ and

I felt really good in my beautiful long Spanish-style dress. It was so kind of Rosamund and so expensive! I even managed my speech without too many hiccups. I'm very pleased with my lovely present from the Lodge and can't wait to see the clock working, it's four golden balls gently rotating and moving back again like the one Pam's got. Everyone signed my menu and we just about managed to lead off the dancing, so our practicing paid off in the long run. We were home by 1am and really grateful to Sue for babysitting. Even Ralph was in high spirits and pleased with me! I think things are on the way up again as far as our relationship is concerned! I pray so, every night.

On holiday the following summer Ralph seemed in particularly good form, as if some big problem he had been working on had been resolved. Although he was more patient with the children, he still maintained a certain distance with Charlotte. During August Rita and David had invited them to stay for two weeks in the cottage next door. This was small and damp and had been bought by Linda's father-in-law with a view to doing it up and letting it out in holiday time but it cost them nothing and suited the Fieldings well as they could do as they pleased whilst meeting up with Rita and David at intervals, so that all round equilibrium was maintained.

Charlotte found it hard to talk to Rita about the things that bothered her, especially as they concerned Ralph, for Rita would hold a biased view on anything that concerned him. Outwardly, all seemed to be well with the family and they made the most of the beaches and woodland walks that were available to them. Ralph's interests lay in an old railway line and station where he walked them for miles along the track, finding a siding with derelict steam engine that the children were happy to clamber over. Charlotte liked to roam around the antique shops and swim in the cold sea. They also found riding stables where she and Jemma signed up for a hack.

Rita and David took them to a local agricultural show with livestock, horse jumping and other attractions that enchanted the children. On other occasions they visited Blickling Hall and a bird sanctuary.

According to Charlotte they all agreed it had been a super holiday but at the back of her mind she felt uneasy, as if everything was too good to be true and asked herself 'Where was the catch?'

Autumn term began for the children whilst Charlotte went back to the office. She tried to ignore the fact that she found both the work and petty restrictions tedious, but the lure of the sports club and all its merits kept her happy. Ralph became more engrossed with his engine at the weekends as it neared completion.

It had taken up the garage. He was proud of the carriage too, with seats and a little door. It was painted red with a grey interior. Once outside in the yard, the children and their friends were photographed leaning out of the carriage and waving.

At half term Jemma celebrated her tenth birthday. She was a beautiful child, talented and intelligent but her father considered further education for girls as a waste of time. He had little time for Jay who he considered a dreamer like his mother and who would never make his way in business and his hopes for him to enter the Whitgift School or Alleyns in Dulwich were not realised and even if they had been, he could not have afforded to keep him there. On this occasion he made a rare appearance at Jemma's party, having come home early from work. This pleased her enormously. Charlotte had made and iced the cake and Jemma and her friends had played happily together all afternoon. She said it was her best birthday ever.

That evening after a glass of cider, their one concession to alcohol, they took a bath together. This was not an unusual occurrence since the blackouts, when they would save on hot water and electricity. Charlotte recorded that she had been telling Ralph about friends of theirs in the village who were on the brink of divorce. Charlotte had said what an awful thing to happen and what would they do now? Ralph had 'looked into space' and then said 'you have taught me what love really is!' She had been nonplussed and at a loss for an answer. That night she had slept well, tucked up beside him but totally unaware that the land mine he had been preparing for the last six years was now ready to be laid at her feet.

CHAPTER TEN

HELL'S GATE

When life throws everything at you, you can cower beneath the rubble or come out fighting; rage, rage, against your pain and let it out or it will destroy you.

The Fire and the Phoenix

On Friday 17th November 1973, Charlotte received the worst shock of her life. On her arrival home, after a busy day, ten-year-old Jemma had pointed to an envelope high on a kitchen shelf. Inside there was a twenty-pound note and a scrap of paper that stated:

'I'm sorry I can no longer hold our marriage together. Ralph.'

Charlotte had stared, transfixed, at the words and then, unaware of Jemma's gaze, had rushed out into the close, her one thought to cry out her bewilderment and to find her neighbour Trich, but she found that Trich was busy with her elderly visiting parents. Charlotte halted, undecided, and then went back indoors, still unaware of the effect that her distraught face and this strange action was to have on Jemma, especially in the years to come. Smothering her feelings for the sake of the children, she tried to carry on as normal, whilst all the time her mind was racing: *Ralph had suffered a brainstorm, Ralph was in trouble of some sort, Ralph was wandering the streets, hurt and in a daze somewhere.* She would phone his brother Eddie when the children were upstairs, to see if he could throw any light on the situation. What did Ralph mean *I CAN NO LONGER HOLD OUR MARRIAGE TOGETHER?*

Eddie's first words on arrival were 'Has he taken his shaving kit?' which seemed odd to Charlotte but she checked and assured him that he had not taken anything that was obvious, although she had not checked everything. Eddie and Pam had come straight away after receiving Charlotte's distress call and were sitting in the sitting room trying to fathom out what could have happened. Charlotte assured them that there was no one else in his life, as she would have known about it from any erratic behaviour. It was agreed between them that not much could be done until Monday morning when Charlotte could contact Brewster's, Ralph's office in West London.

It was a long and agonising weekend for Charlotte but worse was to follow on Monday morning. Cramped into a small side office at work, she phoned Brewster's, only to be told that Ralph no longer worked for them anymore and had taken a job in Newmarket. They did not speak well of him and apologised for the fact that Charlotte was ignorant of this information. She sat motionless, trying to come to terms with this news and wondering what to do next. The girls in the office were staring at her 'What did she think she was doing – helping herself to the manager's phone?' but she was quite unable to utter the words 'My husband has deserted me and I don't know where he is.' Already she felt a stigma attached to these very words and that she must somehow be a failure.

The day passed with a suffocating slowness, Charlotte tight with control and held in emotions but when she arrived home she passed on this latest news to Eddie. Again he could only repeat to Charlotte's chagrin that 'he had another woman tucked away somewhere'.

On the Wednesday morning, a stranger who identified herself as Marion Clark rang her at home and gave her the truth that would rock Charlotte to the very core of her being. 'I thought you ought to know that your husband Ralph Fielding has gone off with my friend's daughter Rachael Simpson. I can't believe what the pair of them have done. Rachael took her two small children to school on Friday morning and left them there, whilst she then met up with your husband and is now living with him in Newmarket. This must have been planned months ago and with calculated precision. It has been going on for years I'm told. We must stop them!' Charlotte's hand was clamped so tightly to the receiver that she could not let go. Rachael Simpson was Ralph's secretary at Bristow's. She felt so sick she could not speak and sat like a stone effigy whilst the other voice droned on. 'My friend is…' but Charlotte was no longer listening. She was too traumatised. It was beyond her belief and beyond her control.

All that week, she had tried to keep things normal for the children and had told them 'Daddy's away on business for a week or two' whilst she tried to grapple with the truth. They were looking forward to the annual church Christmas bazaar to be held on Saturday where they would buy their small presents. Charlotte had walked about in a daze, seeing all her friends' smiling faces from behind their stalls, ignorant of her pain. Her heart almost broke when Jay presented her with his gift for his father. 'Look Mummy, two chisels for his engine,' and Jemma's excited voice: 'I've bought him some hankies for his hay fever.' Charlotte would have to tell them the truth before long. She could not keep up the pretence, but what was she going to say? Her inner voice cried out, 'Oh my babies, my babies, what has he done to us?'

At the end of the first week of strain and worry, Charlotte had lost half a stone in weight and was taking tranquillizers. Her doctor had shown little sympathy with her situation by exclaiming, 'There's a lot of it about,' and 'didn't you see it coming?' If she was looking for comfort, the unkind, or perhaps wise, practitioner was not going to give her any.

Charlotte had further discovered that their joint account had been emptied, but there were no statements around to say how much had been taken, as Ralph always kept strict control of their finances and kept her in ignorance. She did not own her own chequebook. After being contacted by a worried Rita, Brian arrived to help her out with the outstanding utility bills that had yet to be paid. Charlotte was most grateful and let him pay but assured him that she would have to learn to cope with all the household expenses, and what about the mortgage? Brian was concerned but she had told him that she would manage somehow.

Diary extract:

I did a terrible thing today. Jean rang up and sounded so bewildered about what she had heard from Eddie about Ralph that I slammed the receiver down. I couldn't bring myself to talk about it and, for some reason, I blamed her and Bruce for the callous, cowardly, calculating and selfish behaviour of their son. The pain was too great. I would have said something I would have regretted even more. I had to get back at somebody and I took it out on this kind, elderly woman who has always been good to me and the children. Already it seems I'm at hell's gate and breaking the mould. My scruples are all being challenged. How could Ralph have kissed me goodbye that morning and then driven back to pick up his things when I had gone to work? Why? What have I done to deserve this? Is it punishment from God for causing Netta pain?

Ralph eventually telephoned and arranged a meeting for the following weekend with her and the children in a nearby park. Jemma refused to speak to him and Jay wandered off, his twelve-year-old mind still trying to deal with the situation. Charlotte herself was too traumatised to speak as Ralph tried to explain to her his love for another woman, almost beseeching her to see things from his point of view, but it did not cut any ice with her. No blame was laid at her feet and no accusations, but this only made it worse for Charlotte who finally found her voice and asked 'Why then, why, why? And for how long have you been cheating on me?' He had just looked away, unable to meet the hurt in her tear-filled eyes.

Ralph promised to pay the mortgage, for the time being, 'until things are sorted out' but in the meantime she would be responsible for all other expenses and these would be paid for out of her slim weekly wage. He was sorry but he had his own expenses and rooms to pay for in Newmarket. There was no use in arguing; she knew Ralph meant what he said when his mind was made up.

Diary extract: December, Friday.
Jay came back from choir practice this evening with a determined look on his face. He had given up the choir and no longer believed in God. I am devastated. I must be strong for him but find myself asking 'where is God?' I'll talk to the choirmaster; as Jay has always looked up to him, surely he can help? Was it something to do with my spreading out my week's money on the carpet and itemising how it should be spent?

'What are we going to do Mummy?' he had asked.

'How are we going to manage? I could do a paper round like Pip Saunders.'

I hugged them both and assured them that 'it's alright my darlings, we've got each other and I will never, never leave you.'

Jean had suggested that I take Jemma into my bed but I won't do it. If I do, I will never let her go and that could be bad for both of us. Outwardly she is not unhappy and rarely mentions her father, but Jem is deep. She will store up her pain; she is that much younger than Jay and as yet unaware of the ramifications of Ralph's desertion.

During the next three weeks, Charlotte held on as best she could: getting the children ready for school each day and herself ready for work. She would grit her teeth and count the days to Christmas. Rita and David were waiting to comfort and advise her and even the thought of the long drive to Norfolk was not going to deter her from going. It was all she had left to hold on to, but before this, there was the Zurich Wolf Christmas party.

Charlotte had finally spoken of her situation to her friends and work colleagues, who had all been kind and supportive. She now looked to them for reassurance and security. She had tried to keep to a steady routine for stability and to make sure that the children felt safe. Jay had started his paper round and was proud of his contributions to help his mother, and Jemma continued to do well at school. Did she need a Christmas party?

The fever in the office mounted as the day of the party drew nearer. This was a lively occasion and greatly anticipated by staff and workers alike. Charlotte was persuaded to go despite her private reservations that she would 'hate every minute'. She was still too traumatised to imagine that she could ever enjoy anything ever again, but decided to go to please her friend Mavis by agreeing.

It could be said, in retrospect, that the event was both to make and break the pattern of her life and to introduce her to Tom Wilder.

Charlotte set off, with some trepidation, wearing one of her "Ladies Night" dresses and hoping it was suitable for this occasion. She recovered her poise when she met her colleagues who were already there and who greeted her with smiles of admiration. The canteen had been transformed into a dance hall and was alive with lights, music and decorations. Drinks were on the house and Charlotte was urged to exchange her usual cider for a glass of strong punch. Before long, she began to unwind and enjoy the rhythm of the dancing (a mixture of rock and roll, disco and ballroom), and gradually, as the alcohol warmed her, the inhibitions she had so closely guarded for so long began to loosen. She was surprised to see both scientists and managers joining in with the workers and all behaving with 'gay abandon' like the animated groups she had seen on *Top of the Pops*. This was a new concept and one she would never have entertained. She was soon caught up with the wildness around her. This kind of dancing was something she had never experienced before but she found it breathtakingly exciting.

Charlotte wrote of that evening:

I had met Tom Wilder earlier in the year. He had come down once or twice on business for Z.W. He came into the sports club after watching the tennis finals and afterwards complimented me on my game. I remembered him as a big kind Northumbrian who joked and offered to buy me a drink. Now he was at the party. He came in late and was talking to one of the scientists when our eyes met "across the crowded room". The dancing was slowing down and as the Tennessee Waltz started up he came over and asked me to dance. We danced, politely at first, arms held at length, but suddenly he pulled me towards him and held me to his chest, and when I heard the soft lilt of his Geordie accent crooning in my ear like the past sounds of my childhood, I was lost. All the strain of the last month seemed to melt in the warmth of that embrace. I put my head on his broad shoulder and longed to lay all my sorrows at his feet but he had probably seen them already in my face. I decided to keep these thoughts to myself but one day perhaps I'd voice them, if the time were right.

Tom Wilder was a pathologist who worked and lived in the North of England with his wife and two children but would be moving down to join the staff of Zurich Wolf in the new year. He had told Charlotte of his background and that life on their domestic front was not good. They had parted on the night of the dance with an open invitation to meet 'for coffee' sometime in the new year. Meanwhile, he was house-hunting and would be staying down south in a local hotel after Christmas. No addresses or phone numbers were exchanged but Charlotte went home in a daze. The whole evening had woken her up to the fact that there was a life out there and she wanted to have a place in it.

Her employers were generous with their extra days over the Christmas period and she was able to take a week off to include the New Year. The family packed up the Elf with their luggage and set off for Cromer. Charlotte had never driven so far from home as Ralph liked to take charge on long journeys.

It took them five hours as she had to go through the Blackwall Tunnel and Epping Forest before travelling on the A11 to Norwich. They bypassed Newmarket and Charlotte kept her mind on the road ahead. She could not afford to waver. They arrived exhausted but she was pleased with her achievement, while Rita and David welcomed them with a mixture of apprehension and relief.

At last Charlotte was able to unburden herself and tell of all that had happened but she felt drained of all feeling and was still unable to voice her anger. Rita probed gently but there seemed to be little to be told – Ralph had run off with his secretary with whom he had presumably been sleeping for some years. Charlotte supposed they went to Rachael's place during the day while her husband was at work and her children at school; as Ralph was seldom home late and gave no indication that this was going on. Rita refrained from sharing her opinion that she was not surprised but said he was 'a bloody great fool'.

David gave more practical help by outlining his 'budget account' that he used to give to his customers in the bank. This would take care of her bills and allow her to become overdrawn without a penalty being levied. It was to prove a life-saving scheme for Charlotte and she acted on his advice there and then.

Rita and David did their best to give them a good Christmas but the weather was poor and the children sat forlornly on their Victorian chairs, not knowing what to do, whilst Charlotte stayed in her room and tried to write about the bitterness she felt and her thoughts on returning to an empty house and an uncertain future.

Diary entry: New Year's Day 1974
We have been home two days now. It was kind of Rita and David to look after us so well. I wish that they were

not so far away. I was invited to a New Year's Eve do across the road last night but I couldn't face it. I am feeling so low and empty. I just want to crawl away and hide but the children need me and it's back to work tomorrow. My pride refuses to let me admit that I miss him dreadfully, but I'll never, never take him back. I could never, never trust him again. If I feel anything at all, I feel free, free to be independent, to make my own decisions and not to have to ask permission from Ralph; independent is something I have not been for the last fifteen years.

By February her resolve to be entirely independent wavered and insecurity began to nag. She needed a man to love and a man to love her or she would die inside. She loved her children fiercely but they were children and should not be burdened with her anxieties or looked to for reassurance. With this in mind she took a deliberate action, well aware of what she was doing, and sent a note in the internal mail to Tom Wilder.

Tom was quick to respond and phoned her from the lab where he was working late that night. A time was arranged between them and he arrived one evening at Pine Trees after the children were in bed, clutching a bottle of wine in his large hand.

Charlotte, who had been imbibing port and brandy, the delights of which had been introduced to her at her aunt's house in Cromer, was ready for him. She had argued in her head that what Ralph could do she was also capable of and there would be no holds barred. Tom poured the wine and their evening began to the sound of classical music and the clink of glasses. Tom was clumsy in his advances and gave the impression of a starved man in sight of a meal. Had

Charlotte been less inebriated this might have been a deterrent, but she had set her course and meant to see it through. In the process, wine was spilt and Charlotte, emerging later from her sated state, saw in the cold light of sober realisation the debris of their evening, and began to regret the whole sordid business.

Diary entry February 9th
I feel so cheap. How could I have brought myself so low? Is this what I've come to in my efforts to get back at Ralph? In the morning the sitting room was like a saloon bar, bottles, glasses and a stain on the carpet to say nothing of the stale smell of sweat, alcohol and his cigarette. I'm so ashamed. I kept the children out of the room whilst I cleared up and was late for work and feel like death. What am I going to do about Tom? He's going back up north at the weekend but he'll be down again next week. I have broken all the rules. I can no longer pray or go to church. What did I do wrong? I thought it was God's will that I should marry Ralph, a man brought up by decent Christian folk; now the only voice I hear is Netta's, coming from beyond the grave, reminding me of her prophecy that it would end in pain and anguish, but I promise myself daily that there will be no divorce. I couldn't bear the shame. It would be better if he'd died. I would be heartbroken but at least I could hold up my head. Bereavement is a painful state to be in but at least it's a noble one. I tell myself that I did what I did with Tom to prove that I am still attractive to men and that having been so cruelly discarded, I needed to know that I could still be desired and loved, whatever that phrase may now mean.

Charlotte tried to put these thoughts out of her mind while she concentrated on keeping to the routines she had set herself. At the end of the month she would be taking on the new position of P.A. to John Bradley and this would mean an increase in salary on a monthly basis and would help her both mentally and financially.

On Jay's thirteenth birthday they drove into the country for a cream tea in an old farmhouse down by the river. He was saving up for a better bicycle for his paper round and was glad of offerings from Rita, Jean and Annie. Jean had given a warning to Charlotte that the money for Jemma's music lessons would cease when she left junior school. They also asked if she had sat the eleven plus exam? Charlotte knew that she would be unable to afford the piano lessons herself and became angry. This was another unwelcome consequence of her husband's inconsideration. Jemma was doing well and had just passed her grade four. She had sat the eleven plus and passed but the best grammar school was too far away and Cranmer Convent was oversubscribed, two hundred applicants trying for sixty places, so she would join Jay at Southparks High School in the autumn. This would mean a new uniform for her and new shoes for them both. Where was the money coming from? She would start her new post soon but would have to wait until April for her new salary; the increase was not great but the work was more interesting and any extra money would help towards her rising costs.

Another unexpected almost "divine" intervention made itself apparent one day in March, as described in her diary.

Diary extract: March 14th
He had been wandering in the woods behind us for some time, cowed and nervous. If I caught him drinking from our pond he would dash off again,

frightened, with his tail between his legs. Slowly we made friends. I had put out biscuits for him and gradually he began to trust me. There was no collar around his neck and his black and tan coat was matted with dirt. Today, he finally forgot his fear and followed me to the back door, where he sat expectantly. We looked at each other. 'If you want to come in and stay,' I told him, 'you must have a bath.' He cocked his head and swished his tail and I took this to be an agreement. I ran the bath and put in some shampoo and disinfectant. I lifted up this unknown but acquiescent Alsatian and put him in the water. He stood meekly whilst I soaped and scrubbed him. I am not an authority on dogs but guess he is around a year old and probably chucked out after Christmas from the council estate some miles away. He looked all skin and bone but fluffed up well when I towelled him and now gazes at me with soft brown adoring eyes. He ate a large plate of food. He could be costly but I think our shop at work sells special food for dogs. He follows me everywhere. We are two of a kind, both unwanted and discarded by our owners. We have called him Dougal and he was the best thing that could have happened for the children. They were not allowed a dog with Ralph, but now they have in Dougie both a companion and a protector.

Charlotte made enquiries about a stray dog but no one came forward. Already stretched to the limit on all fronts, taking on a dog of any sort let alone a large one could have been deemed as foolish but she knew that help could be found where she worked and that both food and vet services were on hand at a fraction of the normal cost. Besides, the benefits of a guard dog could not be ignored. She could buy sacks of dried food that could be reconstituted, from the onsite shop, and would hunt round for a bed, collar and lead in the local market or jumble sale. Dougal grew strong and healthy with a shiny coat and pink lolling tongue.

While the coming of Dougal was a blessing in some ways and a welcome distraction, it was not long before unhappiness and anger engulfed her again and when the fear, rage and frustration of her life struck her with force, she would make for the squash court where she would slam the ball with powerful venom and give her partner a hard game. Then she would finish, spent, limp and fatigued and take a shower, standing under the deluge, where the final purging would take place and be completed and return her to some form of transient peace.

Tom Wilder was not far from her thoughts and although she had not seen him for some weeks, she knew where he was staying and wanted to resume their friendship. Charlotte knew that again she was making the running but was unbowed. She knew that Tom was waiting for her to make the decisions. She rang the hotel.

CHAPTER ELEVEN

METAMORPHOSIS

The 1970s were a decade of contradictions and tremendous change. Cosy ideals were swept away as Britain was catapulted into a new and modern life after twenty-five years of post-war shortages and menial living standards. There were equal opportunities for all: health, wealth and a home of your own along with easy credit and better job opportunities. But by the mid-seventies Britain was in deep trouble and losing its place on the world stage as the oil crisis in the Middle East took hold. As a result, the British people were plunged into gloom as food and petrol prices soared and the lights 'literally' went out. The miners found their voice and held the country to ransom. Punk rock invaded the airways and anarchy and desecration of family values prevailed. The divorce rate went up, preparing the way for single parenthood and the birth of the phrase "latchkey" children. Rioters held sway and football hooligans ran wild, degrading the country and insulting Britain's most cherished heroes from an imperial past.

Now is the time to take stock and turn frugality and misery into hope. We must become more self-reliant and attack our problems. We must no longer live on our dreams.

Taken from *The Fire and the Phoenix*

With her new salary and budget account Charlotte was able to cope but it left no room for treats or extras. Her relationship with Tom grew and as she regained her confidence, she was able to grapple with the various everyday problems more competently. Tom was an astute 'man of the world' and his feelings for Charlotte were initially based on her vulnerability and her need to be comforted. He saw himself as her mentor, father figure and brother all in one, but was happy to satisfy his own sexual needs and be her lover at the same time. He had told her that she was highly sexed and that this was in her genes. This gave Charlotte some insight into her parents' relationship before she was born. Netta had said she was a love child. Perhaps they had practiced little constraint. Had her mother been his model? Had she too been unable to resist her overpowering needs?

Charlotte was not prepared to disturb Tom's marital state. He had told her that, although his wife had cheated on him in the past, he wanted to maintain the status quo for the sake of his children, and so their affair must be discreet. Charlotte was prepared to take him on at any price and was prepared to sell her soul rather than lose him. This support for her, whatever his reason, gave her the power to hold her own home and family together. She was not proud of her behaviour, but surprised at her boldness in pursuing Tom, albeit he was a willing partner in her game and needed no encouragement.

She wondered where her boldness came from when normally she was self-depreciating and reserved. Ralph had often endorsed this with his sarcasm and belittling attitude towards her. Was she now just trying to survive and take control of her own needs, enjoying her newfound freedom and aspirations, or merely trying to get back at Ralph?

Diary extract: Thursday
Tom came round last night. I was hungry for him. He is still impetuous but I'll forgive him anything! He is so big, he just folds me in his arms, croons in my ear with that Northumbrian lilt and all my troubles melt away! He told me he would be away next week and would return with the family. They have found a house in the next town. Our activities must go on hold for the time being. I told him I would wait however long but how will I feel about sharing him with Lorna? We are bound to meet! Will I feel really hostile or deeply guilty and why am I so careless of my children's happiness?

At times, due to work and over-activity, her health would suffer. She would struggle to keep going and on these occasions she would take to her bed exhausted, believing sleep to be of more benefit than drugs or alcohol. Her constant need to keep the "wheels turning" was due to the fear that not enough activity on her part would lead to depression and despair. As a result, she would take on more challenges, as recorded in her diary.

Dougie is a great asset but there are times when his exuberance is too much! Today he nearly knocked me off my feet when welcoming me home from work. I was tired and laden with bags. He daily smothers me with wet kisses in his joy at my return, while sometimes I have barely enough strength to stand up. My new job is both interesting but also challenging, and I was mad enough to say that I'd love to take up John's offer of a game of squash! John Bradley is the lab supervisor and in charge of running the labs and their requirements. He resembles John Gregson in looks. He is amiable and a good boss to work for. John taught me to play squash two years ago and has booked a court for the lunch hour next week. I don't stand a chance! His large frame just stands in the centre of the court, delivering accurate shots, while I run around in all directions trying to gain a point! Do I need this torture!!! He's a good water polo player too, but I'll give that a miss!

At the beginning of April, Ralph requested a meeting in the local town for lunch. There were things he needed to discuss. Charlotte mentioned that the fence needed mending and perhaps he could make himself useful at the same time. He agreed but told her that he would have to stay for the night as it could not be done in a day. The children ignored him most of the time and there were no tears or requests for him to stay when it was finished. He spent the night on the settee downstairs and looked uncomfortable to be there at all. He told her that she must contact a solicitor because he would not be able to pay towards the mortgage for much longer and that their separation must be put on a legal footing. Ralph assured her that she would receive some sort of housing benefit because of her low wage, and some help towards the rates. Because of her inheritance paying a large deposit on the house, the mortgage was reasonable but Charlotte did not welcome the extra burden and further responsibility. Jemma would now have to give up both riding and music lessons or be taught by less experienced people. Jean and Bruce no longer paid for her private piano lessons. Charlotte still rode with Zurich but this was subsidised and did not apply to family members.

Easter brought a welcome diversion and was spent in Studland with the Appleyards. The four children had a great time on the beach and in the sea with the canoe and Dougal wore himself out racing up and down the grassy slopes of Maiden Castle in the early summer heat. The Iron-Age fort was interesting and the warm wind brought a flush to their faces. Charlotte wrote:

> I was deeply grateful to Alan and June for befriending me since Ralph left us. Sadly they will be moving north soon as Alan has a new job but they have assured me that their cottage in Studland will be at our disposal when I'm able to take the children and that we would be welcome to visit them in Leominster when they are settled. I thank God for my friends; both the Lovetts and the Appleyards have been so kind to me.

Rita had spoken to Brian about Charlotte's need for a solicitor. He gave her an address in Thornton Heath and generously promised to pay the fee at the end of the proceedings. Charlotte wrote:

> I took the day off work and travelled by train as the car was out of action again. I have never encountered a solicitor before, let alone one who specialised in divorce. Mr Stebbings was a large florid man who seemed to spill out over his large desk. He peered at me over his half-moon specs and was sympathetic to my case. I was shaking inwardly with nerves and didn't know what to expect.
>
> He explained that things needed to be put on a firm footing with regard to maintenance and that he would set the ball rolling. I had shown him the note left by Ralph and he had held it in his large spatula-type fingers, shaken his head and then put it away in his file.

I arrived home drained and empty, had a row with Jay and even the thought of hearing from Tom later did not cheer me up.

How could Ralph have brought us to all this?

Brian paid Charlotte a visit and when he saw the state of the Riley Elf, offered to look out for something more reliable for her. The car had let her down frequently and the arduous journey by two buses added to her long day. He also promised to take her out for a meal in one of the smart restaurants owned by his company. Charlotte was flattered by his attentions and kindness but unaware of his motives. Whatever she had learnt from her liaison with Tom, she was still naïve and trusted her uncle implicitly. When he asked her if she was still a member of the Salvation Army she had denied this with the fervour of the disciple Peter of his Lord. She protested arrogantly that she had now grown up and no longer needed their support, thus ignoring the acknowledgement of her debt to their teaching. She denied the God who she said had treated her so badly when she had kept to His rules to the best of her ability, and Who had brought sadness to her innocent children. This had given her a feeling of maturity in Brian's presence and a desire to appear sophisticated. Her uncle was very much the smooth benefactor who drove fast cars and dealt in big business. Charlotte was easily impressed by his lifestyle but had no idea what he really had in mind. Rosamund's illness had worsened and Brian had installed a housekeeper to look after them. He asked if Charlotte could visit her aunt from time to time, to which she agreed. This appeared to be all he wanted from her, for the time being at any rate.

As time went by Charlotte fluctuated between the joy of awaking to her real self and discovering what she had missed by marrying so young and the dark despair brought on by guilt. With the regard to the latter she felt sucked in by a gravitational force, a bewitching upsurge of emotion whenever Tom was around, driving out any sense of pride or decency. She knew where his car was parked and could view his comings and goings at certain times from the women's restroom window high up in the manse roof. Sometimes she would see him walking towards his car and her heart would race as she tore down the three flights of stairs in an effort to waylay him for a hurried message or date for their next clandestine meeting. Now that his family were in town, phone calls outside work were few and far between and office calls were tricky. She had never experienced this urgency or cravings for Ralph.

At times the pain of her new love was so strong that she was bowed down by its very force. Sharing him only added to her stress but she was uncomplaining. Hiding her secret from her children and her colleagues only added fuel to the fire that was already well alight and she wondered how long it would be before she could no longer conceal its flame.

Another part of her revelled in her newly found enjoyment of the things she had been warned against during her teenage years. She experimented with cosmetics, alcohol and cigarettes. She tried eye make-up and mini-skirts but was careful not to look vampish and was happy with jeans and mules at the weekend. The long thin menthol cigarettes gave her a feeling of sophisticated elegance but were expensive and hard to master. Alcohol gave some comfort but was not always agreeable. She learnt to appreciate what was beneficial and not to overdose.

There were numerous dances put on by various lab departments at the sports club and Charlotte, whose only venture into dancing had been strictly ballroom with Mr Scott and the music of Victor Sylvester at school, found that the new fast rhythm came as easily and naturally as breathing. She loved the disco sound and its modern beat. She could forget everything as she danced herself into a numbing oblivion, where only the music and tempo existed. It was as if she was born to dance.

As the metamorphosis continued Charlotte had other ideas to improve her lot. She may not have been strong on the emotional front but she was intelligent, optimistic and resourceful when it came to spreading her meagre budget thinly over a large area. She tackled any job within reason and learnt to solve simple electrical and plumbing problems, use a drill and tools, glaze a window and keep the land drains flowing. These were constantly blocked after heavy rain due to the lie of the land. Meals were plain but wholesome with few treats or luxuries. Jumble sales and markets were frequented and became a good source of cheaper alternatives. Eventually she was to take on foreign students during the summer, tolerated by Jay and welcomed by Jemma, who would bring in extra cash. In the summer of 1975 whilst on holiday in Dorset, she had the idea to write a book. It would be to help others in a similar situation as recorded in her diary.

August 20th 1975

I am sitting in the hollow of the scrub high up on the Purbecks. The children are still asleep in the cottage below as it's 8am in the morning and teenagers need their sleep. Dougie is with me as he loves his morning "gallop" and is nosing around the rabbit holes as I write. It is so beautiful here; so peaceful where only the rabbits and butterflies venture on these grassy flowery slopes. The sky is painted azure and the sea a deeper blue. I sit here with the sun upon my face and I think about my new idea. I have been making notes of all the things I have learnt to do on my own and the ways in which I have saved money. Since re-decorating my bedroom with half-priced Laura Ashley wallpaper I feel a new surge of freedom and a break with the past. The new cheap plywood dressing table shelf looks good varnished and I'm pleased with the result, also the covering up of the ugly old fireplace with tongued and grooved pine. The cheap offcut of shag pile carpet completes the job. I seem to have a nose for a bargain and an eye for what I can do with it. I am buzzing with ideas and will write them down as they occur. They will not all be practical or culinary as some will be on a more personal level; things that have helped me get through the difficult times, simple things like long hot baths and hugging a pillow at night for warmth and comfort. There will also be information about legal procedures and council grants, singles clubs and help with children. I just wish I knew about cars! It could save me a lot of money. Jay changed a tyre on the way down. I don't know where he learnt that but he can teach me! I shall call my book The Fire and the Phoenix! Jemma put it into my head when she asked about this mythical bird. This book will be my Phoenix that hopefully rises from the ashes of things past. It may become part autobiographical at the same time.

The previous Autumn Jemma had joined Jay at Springfield High. Jay, now fourteen, practiced hard to become a rock musician after buying his first guitar. He would "jam" in his room much to the consternation of his mother and sister. This natural progression was to take over his life in time and fill the void left by his father. Jemma, on the other hand, was not progressing under an inferior piano teacher and eventually her lessons were dropped. This did not deter her from practicing as she was accomplished enough to play for her own enjoyment but Charlotte was still angry that she was missing out on proper tuition due to her father's selfishness. In October Charlotte received a surprise that was most welcome but came with a hidden price tag.

Diary entry: 4th October
I can't believe what happened today! I was working in the office when an unknown man asked for me at the lodge gate. The security men told me that he was a chauffeur delivering a car to a Charlotte Fielding from a Brian Mayhew and would I sign for it? I was flabbergasted! It is a white Cortina about eight years old. I'm over the moon! I have yet to get all the paperwork sorted but that won't take long and someone on site wants to buy the Elf! Things are really looking up! I must thank Brian profusely! I can drive it up to Norfolk when we go to Rita's for half term.

The following month Brian arrived for his reward as recorded:

Diary entry: November
I feel let down, humiliated, cheap and degraded. When Brian offered to take me out for a meal in le Gourmet, a smart restaurant in Jerome Street last night, I was all for it but failed to pick up on the knowing looks from some of his business friends when Brian introduced me as 'his niece'. I was stupid enough to down sherry by the glass in an effort to please and then accepted glasses of wine in the same manner. I suppose I was

trying to be sophisticated beyond my capabilities. Brian was the charming host all evening and then drove me home in the Rolls-Royce. He asked if he could come in for a nightcap. By then I was well away and unable to refuse. Barely had we crept in and taken off our coats before he made a lunge at me on the settee, his hands and mouth everywhere. I was so full of drink and shock that I rushed out to vomit in the kitchen sink. I couldn't even make it to the lavatory. This stopped Brian in his tracks and shortly afterwards he apologised and made his exit but not before asking again 'was it the uncle thing?' as if this was what had caused me to call a stop to his advances. I am so stupid! I had no idea that that's what he had in mind. My own uncle! He kept saying that we're not related and it didn't matter, but goodness, I never thought of him in that way and what about poor Rosamund: terminally ill and unable to defend herself? I'm so bloody naïve. I suppose Tom just wants me for sex as well? I overheard one of the scientists say to him 'don't handle the goods if you don't want to buy'. I'm just bloody goods! Every party I go to at the club there's always someone waiting to pounce on me and make sexual overtures of some sort or another. Have I brought this on myself? If so it's not intentional. What is it about me? I don't flirt or lead men on deliberately. I like them as friends. They are less complicated and less critical than women. Was my mother a prostitute? Have I got some weird attraction? Now I'll feel embarrassed when I meet Brian again. I've always been fond of him ever since I was eight when he kindly bought me those books. Now I think he's just like all the rest. All this upset has brought me to profanity.

This I strongly dislike and it's one more step down this thorny hellish path. Even the new feral kitten we brought back from Norfolk can't cheer me up but it's good to see that she's getting on so well with Dougie. We have called her Patty because she pats everything she comes across. We found her on Jemma's twelfth birthday.

Sadly for Charlotte worse was to come. In the spring of the following year, an event took place that was to bring her to the very brink of despair and remorse. On the eve of St Valentine's Day Tom had taken her out for a romantic meal. Later, their passions had reached fever pitch and in their haste, precautions were forgotten. Charlotte became pregnant but due to her mental stress and anguish she miscarried, blaming this on a fierce game of squash, slamming at her demons on all four walls with all her strength. She won the game but not her battle against the fear of reprisals from her children, Tom's wife, and all who knew her if it came to light. In her turmoil she had not thought of the consequences for her unborn child. All that was recorded of her thoughts and emotions of that time are contained in a sad little poem "Remorse":

Remorse

He was born at the end,
At the end of a beginning
That might have been
Had we chosen that it should have been
And who were we to choose?
Send not the bier
So little left to take.
Oh God look not down

For this was our mistake.
You gave him life.

Charlotte Fielding 1976

A draft of an earlier poem written the year before was found among her papers; Charlotte wrote:

I will have his child.
He will not go free of me.
I shall bear his fruit upon my vine.
My lonely days will end
 with his love child
with our love child.
This child, a son, born to be wild and free
Borne upon the tide of our love.
Song of the bird, song of the sea
Song of Summer shall blow thro his hair
And ruffle his fair curls.
Dear God let it be, let it be, while there's still life in me.

During the dark weeks that followed Charlotte was unable to write in her diary or work on her book. Depression engulfed her and Tom kept his distance. Its was not until some months later that a bleak light eventually began to filter through and optimism sent out new shoots of hope.

CHAPTER TWELVE

TRIALS AND TRIBULATIONS

The summer of 1976 was all that Charlotte could have wished for as she recovered her strength. She loved the heat of the long days and the sensuous torpid nights. She lolled in a hammock at weekends, too hot to work, and built a barbecue with loose bricks for "bring your own" parties in the garden. Her confidence in driving through London increased with the new car and extra time was filched with Tom by taking him to and from Heathrow airport whenever possible, as business trips for Zurich Wolf dictated. In July she sold the model train to an enthusiast in the Midlands and in a moment of madness sent half the proceeds to Ralph, while the rest helped towards new school uniforms for the children. During the winter months she continued with the research and writing of her book *The Fire and the Phoenix* but lacked her initial enthusiasm and began to doubt her ability to succeed. Ralph continued to send her maintenance but on a matter of principle Charlotte refused to give him the divorce he requested. He would have to wait the full five years. She knew that she was being vindictive but gave no heed.

In February the following year the central heating boiler broke down and the family were without heating or hot water. Charlotte was desperate but determined not to ask Brian or Rita for help but offered to take on a clinical trial for Zurich that would supply the necessary extra cash. The trial was described in her diary.

Diary entry; Feb 19th

The paraffin stove ran out again last night and the smell was awful this morning. Have heard about a big trial next month and have put my name down. The money will pay off a loan I must get from the bank in order to pay a heating engineer as we can't wait another month. Thank goodness the cold spell is nearly over. I have been relying on hot showers at the swimming pool for a good warm up and hair wash.

March 16th

Had my check up for the trial today. Lots of electrodes and various tests to make sure I'm up to scratch! Clinical trials are not unusual at Zurich and are "on offer" to staff now and then. The "big ones" are less common but pay well. I'm going to be testing amphetamines over a period of six consecutive Tuesdays. John Bradley has given his consent and will give me the required time off work as they are all day. I will be picked up by car from home and taken to Zurich at 8am and then brought home again at 4pm.

The trial includes a slap-up lunch in order to get us feeling sleepy in the afternoon and so testing the effects of the drug designed to keep us awake and "on the ball"! The trial consists of being wired up and then sitting in a booth, after medication, and wearing headphones, listening to bleeps and tapping on a Morse code type machine.

March 30th

Session three in the "torture chamber"! The car arrived at the same time as last week only this time I nearly freaked out. Tom had arrived at midnight the night before and stayed over. He had only just left 10 mins before the Zurich car arrived! Phew!! After being wired up (the electrodes will not stay in my thick hair) the four of us sat chatting and reading papers. About 10am we were given our dose: six tablets containing possible placebos or the real drug but how much was hard to say. We had to stand up to take the tablets in case any rolled down the chair! We then went into the soundproof room, with the large comfy chairs. After we were "plugged in" and our blood pressure was taken we then filled in a questionnaire and began the "bleep" and "tapping" test. These were designed to test our reactions and whether we were extra alert with the new drug. Our pupils were photographed at one stage. At lunch one or two described themselves as being on a "high". I may have had a low dose but I still felt more awake than usual! Lunch was prawn cocktail and beef stroganoff followed by fruit and lashings of orange juice then back in the room for another session until 4pm. I was driven home suffering from a bad headache!

April 6th
Another day of the clinical trial. I started off ok and felt quite happy and relaxed. Unfortunately I must have been given a high dose of the amphetamine because I felt really awful and had to summon help. My heart was racing. It has quite unnerved me for the next two sessions. Went home with a cracking headache which stayed with me all evening. Will I live through it all? What people will do for money!

John just laughs. He's taken part in dozens and walks about as though he's permanently in a daze.

Charlotte was to take on several more clinical trials during her time at Zurich but was quite unaffected by them in the long term. Zurich would not risk any life-threatening situation although some of the more complicated trials could have minor unpleasant effects in the short term.

Finally Charlotte was forced to face the divorce proceedings she had fought so hard against for five years. The requirement had now become legal. On the day, she resolved to make a statement by wearing her trendiest clothes and investing in an extravagant, but eye-catching, hairdo. She was going to show Ralph that his treatment of her had left her unbowed and that she was still an attractive woman. If she must go through the divorce, she would put on a show and impress him with her apparent ability to cope without him. Charlotte noted with some satisfaction that the "other woman" may have been blond and younger but was also plain and dumpy. This gave Charlotte the courage to hold her head high during the dissolution of their fifteen-year-old marriage. She wanted everyone to know that her new life was about to begin and that she was strong enough 'to go it alone'.

In truth, she was far from this ideal and as the months went by things did not get easier. Her children had never blamed her for the breakdown of the family but neither did they condone her turning her back on morality. Charlotte had not realised how perceptive they had become since Ralph had left. They had been forced, by circumstances beyond their control, to be older and wiser than their years and as a result took a high moral stand, especially where their mother was concerned. Rows became more frequent and troubled times lay ahead. Could Charlotte bring herself to let go of the emotional rope that bound her to Tom and glide freely above it all? Not yet.

Jay had reached his seventeenth birthday and had passed his driving test. Charlotte had treated him to a birthday dinner in their local Bernie Inn. It was the best she could afford. He had asked her to break with Tom and told her that she was wasting her time with him. In Jay's view he was no longer the kind man who had taught him squash and snooker but a monster in disguise who could sweet-talk his mother into a false sense of security with his empty promises when all was far from the truth. She would be hurt again.

Charlotte too began to question her motives for prolonging the relationship. Her diary entry for September gives insight to her turbulence.

September
Dreadful row with Jay over nothing in particular. I said it wasn't my fault my life had shattered into a thousand pieces. He told me not to leave the splinters lying around. I knew what he meant. Jemma's started going for me too. I can't bear to hurt them but what can I do? I'm so weak, so dependent on Tom, it's pathetic. On good days when I feel strong I swear I'll give him up but then something happens and I need him again. I'm so lonely for family discourse. My other friends all have parents, siblings, nephews and nieces, where are mine? Are they out there somewhere? Now Rita and David are in East Anglia and Brian's out of bounds, I'm even more dependent on Tom to tell me I'm doing alright. Perhaps one day my babes will understand that it's the only way I can cope. How would it be if I was a drug addict or alcoholic or locked in a loony bin? Would they thank me if I had put them into care or sent them to live with their father and "that woman" who left her own children?

'Why do you love Tom so, Mummy, when he makes you cry?'

Jemma is too young to understand the complexities

of this unfortunate relationship, born of retaliation on my part and sexual desire on his; but now we're in this fog there's no way back or is there? I must find an answer. Dougie has put his head in my lap and is gazing at me with large brown eyes burning with love. He is the most extraordinary dog. He seems to know my every thought. He can still make me laugh.

I won't forget the day he bounded upstairs, eager to join in our lovemaking! We just collapsed with laughter!

There were many more diary days filled with a desperate longing to end the pain the relationship caused, but how would she go about it? They had both tried 'a separation period' but each time they were drawn back together again with a renewed intensity. Both were to blame. Another problem was that Charlotte was becoming more possessive and her sharing Tom with Lorna became more and more irksome. For most of their time together she had kept to the rules, a discreet distance from his home life with no impossible demands to be made. Now she would ask why he had not phoned or where had he been when he promised to call? She could hardly contain her jealousy when his family decamped to Spain for a holiday. 'What about me?' she would demand. 'Aren't I worth taking away?' Tom would tell her that it was expedient. He just wanted both worlds.

New ideas presented themselves as another year approached. She sent off the synopsis for *The Fire and the Phoenix* to a small family-run publishers recommended by a literary friend Anne Johnson, although the manuscript was far from finished. Charlotte also met up with other divorced or separated people in the district and joined their singles groups. Gingerbread was the first of them but there was little comfort to be found. She felt depressed as this accentuated her feelings of inadequacy and loneliness, in spite of being surrounded by unfortunate people in the same boat. Her children were too old to benefit and did not want to accompany their mother on forced friendly "family" excursions. Other singles clubs were either too expensive or too desperate. Charlotte would team up with her friend Anne and they would dance in various dingy venues with unlikely dance partners. Throughout the proceedings, Charlotte would half-heartedly enter into the spirit of the occasion while her mind would be querying the whereabouts of Tom and the date of their next meeting. It was easy enough to juggle the two situations because she still felt safe in her relationship with Tom and her search for a new partner was merely a game. It would take a very special person to prise her away from him. She was prepared to look around but not here, in these dives. Perhaps there was a better way? Would she consider Dateline, the new computer matchmaking agency? Not yet as this was on a more personal level and the cost would have to be considered, but it could be an option, when she was ready.

Tom knew of her threats to leave him but was complacent enough to laugh at her efforts. It was true that she gave him a hard time when Lorna took control. Occasionally, as a result of his deferring to her plans, a meal with Charlotte would be cancelled and a row would ensue, but he would bounce back again and win her over with his good humour or he would present her with some bauble he had brought back from one of his business trips abroad. She would forgive him and they would be back in the old groove, each settling into the usual routine.

Sometimes, as the children grew older, they were less afraid to show Tom their angst. He would stay away and the situation would become exacerbated, with Charlotte torn between the warring sides. One day, Jay called him 'a wanker' and this stopped Tom dead in his tracks. Jay had touched a raw nerve and Tom had withdrawn for some weeks. Maybe Jay had been right?

To distract herself, Charlotte decided to take up the suggestion that she should visit a clairvoyant by the name of Mrs Hardwick. Charlotte wrote: 'I have never been in favour of visiting a psychic but was spellbound by Anne's account of Mrs Hardwick's powers. She had described Anne's husband to her, who had died last year, and told her he was very angry. She said that he was holding up a violin and asking why their son Robert was no longer having violin lessons! Anne said that there was no way that Mrs H. would have known such a thing and it was true, she had stopped Robert's lessons. She told her many other facts as well. I have decided to pluck up my courage and pay Mrs H. a visit. Perhaps she can spread some light on my most uncertain future or my unknown past?'

Diary entry: Wednesday May 4th
Today I went to see Mrs H. Anne had told me to take some cash but it was up to me how much as Mrs H did not set an exact amount for her services. Her house was on a council estate in Peckham. Mrs Hardwick was chair bound and the door was on the latch. She was a large lady and her paisley dress appeared to overflow and mingle with the patterned carpet below. She smiled and held out her hand and asked for a piece of jewellery or the watch I was wearing, presumably for "vibes". I gave her my watch and she held it in her hand for some minutes with her eyes closed. I waited in nervous trepidation. What would she reveal?

Suddenly she clapped her hands over her ears and

shouted 'the noise, the noise!' This apparently was Jay and his friends having a gig somewhere. After a while she opened her button-brown eyes and spoke in a normal voice. She told me that both my children were of good character and that I had no need to worry about them.

With regard to Tom she said that 'like goes toward like', whatever that means and that she could see a wedding and lilies at some far distant date but gave no indication of who the bridegroom might be. She also told me to keep writing as there was money to be made. She remained quiet for a moment and just as I thought she had finished she held her hand up in the air in an attitude of forbearance. 'Your mother is holding a baby. She says he's happy where he is but you must find your twin –' she paused as though searching through a fog, 'he's in America or it could be Australia, odd-colour eyes: one blue the other... a missing person? I'm not sure.' She smiled and returned my watch. Interview over!

I thanked her profusely, paid my contribution, and walked dazedly out of the house. I don't know what to make of her last revelation.

Maybe the "vibes" were wearing thin!

When I told Jemma about the writing, she said, 'I keep telling you Mum, forget Tom and get on with your book.' I need to research legal aid as I'm stuck at the moment. I must press on as I get so easily distracted. Forget about a twin, it's all nonsense. What did she say about my mother? Does that mean she is alive or dead? Was it a Mrs Lytton who came to see me and Netta all those years ago? It's all so odd!

Although work at Zurich progressed and became a stable

background, Charlotte's emotional state fluctuated from day to day. She tried to concentrate on her book that was nearing completion. The publishers Gleave & Gleave had approved the synopsis sent to them in January and wanted to see the finished manuscript, but a missed phone call from Tom or a dispute with the children would set her back again and more time would be wasted.

After a particularly bad evening with Tom, Charlotte threatened him with her intention to join Dateline if he didn't keep his promise to take her on holiday. She finally got her way. He would take her to Spain for a week under the cover of a golfing trip with his friend and ally, Max. Charlotte told the children, now young adults, she was going away with her friend Anne. Arrangements were made and Charlotte was tense with excitement. She stocked the larder, informed the neighbours who would watch out for Jay and Jemma, who were more than able to cope and now thoroughly independent. Jay had started at art college and Jemma her O Levels. They were busy with their friends and many activities and would not miss her too much. Charlotte wrote of the week in her diary.

Diary entry; October 6th
What an emotional rollercoaster! I have just got back from Spain. What a mixture of elation and guilt, but elation won for the most part even tho' the weather was foul and rained stair-rods that flattened pavements and pocked holes in the sand on the beaches. The place was deserted. We frequented bars wherever possible and my eyes were opened to Tom's excessive drinking habits. We had hired a little Fiat at the airport and drove to the local high spots in Marbella. It was my first visit to Spain but the week was to be memorable for our excess of sexual passion, as the rain hammered on the roof,

rather than the scenery. On the last night I threw a tantrum and slept in the spare room. I was already predicting the end of the honeymoon where there had been no wedding. Tom was going back to Lorna and the taste of honey turned to a taste of gall.

Now I'm home I feel so depressed. I have lied to the children and can no longer bear this deceit. I'll write off to Dateline. Surely there must be someone out there for me who is free? It all sounds desperate but what can I do?

For the next few months Charlotte concentrated on her writing and shut out all other distractions, including Tom and rumours of possible redundancy from Zurich which she had ignored for some time. She was determined to finish before the end of the year. Anne Johnson, who worked for a magazine, had offered to type up the finished manuscript for a reasonable sum and Charlotte had jumped at the chance of meeting a deadline. Anne was moving offices in the new year and would not have so much time for Charlotte's work after that. It was the kick she needed.

In November an unexpected distraction came with the news of the death of Rosamund Mayhew. Charlotte records the funeral and family event.

*Diary entry: 2*th *November*

Today was the funeral of my Aunt Rosamund. There is much to ponder about her shortened life. The poor woman has been ill for many years and it is something of a relief to know that she is in a better place. Rosamund has always been good to me and will be remembered for her generous gifts and sparkling personality.

Whilst I'm well aware of Brian's indiscretions, I

was not surprised to hear from Rita that Rosamund also sought comfort elsewhere. What happens to people? They had everything! Ros was so attractive and fun! I used to look up to Brian. He was always kind to me. Why did he have to spoil things the way he did? There were pitifully few of us at the funeral and no sign of the man she had apparently loved. Rita and David had come down from Norfolk and were staying with Anette and Bob. Linda joined us and Brian brought his brother and sister-in-law. After the brief service at the crematorium, we adjourned to a smart restaurant organised by Brian. Here we all chatted and caught up with family news. Myra and Evan were unable to come but sent condolences.

Both Linda and Anette had brought photos of their children which were passed around. They all asked after my two. After the meal we all went our separate ways but I hope to see R & D before they return to Cromer. Reflecting on funerals is a sober pastime. I still miss Netta and Annie. The list of close friends and relations left to me is still precious. I so appreciate the continued friendship of both the Lovetts and the Appleyards. No family members could have been kinder to us over the years. I have a lot to be grateful for.

Again she turned her attentions to her book but this time thoughts of change and the possible redundancy hampered her progress. It had been rumoured last year that part of Zurich would be moving away to Hertfordshire and now it appeared the rumours were true and that the department where Charlotte worked was included in the move. She would have to go with them or take redundancy. Charlotte knew that this would be her most likely option as her roots and those of her children were now firmly planted in Surrey. In addition to this worry concerning her employment, other unpleasant issues had also come to her notice. Over years of neglect, through coping on her own, Pine Trees had become increasingly in need of attention. Her small budget had not made way for major house repairs. They may have to move house in the next year or two. She would have to start house-hunting before long.

In January 1980 she finally sent off the finished manuscript to Gleave & Gleave, the small family publishers who had shown interest in her synopsis. She toasted the occasion with Jay and Jemma who were pleased to hear that *The Fire and the Phoenix* was definitely in the post. Charlotte wrote:

> For the first time in years I got down on my knees and thanked God I had been able to finish it at last and to ask for His blessing on its journey! Jay says he wants to move out later this year and share a flat with his arty friends. He says he will help me move house if the time comes. I don't know whether to be pleased or sorry if he goes, but I won't miss the rows. Dinner tomorrow with Tom. A new decade and new horizons! Zurich Wolf is definitely splitting but not for another year. I feel real change in the air but will it be for the better? Which way will Tom go? He flits between the two parts of the company. Will it be the push I need to start a new life? I am full of optimism.

CHAPTER THIRTEEN

THE OPTIMIST

Charlotte had been in her thirties during the seventies. Her youth and resilience had carried her through the changes and tribulations of that era. There had been little time for punk or politics but it had driven her to write the book that she hoped would help other people in straightened circumstances or personal crisis. At the same time she had also taken pains to point out to her readers that embarking on an illicit affair was not the answer to wounded pride and would lead to further pain and distress. These honest revelations of her personal downfall were to hopefully act as a deterrent, but Charlotte was yet to give up her immoral lifestyle as suggested in her book. The fire still burned and she was yet to become its phoenix. In her efforts to cut her ties with Tom she would take risks in her search for a more permanent and suitable relationship and, with the book finished, she had more time to search.

As the new decade began, under Margaret Thatcher's government, Charlotte looked forward optimistically to challenging opportunities and new friendships. Little is recorded of her actual move to her new home in 1981, but an estate agent's description was that of a small terraced house on the edge of town with a narrow strip of garden. Charlotte noted that 92 Fenton Road was 'dark, and the road noisy' but that it would have to suffice. She now had a little spare money over from the sale of Pine Trees for the repairs and improvements that were needed for the new house and she would enjoy the process of gradually turning it into her home.

The move coincided with further interest in her book. This brought her much joy but celebrations would have to wait until the publishing was a definite possibility. There was too much claim on her attention with her new domestic demands at present. She would keep the news to herself and the children. Her other problem was that the date for the move of Zurich Wolf to Barnet was to be undertaken the following September but she would worry about that when the time came. Meanwhile she kept in touch with her old friends in Pine Trees and made a new one nearby.

Maggie Leighton taught French at Jemma's school and belonged to the local drama group. In August she encouraged Charlotte to go along with her to the auditions for the autumn production of *Marion's Holiday*. Charlotte, always ready for a new distraction, agreed. The South Park Players had been in existence for many years and were fondly embraced by the local residents, who attended their unchallenging and often, unintentionally, comic performances. Charlotte had not taken the audition too seriously but had joined in the reading with 'gay abandon and a nothing to lose' approach. Later in the week she was somewhat unnerved to hear that she had been cast in the leading role of Marion. The Players were a small friendly crowd and welcomed her wholeheartedly into their midst. She soon felt at home with their rather laid-back approach and the promise that 'all really would be alright on the night.'

The leading man, Vince Davis, was older than Charlotte by some years and according to her diary possessed 'nut-brown eyes and a dark brown voice', both of which she found rather attractive. Rehearsals began in various homes and for some weeks Charlotte was absorbed in her role and busy with her script. Tom had turned up once or twice to weigh up the opposition and then retired but not before letting Vince know that he was around. Jay and Jemma took little interest but promised to come to the play when it was to be performed in October. As the time drew near Charlotte was dismayed to find that there would be no hamper of costumes from Fox's in London; it was true that *Marion's Holiday* was not exactly on a par with *Saint Joan*, but she had hoped for some assistance in the costume department. She was to discover that the South Park Players were solely responsible for all aspects of management and that she was expected to find and finance her own outfit. She would scan the pages of her Freeman's catalogue for a smart two-piece and Maggie had offered her a few eye-catching accessories.

Diary entry: Saturday Oct.12th
During the day I laid out the backcloth for the play in the yard outside after scouring about for any tins of spare paint. I started on a sea scene. It was quite difficult as there had been a previous scene of a Welsh dresser that had to be eradicated. Finally it was finished and I felt quite pleased with the result. In the evening, J&J went to the pictures and Tom arrived. I dressed up in the mauve cat suit (Maggie's) and blonde wig. When he came, I hid behind the front door and then stepped out. The effect was amazing! He was quite at a loss for words! Then he decided I looked like an old girlfriend who won Miss Newcastle years ago! He said 'good luck' with the dress rehearsal tomorrow. I think we're going to need it!

Sunday 13th October.
Dress rehearsal. This was truly appalling! Everything seemed to go wrong. Some of the funniest bits were

not even supposed to be funny! Richard was there but not allowed to use his voice. My hat slipped off my wig and I didn't feel it go. Vince kept fiddling about all through the performance missing his cigarettes. Half the scenery was still not ready and we finished around 7pm having started at 3pm. Jemma says she is not keen to see the performance next week!

Friday 18th October

Marion's Holiday
I felt keyed up all day but managed to get through work ok and left a bit earlier as I had the w/e shopping to do. I was already feeling tired and wondering how I was going to manage. Both Jemma and Annette were coming to witness my efforts!

The performance went off ok except for a few minor mistakes. I found I had left a pencil out of my bag and this could have proved disastrous but noticed one on the table. Vince left out half a page and Kate's entrance. Props forgot to put the suitcase on the stage in the last act and I had to carry it on. This threw me as I was supposed to be on the opposite side of the stage to the case. Anyway all was not lost. Annette said she enjoyed it but Jemma wouldn't comment!

Sunday October 20th

Marion's Holiday
Yesterday morning, the day of the play, I woke up with a swollen eye and had to dash round to the doctor. He gave me some antibiotics and said it was sinusitis. Spent the rest of the day in and out of bed. Vince came round

to see if I was ok. I dosed myself up before the performance and took some of his brandy with me in case of emergencies.

It went really well. I was far less nervous than on Friday and really enjoyed the part. There was only one prompt and very few mistakes all through the play. There were about 120 in the audience, an improvement on Friday. Maggie and Frank came back for a drink and I collapsed on the settee, and then later, dragged myself off to the party not expecting to stay long or enjoy it. Maggie made sure I did enjoy it! She's a great friend! We finally left about 2am. Very tired but glad that it was all over! Needless to say there was no sign of Tom. I knew he wouldn't come. Why do I care? I'm having a lazy day today. Jay says he'll help with set destruction at the hall later. He didn't come to the play as he had two gigs this weekend so it's good of him and will take the pressure off me. I just want to do nothing!

We gather from further entries in her diary that the party was held in Vince's flat. She describes Vince as being a widower whose wife died two years earlier from septicaemia. He was a photographer by profession and ran a small studio in Camberwell. He was a warm-hearted man and generous with his hospitality. His mother, now in her eighties, was once an opera singer and still hoped that her son would settle down with 'a nice little widow from the women's institute, who would mend his socks and bake him cakes'. Vince had other ideas and looked around for someone with a bit of style and physical attraction. Charlotte had caught his eye and his imagination. They had kissed on stage. Charlotte had shown little interest in Vince and had concentrated on his shortcomings during their time together on the set, but she was not entirely averse to his compliments or invitations to the local pub. Although she deplored his smoking she could easily be seduced by his beautiful speaking voice; his soft brown eyes and the fact that he was a free agent, although it was rumoured that one of the other players was an interested party. After the play Charlotte agreed to meet him for a meal and get to know him better. Tom was away in America on business and also busy on the home front with his daughter's wedding planned for November.

Charlotte wrote:

> Vince has asked me to go with him to the Isle of Wight sometime next month. Apparently his friend Den runs a small hotel in Shanklin and is celebrating his fiftieth birthday with his wife Sylvia. They have no family but many friends. I am very tempted though mainly because I have never been to the I.O.W. and the thought of a party and a night with Vince in a hotel sounds intriguing! Am I being promiscuous? After all Tom still sleeps with Lorna!!!

Unbeknown to Charlotte at the time, there was another interested party expecting to be invited to the celebrations on the Isle of Wight. Eileen Hislop had been in love with Vince for some time, and up until *Marion's Holiday* would have been his possible choice of partner. Charlotte was quite unaware of any relationship between them as she had not met Eileen. Eileen was a married woman and could not protest too loudly at the change of arrangement. Arthur Hislop, unlike Vince, was a man of means and Eileen enjoyed the luxuries he could afford so she trod the road of infidelity with caution. The weekend of the celebration arrived and Charlotte records the following:

Diary entry: Monday 12ᵗʰ November

Where do I begin? It was a bit of a farce from the start!
We set off early on Saturday morning and eventually
drove onto the ferry at Portsmouth harbour bound for
Fishbourne. V's old car had rattled and bumped its way
in a state of unhappiness all the way down from Surrey.
Just as the ferry docked at Fishbourne and all the other
car engines burst into life, our car was immobilised
with a broken key in its ignition. It broke off as V
turned it! We were stuck in the middle of the deck but
had to wait until the last car had driven off. We were
then shoved, ignominiously, by the crew, onto the
empty road ahead and left like people in a Hitchcock
movie, to say nothing of the dramatic black cloud that
was looming overhead. We set off for a garage a mile
away and as we trudged along, the black cloud suddenly
gave a growl of thunder and erupted mercilessly. I
squelched into the garage more concerned with my
new shoes! Returning to the car with the mechanic, no
key could be found to fit the ignition so the car had to
be "hot-wired". V would have to put two bare wires
together to form a spark to start the engine. It was quite
scary but we drove to Shanklin in pale sunlight,
without more ado; our spirits rising with every mile.

We were now considerably late, still damp and full
of apologies! Den and Sylvie were a delightful couple
who took it all in their stride. They looked at me keenly
and I got the impression they were expecting someone
else. The hotel, now closed for the summer, was small
with loud carpets, chintz chairs and cheap tables. After
a change of clothes (borrowed in V's case) and a light
lunch, they offered to take us out and about in their
sports car. This proved both exhilarating and,

fortunately, uneventful. Everywhere was closed for the season and it was good to get back to tea and to warm ourselves by the gas fire.

In the evening the party began and about sixty people arrived from around the island. Vince was in good form, swaggering about, telling silly jokes and making the most of the food and drink. There was a live band and dancing, followed by cake and celebratory speeches. By the time we got to bed I was relieved to see V flake out as though he were in a coma, sparing me any sexual engagement I might have regretted. In the morning he couldn't believe that he had passed up on this opportunity. I laughed and said 'next time maybe'. We walked around the town a bit and then, after lunch, set off for home in the "hot-wired" car. It was all quite bizarre but somehow the whole scenario seemed to be part of Vince. Rather a damp squib!

When I got home, Jay said a woman rang asking for me. When he told her I was away for the weekend she put the phone down without giving her name. Was there another woman in Vince's life?

A week later Charlotte went to dinner with Maggie and Frank.

November 20th

It was a good evening and I caught up with Players' gossip. It seems that the mystery lady who rang is called Eileen but apparently it's a one-sided affair. Vince is not convinced!! After such a pleasant evening it was a shock to arrive home at around 1am and find no Cortina in the driveway. I shot upstairs to wake a sleepy Jay and ask him what he had done with it and if he was OK. He said that the car was down by the traffic lights with a broken gear lever. 'Came off in my hand!' were his actual words.

November 21ˢᵗ

Disaster day! Jay and I inspected the damage. Need a new gear lever so phoned a few garages and was quoted £14! I walked into work and met some friendly site workers on the way to my block. They offered to weld the lever if I got the other part out of the car at lunchtime. John gave me a lift as I promised him I'd do overtime in the lab. We managed to get the rest of the stick out, then back to work. After work, back again with the newly welded lever. I finally got it fixed in the car with the help of an old boy from the garage across the road. I was so relieved to get it running OK. David has promised me his Rover when he trades it in for a Passat. He wants £500. It's a bit old but well maintained and more reliable than the Cortina. I will pass it on to Jay until it no longer passes the MOT. I don't want to do a "Vince" with it and be stuck somewhere.

Charlotte stayed friends with Vince but the affair was a non-starter. It was to be the first of many intrigues that she would experience in the following year as further revelations in her diaries come to light.

In December the news was given out to her department that the proposed move was once again postponed, as the new site was still unfinished. This came as a reprieve for Charlotte as it guaranteed her employment for another six months at least. Meanwhile, her book had been accepted for publication and for this, she was offered an advanced sum. Once again she decided to cast her net in the direction of Dateline. This resolution was brought sharply into focus when she had a chance meeting with Lorna in Sainsbury's during the Christmas week. Charlotte wrote:

> I'm surprised it has never happened before. We both came round an aisle at the same time, stopped dead and stared at one another. Then Lorna turned round and headed off quickly in the other direction but not before I saw the pain in her eyes. There were no recriminations or slanging matches. I knew that she was aware of me and I had met her several times at social gatherings at the sports club but in those circumstances we both kept up a pretence. Here in the supermarket it was different. It was raw and painful. I knew things had not been great between her and Tom in the past but I was still filled with remorse at the part I had played in fuelling our affair although I never sought to drive them apart. I long to be free of all this pain. I MUST LEAVE TOM.

The following January Charlotte sent off a form to Dateline. She still lacked the courage to end her affair with Tom or tell him of her intentions and, as a result, was doomed to compare her new "dates" with the man she still loved. During the next six months she would be on a ride that would bring her both excitement and despair. She met many men in that time but few in her eyes warranted a second interview. They ranged from a widower who arrived with photos of his dead wife, to a weirdo who described his caning in South Africa. This harrowing account was described in her diary?

> I was quite excited at the thought of meeting Clive in the Waldorf Hotel. He sounded well spoken on the phone and I was pleased to find that he was not

unattractive, tall, with dark curly hair and wearing a smart suit. He ordered drinks and canapés and we sat at a small table in the lounge. He said he was an educational historian and then launched into the most detailed account of his caning in a school in South Africa when he was sixteen. I felt like the guest of the Ancient Mariner, clamped to my chair, as each agonising moment was recalled, and not omitting the sexual arousal of a girl student who was forced to witness this spectacle and who was the cause of his punishment. At eleven o'clock I hauled myself to my feet in mid-sentence and rushed out. I had not eaten and was so mesmerised and demoralised by his diatribe I could barely make it to the station for the last train. I cried on the journey home as the experience had been so traumatic.

Two other memorable meetings filled her diary pages.

March 16th Saturday
I met Tony, initially, last week. He seemed a friendly sound sort of chap and we had things in common. He taught art at a school in Leatherhead. He called for me in his Volkswagen Beetle and we set off for a pub in Oxstead. We chatted about everything in general and enjoyed each other's company. On the way back we stopped to admire the moon, reflected in a large pond and it all seemed rather promising and romantic. Then we got back into the car and he found he was very low on petrol. We then went on a hunt for a garage but by now it's late and the one garage has closed. Finally we run out completely but fortunately close to a phone box. I woke a disgruntled Jay who agreed to pick us up

in his old customised van he uses for his rock group. True to his word, he arrives and we thankfully pile in the front. We are now on our way home when there is a hiss and a bang and the van blows up. Fortunately we are now near a garage on the main road. Jay freewheels it into the forecourt. He is mortified. It is now 1am and we phone for a taxi. Finally we arrive home and Tony is put to bed on the settee but it doesn't end there! After a sleepless night we are all woken early by the ringing of the phone. It is Tony's ancient mother wondering where he is! I then drive him back to his car with a jerry can of petrol. He really is nice but I'm not sure about his ability to think straight! I may give him one more chance!

April 6th Friday

A surprise "throw up" from the computer. A date liner called Colin Spencer-Wright rang today. I knew a Spencer-Wright at junior school, but he was a senior boy who sang solos in the school chapel. I particularly remember the carol services there. This chap has a wonderfully deep cultivated speaking voice and has given me an address in Chelsea. We have made a date for next week. I must find the A to Z.

April 13th Saturday.

It's extraordinary! Colin is the same Spencer-Wright from school. After he left the senior boys he went on to university. He is divorced and deals in property. He showed me round his smart terraced house from top floor to cellar. He said it was on the market and sparsely furnished. We went to see a film in the afternoon, an old classic at the Everyman, and chomped through a bag of sweets. Colin is large and jovial and drives a big car, rather like a smart landrover. I have invited him to visit us in Surrey in a couple of weeks' time. When I got home Dougie looked at me reproachfully. He had been shut in all day as neither of the children had been around. He's getting problems with his hind legs and has a job to get up. I must take him to the vet next week.

April 29ᵗʰ Monday
I'm really annoyed with myself. Tom came back from Bratislava and we met at lunchtime. We were larking about in the bedroom when the phone rang in there. On hearing Colin's deep dulcet tones booming in my ear I panicked and said 'wrong number' then I grabbed Tom and rushed him downstairs and out of the back door with the excuse that Dougie needed letting out and a walk. Tom seemed rather surprised but went along with my ploy. I can't handle two-timing! I'll have to give up one or the other but which one?

Later that year Charlotte was to find out. In September she recorded the first signs of change that would affect her life during the following year.

September 9ᵗʰ
Have just got back from the vet. Dougie has a disintegrating spine and his back legs keep giving way. Mike says when it gets too difficult for Dougie it will be kinder to put him down. This fills me with sadness as Dougie has been such a loyal and trusty friend, and guardian of the children when they were younger.

Another depressing thought is that I may be losing

Tom. Since he found out about Dateline things have not been good between us. He says that he understands my reasons but that it's still hurtful. I said 'what's the alternative, I need stability in the years to come?'

I had agreed to meet him in the Crown and we sat a little apart like two strangers, but watching each other's moves out of the corner of our eyes. He seemed depressed and hunched, withdrawn into his shell. There were no more recriminations. I tried to explain things better. I felt very sad about everything, I just wanted to get away from all the heartache of hurting others and getting hurt. Why is love such a tormentor?

CHAPTER FOURTEEN

GATHERING CLOUDS

1983 was a year of deep uncertainty. Both Jay and Jemma were growing up and wanting independent lives. Jay had found a flat to share with his friends and Jemma was starting at Sussex University. Charlotte was proud of her children but knew the pain they had both suffered over their father's desertion and the subsequent dissolution of their parents' marriage. Jay had become seriously dedicated to his music. He was the bandleader and put this ambition to succeed above everything else. He had learnt early lessons in frugality, sobriety and the benefit of hard work. He later studied computer graphics and went into the art industry. Charlotte wrote: 'He looks so sad, as if all the cares of the world are on his young shoulders. Jemma too has done well with her exams but has been psychologically damaged by events, and the discovery of the fatal letter from her father all those years ago and the disastrous aftermath still haunts her; as though she herself had brought about our downfall. Despite the rows over my relationship with Tom, they are mindful and tolerant of my weakness and the reason for my dependence. I have let them down but through it all we get by, and I'll miss Jay when he goes.'

There were to be further upsets for Charlotte during the coming months as the company's move to Barnet was now scheduled for July and a decision would have to be made whether to move with them when the time came. There was no news from Gleave and Gleave about her book and her savings were diminishing. In May Charlotte and Tom reached a point of no return. The clouds that had gathered over their relationship in the preceding months were darkening. Charlotte's demands on Tom had increased and she describes one particular fatal evening in her diary.

May 19th

I'm so churned up but I must write it down. I'm still angry and can't sleep. The evening started off well. I wore my prettiest top and the necklace he brought me back from Prague. He complimented me on my appearance, but he had put on weight since he had been away, and his face looked puffy. He appeared agitated but after several pre-prandial drinks, and by the time we were seated at our table, he had settled down. Then he told me that he couldn't keep his promise to take me to Mike's to say 'Goodbye' to Dougie because Lorna wanted him to finish some petty DIY. I exploded. It was probably not helped by PMT but that was no excuse. As the waiter came and went with our order so my venom was released in bursts of fury, held in at times in deference to the waiter. I accused Tom of having his own way in everything. Tom told me that we could never be together permanently, because Lorna was a growth on his shoulder that couldn't be ignored or removed. I got up from the table with the pretext I needed to go to the ladies', leaving him staring into his wine. Suddenly I had realised that this was the beginning of the end. For the first time I saw clearly where it all was leading. Absolutely nowhere. I called a taxi from reception and, without further explanation, went home. Dougie met me, having got painfully to his feet. He wagged his tail as I came in. I cradled his head in my arms and cried enough tears for both us, into his fur.

The relationship was now crippled. There had been many "fallings out" and getting back together again, but this time, it was serious. Charlotte was in a deep depression. This had been heightened by Jay's departure and the loss of Dougie. Only Jemma remained to keep Charlotte from self-harm, but she was taking time out from her studies at university. During the week, a letter arrived together with a poem written in Tom's hand. This caused her even more distress as she realised for the first time, on reading the poem, that he really had loved her. The letter informed her that he was going away in July when the company split. He had been offered another job in Oxford. He had refused this same offer some years ago in order to stay near to Charlotte but now he had no choice. It was better for her that she cut the cord that bound them and made a fresh start. He wished her all the best for the future.

Tom's poem

A look, a smile, some chosen words,
And time began for us – promises
Of things to be, easily made amid
Discovered senses and bewildered joy
When love and life soared high, and dipped again
And came to rest, contented, breathing, warm.
Momentum unimpaired in early years,
Shy glances held to spark the flame,
And touch, to race together once again.
Time passes, and deep knowing thoughts
Now transferred complacently? Perhaps not.
Love still came as surely as before

Indeed more certain in the form of life,
Briefly, but so sadly lost – how long ago.
Recent years and gathering clouds unfurled
To show so clearly flaws in future paths
Committed words of long ago abused,
Where is the life together? Not here, not now.
Emotions masked yet surely felt,
And still with moments softly close,
Held fast the dying lips of love.
Many years, and one, the last, born
Of dark angels who demanded choice
A trial of our sweet life, now
Embittered by its inevitable close.
Memories now and many yet to come
Like needles pricking mind and body both,
Exquisite pain.
The Spring has gone – for me a troubled shade,
For you I wish the Summer, and a love that will not fade.

June 21ˢᵗ

After reading Tom's poem again, I wanted to reply in kind and send him a poem. It finally came into my head last night after weeks of missing him. I have typed it up and taken a chance by putting it through the internal mail. It is unsigned should anyone else read it.

The poem seemed to come from nowhere and I'm not sure that it says all I want it to say or is worked on sufficiently but that's how it is. I'm already missing him as it has now been weeks since I saw him but I'm trying to keep to our inevitable decision. I realise that I have been selfish in wanting all of him when it was not possible, and who's to say that we would have been happy together all the time? We both have a side of ourselves that we try to keep hidden that is unattractive at times. Also, I would have had Lorna on my conscience and I alone know how it feels to be rejected.

The truth is, that a lot of available divorced people I have met are sad cases; sometimes dull and boring, 'tho I'm unfairly comparing them with Tom's good humour and intelligence. This has woken me up to the fact that maybe I had been dull and boring during some of the earlier years of our marriage; but that was mainly due to lack of funds and a chance to take on new challenges and meet new people. I had given up my nursing and there had been no going back. The children had become my vocation. Whatever Ralph had felt about me, his cowardice was not the way to treat me or cause the suffering to our children. I have learnt so much more since then about life after he left. Joining Zurich was a change of gear for me and I know now that I have the resilience and the willpower to go on whatever happens, especially if I follow Jay's philosophy of 'let go and don't look back'.

I'm seeing Stella next week. The Lovetts have been good friends all these years and although neither of them condoned my relationship with Tom, neither have they ever sent me away. They have a true Christian spirit and I should learn from them.

Charlotte's poem

'AND THEN I MET YOU.'

Spring tides of adolescent youth have come and gone;
cruelly crushing, bravely flushing out dumb shyness.
Hot tears had cried for the passing of sweet innocence

but as sap gives rise to blossom, so my awakened senses
reached a new maturity, waiting for fulfilment;
And then I met you.
Our steamy passions rose unaided, writhed un-sated.
Love stalked the stalker, shook the marrow,
swelled and burst, a waterfall of pain unheeded
of joy embraced, held softly, softly, lest it break
upon the coldness of reality. A winter of despair.
Where are you now?
There will be a passing of the years; other loves, and
a watering of time to cool the memories of you;
before my cradle of earth rocks them into silence.

The following month two letters arrived for Charlotte that would jerk her out of her depression. The first confirmed her resignation from Zurich and the promise of a generous redundancy package together with good references for a future employer. Charlotte wrote: 'I shall be leaving Zurich at the end of next month. They are already planning a leaving do to be held in the sports club. I'm sad to be leaving but I can't say that I liked the new site when we visited or the proposed re-arrangement of workload that is being prepared by the new management. I'll miss the sports club but may be able to continue as a "guest" with luck and I'll be sad to say "goodbye" to Mavis and my friends who have helped and supported me all this time. I'll take my chance on the job market although this is not good at the moment. I'll just have to take the risk. I wonder if Tom will be at the do? I haven't seen him for six weeks now that he's in Oxford.'

The second letter informed her that she had won a trip to Greece with the tour operators *Seascape Singles Holidays*.

Diary entry July 15th
I can't believe it! My silly slogan has done the business!

'Seascape Singles, isles in the sun, join our numbers for freedom and fun.' Not exactly Keats but good enough to win a holiday in Spetses! It will be at the end of September so plenty of time to get organised and it will give me something to look forward to especially if I'm out of work!

Charlotte worked out her final days of employment with a mixture of sadness and optimism. She had made the decision to leave on her own and she was not afraid to take her chances. There were parties and presents and promises to keep in touch. She vowed that she would not be bowed down by the enormity of redundancy and a serious lack of skills that may be demanded in a new workplace. She was in a precarious position. At Zurich life had been cushioned by the help of friendly employers who had been prepared to train her to their requirements. There would be few, if any, employers who would be looking for a candidate with scientific knowledge in the nearby town.

Diary entry July 31ˢᵗ
I have finally left Zurich Wolf. I am completely at a loss to know what to do next. ZW has been my home for ten years. It is where I finally grew up. The people there were my family. Now I must stand on my own two feet: no job, no prospects and above all no Tom; but thankfully Jemma is still at home for a little while longer and my book may be coming out at the end of the year; edits pending but it won't keep me in clover and promoting it will be hard! The big leaving do is next week and I'm in turmoil. I don't want to miss it but what if Tom is there?

August 6ᵗʰ
Tom was there. So was Lorna. I had to leave the party as I couldn't stand watching them both; she'd had too

much to drink and he was laughing and joking. He caught my eye once and we just stared at one another, then I crept away. I came home early and found Jemma entertaining a new boyfriend. She looked happy and it cheered me up plus the fact that we are off to Norfolk tomorrow.

Most of August was spent in Norfolk with Rita and David. Charlotte and Jemma went by train from Liverpool Street to Norwich and then took the branch line to Cromer where David met them in his new car. David had offered his now redundant Rover to Charlotte at a reasonable price and the plan was that she would drive it home when the holiday ended. Charlotte wrote about 'a peaceful time and a good opportunity to recharge batteries and enjoy quality time with both Jemma and Rita.' Rita took them out and about and they revisited the places they knew well and one or two new ones, including the Blickling Estate and Fellbrig Hall. During their stay both Linda and Anette arrived with their husbands and children, renting a cottage nearby. It was a happy time and they were sad to leave, but this was tempered with the excitement of driving a classy "roadster" home.

In September she signed on at the local job centre and Jemma went back to university. In the meantime, Charlotte took to decorating her bedroom and awaiting both her holiday and the publication of her book. I have set down Charlotte's own record of her time in Spetses.

Holiday Spetses

Friday and Saturday: September 7th and 8th
Jay drove me to Gatwick and told me he would look out for Jemma while I was away. I still wonder at the

magic of winning this holiday and feel that everything seems right for me after the last few months of stress. Having said that, my fear of the unknown almost overwhelmed me and led to panic stations when Jay left me in the middle of an almost hostile company of strangers. The comet took off at 11pm and while people all around me dug into cottage pie, I contented myself with a glass of tonic water, still too nervous to join in. Sleep was impossible although I was tired beyond belief. After over three hours we touched down in Athens at 5.15 Greek time and boarded a coach, where once again I tried to sleep. This was not difficult for my fellow passenger, a woman of about my own age, whose head drooped repeatedly on my shoulder.

My first glimpse of Greece emerged through pale dawn light: gentle hills gave way to steeper mounds and as the large orange sun emerged, the scenery took on colour and shape. I was enthralled; my tiredness forgotten. The roads became steep and winding, olive trees and pencils of cypress dotted the landscape. Small flat-topped villas gleamed in the sun and donkeys ambled past flicking stringy tails, burdened with I knew not what.

We stopped at 8am to stretch our legs in some remote little village where we surprised the sleepy inhabitants who appeared unused to coachloads. We sampled the local coffee (strong, sweet and almost thick), and then the only loo. This required two feet placed squarely on boards provided, adopting a squatting position and then aiming hopefully for the void at the bottom! Sheer desperation! The road by the taverna spanned the Corinth Canal and we all peered over the rail into the water below. One of the others dropped their coffee cup into the water to see how long before the splash. We all laughed and felt happier with each other.

After another spell in the coach, negotiating steep bends channelled in the rock face, we arrive at Kosta, Porta Heli where we boarded a boat for the relatively short trip across to Spetses.

Spetses is a rocky green island dotted with various-sized buildings rising in tiers and facing the sea. The Dappia, or harbour, is the main hub of the town and bustles with boats and small craft. The square is alive with taverners and restaurants, packed with chairs placed under shady awnings, and facing the sea. Pony traps whiz past in an alarming fashion bearing passengers to the farthest parts of the town. These are the island's taxis. Mopeds and bicycles join the traffic; bells ring and hooves tap consistently along the cobbles of the promenade.

After leaving the boat, the group was divided up and most of the others moved off into different parts of the town to find their lodgings. As the package specified 'rooms only' these could be anywhere and turned out to be in small private houses which was unexpected. Two of us followed our guide away from the main thoroughfare and along a narrow road that petered out into an earthen track, finally stopping at the top of the hill beside a small villa. I was to be billeted with Alison, my fellow passenger who used me as a cushion on the coach, in a separate room next door. We were left with the instructions to meet at Yannis at 7.30 for dinner. After a cold shower and a change of clothes, we went back down the hill for coffee and a quick survey of the shops available; then back to the villa for three hours' sleep.

The fourteen members of the "singles" crowd

were a mixed bunch that was fairly restrained and polite. Some had come as a small group and some, like Alison and me, on their own. The girls outnumbered the men and the latter appeared to be already with partners but time would tell. The meal was served at a long table and consisted of stuffed toms, pork kebabs, salad, bread, wine and various fruits. Cost 250 drachmas and a very good introduction to Greek food.

At 9pm we assembled on the Dappia to watch the enactment of 'the defeat of the battle of the Turks', an annual event much celebrated by the Greeks. A model sailing boat of the 1800s was anchored in the Dappia and apparently a mock battle was to ensue and total destruction of the boat (representing the Turks) would be carried out. It commenced with torches being spaced around the jetty and boats could be seen with red and green lights sailing in from four directions. Many loud explosions could be heard imitating the battle and then a lone rowing boat rowed out to the "Turkish" boat with a man holding two torches. When they reached the boat it was set alight and a loud cheer went up from the crowd. After that fireworks went up over the harbour and the reflections in the sea were very beautiful. The enemy boat burned for nearly an hour. Finally it was all over and we went in search of some "ouzo" and bed.

Sunday
The dark cool room of the villa gave no hint of the sun outside but on opening the shutters the sea sparkled under a deep blue sky. After a cold shower (no hot water!) we drank chocolate milk and ate the biscuits we had bought yesterday, sitting on the balcony and enjoying the view. Then collecting our swimming gear

we walked down the rough hill to the Dappia and boarded a boat for 'Anagari beach, best beach on the island' or so the tanned Greek owner informed us. The journey took three-quarters of an hour as the beach was round the other side of the island.

The beauty of this beach lies in the pine-clothed hills that sweep down to a small bay. The beach is shingle and we were glad of our beach mats. There are several large villas on the top of the hills, commanding a beautiful view. Otherwise the place is deserted except for a taverna where grapes hang from the ceiling. We dozed through the morning and then, after a salad lunch, again in the afternoon. Apart from a refreshing dip in and out of the sea, we were too tired to read or explore.

The boat called for us at 4.30 and then after going back to the villa to change, we met the others in the restaurant and tucked into a fish dish and baklava. Finally I fell wearily into bed.

Monday
Today we had no breakfast with us at the villa so went to the Dappia for bread, marmalade and coffee but rather expensive. Bought pc's and stamps, fruit and chocolate. We decided to go to Lampara beach which was about ten minutes' walk and rather pretty, passing the Anagari boys' school of John Fowles' *The Magus* where he was a teacher. The beach by the Lampara Beach Club taverna, run by an English couple, was spoilt with rubbish so we moved along to a more scenic spot, but the taverna was useful for cold drinks. Alison kept in the shade of the eucalyptus trees and produced a picture with her pastels. I was too lazy and even reading *The Magus* that I had brought with me was too tiring.

In the evening we all gathered on the Dappia and boarded boats for a collective barbecue. Others would be joining us from different groups. We had been told to bring our swimming gear if we fancied a moonlit dip. The trip took about half an hour and as dusk fell the sun was setting over the sea causing the water to turn pink and turquoise, really beautiful. As we sat on deck I took the opportunity to overtly study our group. Alison I already knew had an amour back home in Ireland. I couldn't believe that this slight, mousey, forty-something-year-old woman could not only lie topless on the beach, but have some kind of "mystery man" she is keeping secret tho' why she is on a singles holiday I don't know but it's none of my business! Shirley was large, attractive and good fun. I hope to get to know her better. Her friend Debbie came with her and brought Peter, her man of the moment. Peter seemed uncomfortable in her somewhat domineering presence, and looked at me with embarrassment as his apparent shortcomings were brought to light. I feel myself drawn towards him sympathetically as Debbie is a little harsh and critical. The others in the group are younger and noisier so we have little in common, but they all seem a friendly bunch.

By the time we reached the beach it was getting dark but we all went in search of dry wood and then gathered round for sausages and Retsina. Then some of us took the plunge before the meal. It was beautifully warm and the fire was welcome when we came out. After the meal of barbecued chicken, potatoes, salad and bread followed by melon, we sang songs and some went back into the sea for another swim. One girl was stripped in the water and brought out naked in front of about a hundred people.

About midnight we clambered back into the three boats and made the homeward journey by moonlight.

Tuesday

We both felt fragile with stomach cramps and put it down to too much Retsina. Spent a quiet day. I wrote my postcards out on the balcony and my precious stamps blew into the garden below. I longed to send Tom a postcard but I didn't know his new address. I have tried not to think of him but felt vulnerable today for some reason. I still miss him. Anyway, what would be the use? I wouldn't have signed it.

Both of us ate very little all day and had a poor night's sleep.

Wednesday

We decided to go to Anagari beach by bus but firstly we would call in at Hotel Faros and report our continued lack of hot water to our tour operator who appeared sympathetic. After rolls and coffee (I had declined an egg, unlike Alison, as I still felt queasy) we queued for the bus. As we waited we watched a wizened old woman in black hang out a line of small squid and suchlike to dry. They looked quite gruesome and inedible. Finally we boarded the small bus and the ride was quite an experience as it jolted and rattled over the cobblestones, jammed to capacity. Alison and I stood the whole way, hanging on for dear life and trying to see as much of the scenery as we could.

We had a super day on the beach: swimming, sunbathing, searching for pebbles, painting and exploring. I came upon the villa of Concis and a large notice, 'private property'. I found wild cyclamen and enjoyed diving off a rock into deep cool water in a secluded cove. After a final swim we caught the bus back at 6pm.

We met the others later at Yanis, and then a leisurely walk back up the hill and bed!

Thursday
Washed hair in cold water but it dried very quickly. After breakfast in town we decided to walk a little further round the island. Packed up paraphernalia and, wearing as little as possible, we set off up the winding hillside and followed a tiny path that finally dropped away into a small sandy cove. Spent another lazy day reading etc. and lunching modestly on biscuits, apple and mineral water, before packing up and leaving around 6pm.

This evening there was to be a "fondue party" at the Lampara Beach Club run by the English couple with their two very skinny children. We set off at about 8pm and walked the twenty-minute journey in a leisurely manner. We watched others arrive in buggies like Cinderellas at the ball (except several wore blue jeans!).

It was a very pleasant evening and the company was good. Eight people sat around a circular table and dipped squares of meat into the boiling fondue pot. The meat was quickly cooked. The wine was unlimited and English and American "pop" music blared out from the disco area. We all enjoyed ourselves and some made new acquaintances; I left a leering man called Rick, with a purse on his hip and medals dangling, to Alison whilst I found a softly spoken dark-haired man called Ross to dance with. Hope I see him when we go next time. He's not in our group. We finally tottered up "the goat track" back to the villa in the early hours of the morning but felt good.

Friday

Did the usual "shop" bit and spent longer than usual, looking for presents. Eventually staggered off to our "special" beach again and sunbathed topless at a discreet distance under the fir trees. The day oozed slowly away until it was 4pm and time for the boat.

We decided to go to the roof restaurant again for dinner and on the way bumped into our friends from the next villa. Debbie and Peter were going back to change but Shirley was left so we suggested she came with us. We were just finishing our meal when Rick appeared and came over to our table, medals swinging. Fortunately, Shirley took charge and rescued us from him and we disappeared quickly into the English-French coffee place.

We all decided on an early night so went back to read my book.

Saturday

Shirley had suggested that we go to Paraskivi beach, round the corner from Anagari, so we all met at the coffee shop and after breakfast set off for the boat. I had bought a mask etc. to try a little snorkeling. This small but beautiful beach turned out to be almost deserted. A dear little church was the only building to be seen. No taverna or kiosk. We decided that this might well be a nudist beach but only saw people topless.

Spent a long lazy day swimming, sunbathing – too lazy to explore. This beach is mentioned in *The Magus*, also the church. Peter joined me when snorkeling but we did not see much except for a few interesting fish and sea urchins looking like black round porcupines.

Later, we all had dinner at the French restaurant;

steak au poivre, salad and fruit and then back to Shirley's for gin and tonic.

Slept well!

Sunday

Awoke to loud chanting which rang round the villas. This was a service from a nearby church that was "relayed" through speakers. A second church further away seemed to "answer" the chants. This went on for about an hour. One previous day we had come upon a service in a square. The churches are very small and only the priest seems to go inside. The congregation all stand around listening. Little windows open out and people pass by and receive blessing. The priests wear long black robes with round flat black hats and veils.

Spent the day on Anagari beach and took Shirley who had not been there before. Got to know her better. She owns a boutique in Ruislip. She is good fun with a super personality. We all took photos of one another.

On way back I decided to phone home. It was lovely hearing Jemma who sounded just around the corner.

We went to Cappricio's, a beautiful restaurant only open for one month. Lots of bamboo tables, with cream umbrellas, Habitat style. We all had the "buffet", which comprised of bowls and bowls of different salads on a circular table hung from the ceiling on ropes. I wore my new cheesecloth dress to show off my tan. It was all very enjoyable.

On the walk home, there was a definite change in the weather. There was a strong wind, and a lowering of temperature. Unbelievable! Went to bed and read my book.

Monday

Weather very cold and grey. Wore jeans and jumper for the first time. Slept late. All met for breakfast and decided to go on 2.30 boat to Hydra.

Hydra is a very steep island rising out of the sea. It is very rocky and not so green as Spetses. Because of its steepness the harbour is very picturesque as the villas rise sharply all around. Only donkeys are used here – very much beasts of burden. We saw them loaded with bricks, wood and the usual bags of produce. The shops all around the harbour were large and beautiful, lots of jewellery, craftwork and paintings, sponges etc. I bought Jemma a silver dolphin bracelet; I hope my money lasts a few more days! We took lots of photos and the locals told us the bad weather would be short lived.

Back on the Dappier for Mousaka and honey balls inside the rooftop restaurant. Hope the weather is better tomorrow.

And so to bed, with John Fowles and *The Magus*. Not a lot happening on the romantic front but it's wonderful being here on Spetses.

Tuesday

Opened shutters to clear blue sky and breathed a sigh of relief, but air seemed cooler. Washed hair in the usual cold water and sat on the balcony to dry it. Fairly successful. Went to bank to change last of sterling but the rate had dropped. Very bad news! Missed out on scrambled eggs and had yoghurt from supermarket instead, also bought apples, biscuits and nuts for lunch. Then took the boat to Zogeria.

This turned out to be a charming little cove with interesting rocky walks and pools etc. The sea felt extra warm and both swimming and snorkeling were super. Met up with some other English people and all had a super day. Gave away my pastel picture to one of the women who liked it and was quite delighted. She said she would frame it when she got home.

Sat on the prow of the boat on the homeward journey and then a slow meander back along the Dappia with a Cornetto. I feel so at peace here and alive at the same time. Every day is precious.

Usual buffet at Cappricio's and then sat talking and drinking until midnight. Walked back under a very velvety sky and saw the Milky Way. Really superb!

Wednesday

A very eventful day! We caught the early boat and went back to Zogeria and others joined later. There were seven of us camped out at our usual site by lunchtime. It was a very hot day so lots of swimming etc. About 12 midday a large yacht came sailing in and anchored in the bay. Very smart! We all watched with interest. Three of us decided to swim out and say 'hello'. It was further than we thought but we reached the ladder and climbed aboard. We were welcomed on deck by twelve Swiss fellows who offered us drinks and the champagne flowed. They were all very friendly. It was very smart inside and was powered by a Rolls-Royce engine. We were told it was a British boat! They had a motor launch suspended from metal stays that they lowered into the water for water skiing and a diving platform that hung out over the sea. We saw a chef laying out places on a large oval table. Finally, as lunch was about to be served we said 'goodbye and thanks!' I actually dived off the board. It must have been the champagne. The swim back was very refreshing and a sleep in the shade followed. Soon it was 4pm and time to board the boat back.

All decided to meet up and go to Twins Disco after a meal at the barbecue restaurant. Ate kebabs and more honey balls. These were kind of doughnuts dipped in syrup.

All felt too tired to go to disco so went back to villa about 12 midnight.

Thursday

Last full day! Once again it was back to Zogeria but this time disaster struck. However, this may prove to be fortuitous? Alison and I went on our own as the others were shopping and catching up on chores and getting ready for going home tomorrow. I wanted to squeeze every last ounce out of the sea and sun before departing for cooler shores and taking up goodness knows what in the employment line.

A couple of small boats were anchored in the cove. One of them was very like the Lovetts' boat *Little Eagret*. For something to do and because of the adrenalin of yesterday, I decided to swim the fair distance and investigate. Just as I approached the yacht I was stung by a jellyfish. This sent me into a panic that was then followed by agonising cramp in my left leg. I yelled and spluttered and was mercifully heard by a man on deck who jumped in and pulled me onto a dinghy that was tethered to the yacht. He went to work on my leg and eventually the pain departed but not the pain from the sting. It was just above my right breast and hurt like hell. Another man had joined him and before long, thanks to them, I had recovered. Ian, who had rescued me at the beginning, then powered me back to the beach, where Alison lay, unmoved and asleep underneath her straw hat. She had been ignorant of the whole episode. Ian departed soon after but not before making us promise to meet them for coffee in Pharo's coffee bar tomorrow morning when they come ashore for provisions. He seems quite genuine and I'm tempted to do so as I'd like to know more about him. He lives in Surrey and runs his own business near Gatwick, not that far from me it seems. It could be interesting if he's unattached!

Missed out on the last disco at Lampara and decided on drinks with Shirley and the others at Cappricio's instead. Went to bed speculating about Ian and trying not to notice the ongoing pain caused by the sting on my boob! Home tomorrow but the journey will be in the daylight so much to see.

CHAPTER FIFTEEN

A RAY OF HOPE

On her return from Greece another unexpected piece of good fortune arrived in the post for Charlotte. This came in the form of a note together with a substantial cheque from her aunt, Myra. According to her daughter Anette, Myra had come into the money via her Premium Bonds and wanted to share her win with the family. Charlotte was amazed as neither presents nor cards from her aunt usually came her way but the gift could not have come at a better time. The mortgage and bills still had to be paid and at present she had no stable income. The good news counteracted the less happy prospect of Jemma returning to Sussex University at the end of the month. Whilst Charlotte was proud of her daughter and her achievements she would miss her energy and company at home. During the long summer break Jemma had worked in bars and restaurants and saved up for her own expenses. Next year she was hoping to go inter-railing with two of her close friends.

Meanwhile, Charlotte had signed on again at the job centre and awaited the results of her form filling and interviews in the hope of gaining employment. She had joined another, more prodigious, theatre group, "The Four Seasons Playhouse" and had auditioned for a part in J B Priestley's *When We Are Married*. She also decided to try a course in sculpture for beginners, advertised in the local paper, to be held in the art college in October. There would be two daytime sessions and the fee was deemed as reasonable, as it would be reduced for concessions. Charlotte, who admired Rodin and Michelangelo, had longed to try this three-dimensional form of art for herself. It would be a new challenge but before this was to take place, another opportunity presented itself.

Diary entry: 28th September
Drove Jemma to the station with all her gear. After hugs and fond farewells subsided into coffee shop feeling low. Got up to leave and saw Ian (from Spetses) pass the window with another man, talking earnestly. I couldn't believe my eyes. In the car park I saw him again, this time on his own. He recognised me and came over and after our initial surprise at seeing one another (with our clothes on; his joke) he expressed regret that we had not met them both for coffee in Pharo's and had I time for lunch now? He looked so keen and appealing that I agreed. I had felt guilty about not meeting him on the Dappia after he had probably saved my life; but the morning had been a hectic one with last-minute chores and packing, so it would be churlish to refuse him now. He took me to a curry house and, over a rather hot curry, reminded me again of his position. He is an MD of a small engineering firm that makes parts for propellers and lives near the old airport in Purley. He is divorced from his Swedish wife Ingrid, who wanted to go back to Sweden for good, taking their teenage son, Seb, with her. Ian is older than me by some years, with slightly thinning hair but not unattractive; medium build with wide shoulders and narrow hips, wonderfully tanned when I last saw them in action in Zogeria! He has a warm smile and sharp blue eyes that miss nothing. I felt

drawn towards this seemingly genuine and intelligent man and have agreed to meet him again when he gets back from a business trip in Germany next month. What have I got to lose?

During the weeks that followed, Charlotte rejoiced in the freedom that life now presented. Her aunt's gift had taken off the immediate pressure of unemployment for the time being and she cast about for fresh ideas and inspiration. On the home front there was gardening and decorating to be done, both of which had been neglected. Her audition for *When We Are Married* with the Four Seasons had been successful and rehearsals were already underway. The sculpture course would broaden her artistic horizons and began on October 17th as described in her diary for that day.

Diary entry: Thursday
To state the obvious sculpture is so very different from painting! It involves physical as well as mental effort. Today's class began in the annex of the art college in town. My first impression was that of a marvellously large, light room filled with turntables, pedestals, and benches, under which were bins, sacks of plaster, clay, lumps of wood, stone and metal. It was awe-inspiring! An adjacent smaller room was used solely for applying plaster. Years of student effort could be seen stuck to the walls, ceiling and floor. This was the result of them covering their work, in order to make moulds, with a liberal coating of the "wet stuff". Apparently this is applied at a distance by hand using a flicking movement of the fingers. Sounds fun.

We have a female sitter named Pat. Seven of us stood round in a semi-circle with our turntables and lumps of "thrown" terracotta clay. This is achieved by throwing the clay down hard for five minutes or so and then adding "grog" to help with the firing later.

Callipers were used to measure the circumference of the skull and details of face etc. I found working with this media much easier than I thought I would and have even managed a likeness to the model Pat. I'm really looking forward to getting on with it next week. They are a friendly group of mixed age and ability but not much time to get to know each other as we have been so engrossed but maybe next time.

Charlotte almost missed her class the following week as the clerk at the job centre informed her that the commercial technology course that she was eligible for would begin in a few days' time. She had previously sat an elementary test to qualify for this and was waiting to hear when the eight-weeks training course at the Lambeth Skill Centre would start. Fortunately for Charlotte it was postponed until the following week and she was able to finish her portrait head sculpture.

Diary 24th October
An air of anticipation prevailed in the annex. We were to perform a lobotomy on our leather-hard sculpture. We sliced off the top of the head with a thin cheese wire and then proceeded to scoop out the soft clay inside. The walls must be of even thickness all round. After this the top was replaced using sticky clay called slip to seal the join and make the edges good. Air holes were made in the ears, nostrils, and hair to allow the steam to escape during firing (or it will blow up in the kiln!) and now we must leave them to dry out thoroughly before they can be fired. All this was nerve-wracking in case of

collapse! I made a new friend over sandwiches at lunch.

Wendy is a mature art student at the college so not so much a beginner. We both agreed that we should be modelling Jason, one of the other "would be" sculptors, who has the head and body of a Greek god. We were still giggling when we got back to work! Wendy says she'll come for a drink when we collect our heads in a month's time, if they're not in pieces that is!

Charlotte found that she was to enjoy the commercial technology course more than she could have imagined, as office routine work generally figured low on her agenda. It was a fair drive each day to the centre but her petrol was paid for by the DHSS. Although she had been happy at home with her domestic workload the course was a stimulus and gave direction. It would equip her for the technological age that was burgeoning. It appeared that modern clerical skills could be interesting and challenging with this new science and Charlotte was always keen to try new experiences. The void created by her giving up her responsible career as a nurse still haunted her although she knew in her heart that she was too sensitive for the demands that this noble position expected. It saddened her that she had been unable to support herself financially to take up other professional opportunities that would have taken years to complete. She comforted herself that she had done all she could for her herself and her children under the circumstances and she would make the best of what was on offer now.

Her typing skills were below average but her grasp of computer programming was good. In her free time she took advantage of practice sessions and typed up a play she had written some time ago, using the new software. This was far less laborious than using her ancient typewriter at home. The course finally finished two weeks before Christmas.

December 11th

Ian was kind enough to take me out to dinner tonight and congratulated me on my new diploma. I said it was hardly rocket science! I was more pleased with my sculpture which survived the kiln and stood on the bookcase, casting a benevolent eye on the pair of us as we later canoodled on the sofa and listened to records. Ian is a lovely man, gentle and patient; so different from Tom—no demanding passion but there is a flame waiting to be ignited. Since going out together we have been treading warily, not to rock the boat so to speak. Sailing is his hobby when he can get away and he and Greg Lawson are joint owners of Caprice. He says he will take me out on the water in the spring when she comes out of dry dock. Thank goodness I know a bit about it all as I've sailed on Little Eagret many times with the Lovetts.

I'm thinking of inviting him down to the cottage in Studland for a romantic weekend. I must check this out with the Appleyards. I have my own key and they are always urging me make use of it when I can and 'air the place!' They don't use it much in winter.

The new year was filled with hope as life took on a rosier glow. Charlotte and Ian continued to build carefully on their relationship; the play was imminent and her book would be published in March, according to a letter from Gleave and Gleave. They apologised for the delay but said there had been a fire at the printers.

After a successful performance of *When We Are Married* Charlotte, buoyed up by euphoria, mentioned her idea of a long weekend in Dorset to Ian who readily agreed and a date was set in February. In the meantime Rowena's Recruitment

Agency sent her out on temporary assignments into various offices and Charlotte was to develop more confidence in the process. She did not take too kindly to losing her freedom and found office routine irksome. It was a far cry from her time with John Bradley and Zurich Wolf where rules were less rigid and the sports club beckoned. She had bought a bicycle with Myra's money and cycling to work each day was her only form of exercise. It was also cost effective. The following month she took a few days off and drove down to Studland for the romantic break she had promised them both. She was taking a risk but she hoped to get to know Ian better in the process. She gives an account of the outcome.

February 12th STUDLAND
Things went wrong from the start. Due to problems at the plant Ian couldn't get away until Saturday so we would have to drive down separately. I had planned to leave after work on Thursday but the forecast was iffy. Finally I decided to take the plunge and drive down anyway. February is not the best month to go anywhere and by the time I reached Ringwood, snow was falling. Battled on as the flakes got larger and after hours of driving finally caught the last ferry in Sandbanks. Fortunately this was still running ok and drove aboard. The chains cranked and groaned as it ploughed across the dark water in a myriad of snowflakes. Drove the final miles to the cottage in a sweat as the car headlights were malfunctioning for some reason. Worse awaited me. I had picked up the wrong key when leaving home and couldn't get in. I decided on a drastic measure and broke a window round the back. Having managed to gain entrance I was now disorientated and couldn't find

the cupboard that held the meters and switch for the lights.

After stumbling about I then discovered that the power was off in the village anyway. I was to be marooned in a sea of "bible black". Fortunately, with the help of the thin beam from my torch I found candles and matches in the same cupboard. I managed to get back to the car but had to bring bags and provisions through the back door. I tried to light a fire in the grate but the kindling was sooty and damp. I then gave up, ate some bread and cheese and drank half a bottle of my precious wine by candlelight. I then creaked up the stairs into a freezing bedroom. Just then the lights came on and I breathed a sigh of relief. Tomorrow I must phone both the garage and Ian. It's madness coming here in the winter when there's no phone or central heating and right now, no hot water! What will Ian think?

Friday
Found garage and friendly man. Said it was some kind of electrical fault and I would have to leave the car there until Monday. Phoned Ian from same callbox and great news he can come latish tonight. Told him to bring sweaters! Walked three miles back to cottage. Snow almost gone. Cleared up broken glass, blocked gap in window with cardboard, and laid fresh fire. Prepared French onion soup and coq au vin. Turned up the two electric radiators and lit fire. By the time Ian arrived it was blazing and the place was warm and cheerful. Added to this was the aroma from the casserole and my Gardenia bath oil, both of which I hoped he would appreciate!

After the meal and a bottle of wine we sat by the fire on the saggy settee wrapped in each other's arms, almost putting off the inevitable moment we were both edging toward. Then, without being aware of how it had happened, we were on the hearthrug and enjoying each other in a slow and deliciously loving way. Afterwards he thanked me shyly and told me it was a long time since he had been loved so tenderly.

Saturday

Drove into town and bought glass and putty to repair window. Also bought ingredients for tonight's curry – Ian's particular speciality that he would be cooking later. Enjoyable lunch in pub in village by huge log fire, then a walk up on the cliffs to Old Harry Rocks and back again to the cottage for a long evening; replete with good food, wine and the newfound pleasure in each other. Afterwards Ian told me how he missed his son Seb who will be seventeen in July. He has been living with his mother in Sweden for four years but now wants to come to study in England next year. I told him of my hopes and fears for Jay and Jemma. Broken homes. It's so hard on the children and could the perpetrators of this selfishness be really happy? If so, where is the justice?

Sunday

Woken up by church bells but both happy to stay warm in bed. After bacon and eggs for breakfast, set off for Kimmeridge later in the morning but it was cold and bleak on top of the cliff and after a walk to the folly, got back in the car and found a pub for lunch on the way home then back to the cottage for tea and lardy cake. Ian had to leave at six and I will pick up my car tomorrow morning. Although our romantic weekend is over we are now on a firmer footing. Both of us enjoyed each other's company and I appreciated his gentleness when we made love; so different from our quick breaks at lunchtime in the past when Tom and I would fling clothes and shoes to the wall in an agony of haste in order to satisfy our wanton desires. Perhaps I'm getting old??

When Charlotte arrived home she rang the agency for her next assignment and was asked to call into the office. Rowena told her that a six-month position in London was on offer to cover an employee's maternity leave. She was to report to the office in Argyle Street for an interview on Thursday. The business was concerned with the movement of cloth from an Italian manufacturer based in Milan to M&S and other clothing companies in Britain. Her new skills on the computer ticked the boxes required. Nevertheless, Charlotte's heart was beating nervously at her interview with Colin Halliday. The whole set up was on a higher level than her other jobs had been, with no room for error, as accuracy was paramount. Charlotte wrote: 'Everyone here is friendly and helpful. They seem a happy crowd and who wouldn't be; we are in the heart of the West End with Liberties round the corner. The journey will take some getting used to but the pay and benefits are well worth it!'

In March Charlotte was thrilled to receive ten free copies of *The Fire and the Phoenix* as agreed in her contract but even so she hugged them to herself, still marvelling at their very existence and savouring the moment before informing family and friends. She had been asked to promote the book on local radio but had felt unequal to the challenge, however had given an interview for the local paper. In April she publicised the event by throwing a party with the help of the final financial instalment paid by Gleave and Gleave.

I really pushed the boat out! Jemma was home for Easter and helped with the food and decoration. We cooked a whole salmon and made coronation chicken. There was ham, pate, prawns and various puds. Jay organised the music and friends brought drink. Ian arrived with two bottles of champagne. He was accompanied by his son Sebastian, a tall blonde young man with Ian's eyes. He was on holiday. Also it was good to see Ian's friend Greg Lawson with them. They got on well with the Lovetts. We were short on family as Rita and David were unable to come, also the Evans and Brian but Anette and Bob were there, also friends from Z.W. and South Park Players. It was a great evening and there were still people around next morning at breakfast! I gave one of my books to Anne Johnson who had helped with the typing of my manuscript as she has connections with the world of journalism and it maybe helpful.

Tuesday
After a hard day at the office and crowded tube trains, came back to find among the post on the mat, a card with a smudged post mark. *Congratulations on The Fire and the Phoenix. May it do well. Tom.* I sat down suddenly on the stairs. In my euphoria I had quite forgotten him, not that we kept in touch but he had been my inspiration. He must have heard the news from someone else. I wonder how he is? Could it be an Oxford postmark?

In early May Ian suggested that she met him in Paris where he had business to discuss in Montparnasse along with a work colleague. He would be busy for a couple of days but would be free at the weekend to take her around. An arrangement was made that Charlotte would make the outward journey on her own but then they would fly back together on Sunday. She did not want to compromise him by staying at the same hotel and chose a smaller one also on the left bank. She describes her first time experiences in the romantic French capital.

Diary: Thursday May 3rd
My first port of call will be the Musee Rodin in the Rue de Varenne tomorrow. I was very fortunate on the way over on the hovercraft to meet a very friendly Swiss lady who gave me some good advice. 'Buy a carnet, a book of ten tickets, it's the cheapest way to get around the metro. Always look for the destination at the end of the line for the direction you want to travel in. Correspondence is the French word for connection.' Finally she told me of the three tier prices in bars and restaurants and finished with 'Your first time in Paris? Beautiful.'

My confidence improved as I boarded the sleek train from Boulogne. It sang a gentle song as we sped through the French countryside. At the Gare du Nord I bought my carnet and then with steely determination plunged into the depths of the French Metro. I was struck by the efficiency of the French and it was all as the Swiss lady had described and I arrived at my destination. The Hotel Maxim was situated down a narrow street close to the metro Solferino. The hotel was tall and narrow and I was amused by the lift that was about the size of a single wardrobe. I just managed to squeeze myself and suitcase inside as we were both whisked up to the top floor. The room was long and narrow with a French window at the end that I opened and looked down on the street below. The air was warm although it was early evening. I sat on the bed and sighed contentedly. I had arrived. When I had washed and changed I went out in search of a café and phone.

Friday May 4th
In the morning I sat in the small dining area and ate my continental breakfast with the air of a millionaire. Afterwards I took the metro to Invalides and emerged from the night world of the underground into a burst of spring sunshine with the sense of achievement reserved for a mountaineer who has reached the summit. The Musee Rodin was a short walk away.

Chestnuts and lilacs were in bloom as promised and the splash of red tulips painted the grass around his immense sculpture of *The Burghers of Calais*. I walked in the gardens and dawdled among these huge green bronzed giants. Hesitatingly, I reached up and held a cold bronzed finger, or rubbed a naked toe, polished to brilliance by others who had passed this way and wanted to share in the moment. I marvelled at the hugeness of muscled limbs and the detail of feet and hands.

Inside the museum were many of his famous works. White marbled lovers, entwined forever with the blessing of the Master; the terracotta portrait of the Girl with the Hat and numerous busts and torsos. Sometime later I came out feeling fulfilled and inspired.

I crossed the wide road at the Pont Alexandre where the traffic was slight and made for a café. I was hungry and ordered omelette and coffee. I sat watching all around me and for the first time, to drink in Paris. I had not told Ian of my fear of travelling alone and of my limited schoolgirl French. I am still so naïve about things but my self-esteem is rising. After a good rest I re-crossed the road and began to walk along the banks of the Seine. It was beautiful; trees dipped gracefully into the water which had risen considerably and houseboats coloured the dull surface. After several *"ponts"* had been passed, I noted on my map the Louvre to the left of me. This immense building was set off the road and was humming with life. I joined the throng of people and marvelled at the paintings which I had only seen as small coloured squares in books. I became one of a tight packed crowd and struggled for a better view of the glass encased *Mona Lisa,* the alleged most famous painting in the world. Tired of such greatness and with still much to see another day, I collapsed on a grassy bank outside, together with many others and felt the warm sun on my face.

Refreshed, I continued my walk beside the Seine, dawdling over the many stalls which lined the embankment. These displayed prints and other bric-a-brac. Crossing to the other side of the street I found that many shops were open and stalls of brightly coloured plants and flowers made a profusion of colour in the bright sunshine. I was surprised to see, mingled with the plant stalls, cages, stacked high with clucking chickens; rabbits and other small animals accompanied them. Finally I subsided into a welcome chair outside one of the cafes and lingered over a cool drink, tired but content. I could see the spires of the Notre Dame across the water, dominating the small island of her birth but her secrets could hold for another day. All around me Paris buzzed with life and the now familiar 'toot toot' of the traffic played upon the ear. To the newcomer, the ways of the French traffic can be very daunting. Unless you take care you can be mercilessly mown down by a small Citroen or scooter.

Back once more in the relative calm of the metro I made my way back to the hotel. At the exit I was amused to see two youths vault the automatic barrier and an elderly lady squeeze firmly through it in the close wake of a proceeding passenger before the gates shut. I took the tiny lift up to my room and flung myself on the bed hoping to wake in time to meet Ian for dinner.

Later, over our *Cul de Veau Poele a la mode d'artois* in La Cupole *w*e discussed the places to visit tomorrow. I was keen to go to Montmartre and the flea market in Port Cligncourt, both in opposite directions and Ian chose a walk in the Tuileries gardens, the Musee D'Orsay and a *bateau* on the Seine. I said we will have to come again to fit it all in! He laughed and raised his glass of *Gevrey-Chambertine* and said 'Why not?'

CHAPTER SIXTEEN

IN THE MIDST OF LIFE...

In July Charlotte's employment in Argyll Street came to an end. The occasion was marked by a meal held in the Trocadera Restaurant in Shaftsbury Avenue. There was much merriment and, to Charlotte's conservative way of thinking, a silly show of 'bread throwing' and other 'unexpected behaviour' by her boss and fellow workers but she appreciated their good wishes towards her and she would miss their friendship. She had spent her lunch hours, over the last week, in Oxford Street availing herself of the sales, and had invested in as many new clothes as she could afford, as there had been plenty to tempt her.

On her return to Surrey she decided to take a few days off and join Ian and Greg for some sailing over the following week. The weather was changeable but warm enough and they proposed a trip to the Isle of Wight and possibly the French coast. Her book was making slow progress in spite of various promotions but Anne Johnson had passed her own copy of *The Fire and the Phoenix* on to her good friend and editor Mary Kemp. Mary ran the publication *True Grit*, a relatively new magazine that dealt with real-life situations. There was a possibility that Charlotte's book could be given a review.

Diary entry 28th July
Had a great day on Caprice. First we stowed our stuff on board; filled water containers and checked fuel.

Then, with the engine running, hauled in the fenders and slowly backed her out of her mooring in the marina, between two large yachts. *Caprice* is a 40ft yacht, well appointed, with four berths. Seagulls screamed over our heads and the smell of seaweed and salt was a heady mix. As we got underway, the sails were hoisted and the engine cut. The mainstays twanged and the boat seesawed in the wash of a passing motor launch. Cloud formations scudded across the sky as we flew along in the bright sun and cool breeze at 5-6 knots. I enjoyed the tug and pull of the tiller under my hand whilst at the helm and the satisfying tick and click of the winches as the ropes were tightened around them. We made it to Cowes in good time, moored her to a floating pontoon and then went into the clubhouse for lunch, all three of us famished and windblown.

Over lunch both men told me of their narrow escape in the 1979 Fastnet Race when they had sailed out as crew on a large yacht in brilliant sunshine only to be bruised and battered in the awful storm that blew up around them. They had been lucky to survive as many did not. They are both planning to take part in a race next year, in America, but I'm opting to keep warm and dry at home!

I'm just a fair-weather sailor.

There were several more happy days spent on the water as Charlotte and Ian delighted in each other's company. Greg was happy to acknowledge their relationship and generously gave them space where possible. Normally he was a quiet man with an air of sadness about him but he enjoyed sparring with Ian on the boat and usually won their dangerous game of "man overboard" that involved dexterity in bringing the boat round single-handed to accomplish the "rescue" of the one in the water in record time. Charlotte wondered about his circumstances but was too timid to ask.

The agency continued to give her temporary work with a view to finding something more permanent nearer to her home when a position arose. Charlotte had enjoyed the benefits of the London job but was not keen to travel so far as this impinged on her evenings that she now reserved for drama and sculpture, both of these appealing to the creative side of her personality and vital to her wellbeing. Since returning from Paris she had signed up at the art college for evening classes where she was reunited with Wendy who was also on the same course. Charlotte found she had a flair for this art form and that it could be therapeutic.

In August she visited Rita and David for a few days and basked in their organised home life and her aunt's country cooking. Rita was not a motherly figure but she was practical and energetic for her age. David, some years her senior, was becoming frail but kept cheerful. Charlotte visited the stables and enjoyed a hack along the cliffs at West Runton. It was a year since she had been riding as this privilege was forfeited when she left Zurich Wolf. In the evening Rita and David took her to Norwich for a Chinese meal to celebrate the success of the publication of her book. They were proud of their niece and offered to help with promotion where possible. Their eyes opened wide and they hung on every word when she told them about Ian and she promised to bring him with her next time.

Back home things had not improved on the job front and there seemed to be little on offer in respect of suitable permanent work. Moving around different offices had its upside when the work was of little interest or repetitive but Charlotte was missing the companionship of her former work colleagues and a sense of belonging. The temporary posts were not always well paid and she was still trying to make ends meet. Whilst attending the art college one evening, Wendy mentioned that lodgings were needed for two teenage male engineering students who were attending the college during term time. Charlotte would have to decide quickly if she was interested in taking them, as Wendy herself would put forward her personal recommendation in her role as placement officer. They would require bed, breakfast and an evening meal. There was little time to prepare their bedrooms, as they would be arriving the following month. Charlotte discussed the matter with Jemma who was quite happy to tidy away her girlish clobber in exchange for a small percentage of the takings. She would still be in Sussex during term time and would return to her room in the holidays.

The next four months were busy ones for Charlotte but she was high on adrenalin trying to keep all her projects under control. The students, both from Kent, travelled home at weekends and this left time for her and Ian to meet up before the following week began again once more; so she was working for the agency, shopping and cooking for the boys and then out in the evening in a whirl of rehearsals or some other deadline.

In December she received the very exciting news that the publication *True Grit* had offered to publish *The Fire and the Phoenix* as a serial commencing in February. Charlotte wrote: 'I'm so lucky. It's most unusual as this happens so rarely and it will be such a promotion for my book. I'm overwhelmed!'

Christmas was spent with Jay and Jemma and their respective partners. Ian had promised his son Seb that he would spend Christmas in Sweden and Charlotte had felt a twinge of uncertainty that he would become reunited with Ingrid and that she, Charlotte, would be left out in the cold. Ian reassured her that this would never happen and that he would be back for the New Year. He wanted to bring Sebastian to London the following Easter to start an architectural course at the London Polytechnic, and Ian needed to sort out the details. He promised to take Charlotte to Wales on his return to walk in the Brecon Beacons and later in the year to Florence, because she wanted to see the work of Michelangelo and Raphael. Both of these ideas filled her with joy, together with the anticipated serialisation of her book. She wrote: 'I'm almost afraid of too much happiness, I'm not used to it; surely something will go wrong?'

Among Charlotte's Christmas cards was the usual round robin from Graham and Jill Prior in Los Angeles. They had kept in touch by this method at Christmas, promoting their good works and family triumphs. Charlotte had felt slighted by them over the passing time, as they had gained in status whilst she had fallen, and she felt that a personal letter enquiring after herself and her children would have been kinder. This year Graham had scribbled on the bottom of the printed page 'coming to UK in October and hope to see you!' She paid little heed to this information, as they had promised a visit before in previous years.

Soon after New Year, before the boys arrived back from Kent for the new term, Charlotte and Ian went to Wales for a few days. Members of Ian's family lived in Cardiff but they decided to stay in a small hotel on the outskirts of the city. Charlotte wrote:

Sunday January 22nd
Set off for Wales down the M4 and drove over the Avon Bridge and into Cardiff. Our hotel was just outside of the city in an attractive part of the suburb. We looked out on a rather lovely castle on the other side of a mountain that reminded me of a German schloss on the Rhine.

After an early lunch we set off for St Fagan's Castle and the Folk Museum. We wandered about in the grounds looking at some very old Welsh farmhouses which had been brought down from all over Wales and put together for people to view. Some were very primitive and we then went to the museum and looked at the usual things: farm machinery, tools, furniture etc. We then drove to Llandough Cathedral and listened to evening song. The singing was lovely – and so was the architecture. There was a large Epstein statue in the middle of the cathedral to hide the pipes of the organ. The setting outside was beautiful. Finally we drove up a very steep mountain road to a pub called The Traveller's Rest, not surprisingly as many people had been caught in the snow and been forced to stay the night! Fortunately for us the weather was cold but dry. We drove back to our hotel in the dark and enjoyed a meal by a good fire.

After we had made love and lay warm in bed together, Ian told me that I had no need to worry about Ingrid and that as far as he was concerned I was everything to him. I told him I was scared that something would go wrong, as I was so happy. He just held me close and said, 'I'm here for you now. You must trust me.'

Monday January 23rd
In the morning we lay in bed and wondered what to do, as the weather was a bit grey and overcast and the forecast poor. He knew I wanted to go walking over the Brecon Beacons. He ran a bath for me and then dressed me up in some of his sailing gear as my weekend wardrobe was inadequate for the task! It was marvellous up there. Not a soul in sight. The ferns looked salmon pink and the pines a dark green. Everywhere water was

falling in small and tall waterfalls. I tried to take some photos. We crossed over a shaky log bridge and at one stage we had to get across a fast-flowing stream about five yards in width. We couldn't find a bridge so Ian found some rocks and we dropped them into the stream and made steppingstones. It was a bit nerve-wracking but he helped me across. My large waterproof trousers hampered my progress. Just as we overcame this calamity, Ian went down into a bog. We had been walking for hours and I was quite exhausted and unfit. Finally we collapsed in the car and removed all our wet things. Ian had thoughtfully brought dry socks and anoraks.

We drove to a tiny pub on a mountainside where we downed a welcome drink and thick sandwiches. The pub stood on an old railway station where the men from the mines used to alight. On the way back in the rain, I took in the sights of Aberfan (you could see where the tip came down into the school). I saw the Rhonda Valley surrounded by slag heaps. I saw Merthyr Tydfil and saw how depressing it was. It made me realise how I had taken coal mining for granted without counting the cost of how and where the families live out their frugal lives. They give everything to the job of keeping the country warm and the wheels of industry turning and take pride in their heritage. Where will we be without them?

Another huge meal by the fire, and then wrapped lovingly in each other's arms at bedtime. Home early tomorrow and then back to work. It's been a great few days.

The next few months took on a routine aspect as Charlotte relaxed into calmer waters where her life was concerned. The agency found her work of a more interesting nature; the magazine *True Grit* was serialising parts of her book, the students were bringing in extra cash and her life on the romantic front continued to grow. Jay was making progress with his band and Jemma was in her last year of university. Charlotte maintained her creative pursuits and was working on a bass relief of a surfboarder for a sculpture exhibition in September. The Four Seasons were producing Lorca's *The House of Bernada Alba* and Charlotte was given the part of Angustias, the eldest of the five of Bernada's daughters, to be performed at Easter.

Diary entry March 13th.

I'm beginning to think I have taken on too much. Some days I have a job to keep up with everything. Today was spent staring at the computer screen for so long that I got a frightful headache. I then arrived home and found I had left tonight's meal in a bag in the office. I then went back out for fish and chips for the boys instead. This made me late for my rehearsal and then found that I'd left my script at home! Fortunately I managed to cope but it's not long now until the performance – two weeks! I have also offered to help to paint the scenery depicting a Spanish courtyard. Lots of scope but it will take two Sundays. It's a dark play, full of sexual repression but challenging. On a more positive note, last night at sculpture I managed to make a plaster mould for the bass relief. It's surprisingly heavy as the surfboard sails are quite proud. Next week I'll clean out the clay and leave the plaster to dry before casting it in bronze resin. The tricky bit will be chipping off the plaster to release the then-finished work. Wendy is casting a pair of March hares, much simpler as there is less rebate so this should be easier. Why did I go for a more difficult subject!

Ian is making plans for us to visit Florence in May. I will have to make provision for the boys as it will be term time. I'm excited at the prospect of seeing more sculpture: Donatello, Verrocchio and Michelangelo to name a few also frescos by Fra Angelico and paintings by Raphael. I get scared some times that all this excitement might cause one of my "glitches" when I seize up completely and go into a kind of meltdown anxiety state. It has happened before.

Unfortunately for Charlotte her prediction was justified and a week after the successful production of the Lorca play she suffered a minor breakdown. Fortunately the students were not due back to college for another two weeks and Jemma came to her rescue. It was not the first time that her daughter had picked up the pieces but this time her mother's anxiety state was due to overwork and not due to depression or loss of self-esteem. Charlotte was adamant that Ian should not know the real cause of her illness and told him she was suffering from a viral infection. She had always believed that mental problems were a sign of weakness and she would not admit to this failing, should it be so, not even to herself. Ian assured her that the proposed trip to Florence would banish the infection and she would thrive in the culturally sound climate of this famous city. He was busy at work and also preparing for his son Seb to join him at the start of his new term at the Polytechnic.

Charlotte was not paid by the agency for her absence from her temporary work but her book was now bringing in a little more revenue and this kept her from worrying. She would get back to work as soon as possible.

By the end of April her health had picked up and she had resumed her duties. She began to look forward to her Italian trip booked for the second week in May. This was a good time to go away as they would avoid the crowds. Maggie had agreed to take over the boys for the week and so all was set. Charlotte records some of her experiences in her diary entries.

Monday May 14th

These diary entries have been transcribed from my brief notes, scribbled in tiny writing; first on both sides of a blank envelope and lastly on the back of a paper napkin! I had forgotten my diary! I hope I can make sense of both of these desperate measures!

Good flight to Pisa and then train, about one hour to Florence. Arrived at hotel at 10pm. Ground floor room with en-suite bathroom complete with Victorian bath!

Tuesday

Buffet breakfast with a good food selection and then set off on foot for the Piazza de Michelangelo, a high point overlooking Florence and the Arno, where a copy of the sculptor's *David* stands tall. Visited the church of San Miniato, a very pretty romantic 11C church with green marble façade. Apparently Michelangelo saved it during the siege of 1530 and built a fortress around the site. We enjoyed lunch in the Boboli Gardens and walked back via the Pitti Palace and over the Ponte Vecchio, the oldest bridge in Florence. This was quite delightful; tiny boutiques each side and wonderful views of the River Arno and surrounding hills. I love the tall Cyprus trees, so typical of the landscape. Back to the hotel, exhausted, as the temperature was over 80 degrees! The air conditioning in the room was poor, so a sticky siesta. After showering, I put on my orange dress; then went out to Travitorri 'Roberto' for an excellent meal, particularly enjoyed the starter of canalloni with spinach and cream cheese. After a walk around town finally got to bed about twelve midnight!

Wednesday
Walked to the Pitti Palace this time to go into the art galleries and I discovered Raphael. Wonderful paintings that lit the wall with colour where dingy brown was the norm. The collection includes works by Botticelli, Titian, Rubens, Velasquez and Murillo. Went dizzy looking at the frescoed ceilings and then down at the wonderful floors, fantastic marbled inlaid tables and other delights. Walked in the Boboli Gardens and found a shady nook for our picnic lunch. Once again the temperature was in the 80s and even the Italians looked hot! Back over the Ponte Vecchio, where I lingered among the boutiques. We looked at other marvels to be visited tomorrow then back to the hotel for another welcome siesta, cooler this time, bath and then out for our meal. Walked back over the other side of the Arno, then bed at midnight.

Thursday
10am. Walked to the centre of town to see the church of San Lorenzo to visit the New Sacristy and Michelangelo's original work for the tomb of Lorenzo. Went inside the vast *Duomo*, wonderful from the outside but very dark and lifeless inside. Viewed the *Doors of Paradise*, named by Michelangelo who was so impressed by them as a young boy, but sculpted by Lorenzo Ghiberti. These face the cathedral's main door, on the Baptistry, which is reckoned to be the oldest building in

Florence. They are very beautiful and depict the Old Testament in ten framed squares, the light gleaming on all of them. Visited the Casa Buonarrotti, Michelangelo's home and museum and saw his early works which were very inspiring; especially the *Madonna of the Stairs* and a carving of Christ on the cross with a marvellous delicacy of touch, giving such an expression of suffering on the face. We ate our lunch in the Piazza Signoria, by the Neptune Fountain. We then went into the church of Santa Croce. This is a lovely church, very big and cool. The tombs of Michelangelo, Galileo and Machiavelli are all here. Inside are two frescoed chapels. Back over the river for a rest in the Boboli Gardens then on to the hotel for rest and shower. The Uffizi tomorrow?

Friday
The Uffizi was closed for some reason so we decided to take the bus to Fiasole. This is a very beautiful little town situated on the highest point overlooking Florence. We had to change buses en route, which was tricky but the ride was quite delightful as we wound up the hill, bordered with beautiful gardens and villas, arriving at the central square. We walked all round and visited the "Roman remains". It was very interesting. They were so advanced with their knowledge of underground heating pipes etc. The remains showed that they were the municipal baths and theatre. It was lovely to see so much greenery after all the concrete of the city. Unfortunately we were given a poor meal at an incorrect price in a *trattoria* in the square but we didn't let it spoil things. Finally we caught the bus back. It went round the entire town at breakneck speed. The traffic here is crazy, constant sirens, hooters and squeals of

brakes. We were quite exhausted when we arrived back at the hotel.

Saturday

We spent the morning window shopping and present buying. The Bargello Museum was closed so went to the church of San Spirito. This is ugly from the outside but magnificent inside, rich with paintings and art treasures. Found a copy of Michelangelo's *Pieta* from St Peter's in Rome and *The Risen Christ*.

We finished our holiday with a superb meal at Alfredo's. Going back tomorrow via Pisa. We can't leave without seeing the leaning tower! Ian has been my tower! I'm so happy with him. He shows me such love and consideration. I have not experienced this before, not since Netta took me under her wing when I was a child, but that seems a long time ago now. Ian says we should get together permanently but he has to think of Seb, so we must be patient. I don't mind waiting, as I read somewhere, 'the best is yet to be!'

Sadly for Charlotte this dream was not to be fulfilled. Her hopes for a shining future with the man she now loved would be dashed just three months later. In mid-August both Greg and Ian had travelled to California for a sailing adventure with Greg's brother Simon. He had invited them over to help crew his yacht *Pegasus* in a race held there.

Since their holiday in May Charlotte had been busy with her book that was now doing well as a result of the serialisation in *True Grit*. She was on a high and prepared to take on interviews for the local media. She had also started writing her next book, *O is for Orphan*. Ian had given her a word processor, redundant from his office, before he went away. The recent stability of her life had given her the resource to start writing again. In addition to these pursuits she had spent time helping Jemma move into a flat with her best friend Sally. Jemma had graduated with an honours degree in English and was looking for work as an editor with a publishing firm in London. Both Charlotte and Jemma had spent a pleasant weekend in Norfolk and it was on her return to Surrey that she had taken the fatal phone call.

Charlotte heard the news from Greg, his voice cracking and crackling on a bad line from the States. All Charlotte could take in was that Ian was dead, drowned in a terrible accident. Greg went on to tell her that he and Simon had been picked out of the sea by a passing vessel, together with one other sailor. It appeared that a storm had blown up and they had battled against giant waves before *Pegasus* was hurled onto the rocks of a small island. Most of the crew were thrown overboard but not all were recovered. Ian's body was one of the missing.

There are no diary entries to record the horror and anguish that Charlotte was to suffer over the next few months. She retreated into her inner self and proceeded to go through the everyday motions of living in a mechanical fashion. Jemma was no longer at home and she resolved not to call on her daughter's good will as she had before. Instead she took medication and continued to look after her students and work for the agency but she gave up on her writing and evening pursuits and avoided both friends and neighbours. She was in 'another place', one that was dark and lonely but safe.

One rainy day in October, she was jerked temporarily out of her torpor, by the appearance of two unexpected visitors.

October 16th Saturday.
The front door bell rang and I was in two minds whether to answer it. I dragged myself downstairs, annoyed at the intrusion, to find Greg and Sebastian

standing on the doorstep in the rain. I hugged them both in turn and then burst into tears. I was so glad to see them.

Greg had lost weight and seemed much older. Seb was pale and hollow-cheeked but gave me a warm smile. I see Ian's eyes. He sat on the settee and awkwardly folded his long limbs. Greg gave me a parcel. It contained some personal belongings of mine that were left on *Caprice*. There was a record album that Ian and I had bought together and I started to cry again. Greg said there was also a present for my birthday that Ian had bought in advance in the States. He laid it on the bookcase. I would save it until later.

Greg told me that he had been in California staying with Simon who was suffering from post-traumatic stress after the accident, and the feelings of guilt because he had survived. Greg said that Caprice was being sold and that he no longer wanted to sail without Ian, his long-time friend and sailing companion.

Seb told me that he was looking to share a flat with fellow students in London. At the moment he was lodging with Greg who was teaching again. Greg said that he wouldn't be around at Christmas as he would be in California. I asked Seb if he was going to Sweden for the holiday but he said he was not keen as Ingrid's life had changed. Seb said that she had met and married Henrik Nilssen in February and appeared unmoved by Ian's death. This had caused Seb much pain and heartache as he had been close to his father and in no way fond of Henrik. I asked him if he would like to spend the time with us; Jay, Jemma and partners.

His face lit up and for some reason I felt that a cloud had lifted and a thin shaft of light had touched me.

When they had gone I opened my present. It was a necklace and with it a card that said *I chose this for its translucent colour, the colour of the blue Aegean Sea and the colour of your eyes that looked and smiled at me when first we met. It comes with all my love. Ian.*

Later I wrote this poem:

ANOTHER PLACE

With you…
it was another place, a different time.
Wine-rosed days carpeted with dreams
anticipated, held, squandered, re-captured.
An infinity of star-pricked nights
stretching out, time without end
immortalised in passionate fire, burnt out,
refuelled, strong again, a Phoenix
in the midst of sudden vulnerability.
Age unknown, unfelt in breast or limb
no peak too high for soaring heart
or flood too deep to quench the flame.
No bone to rub on bone but light of step,
a surety of mind, no shadow at the edge
to creep across this emptying glass,
scarring the brain and dimming the eye
and shaking the fingers as they strive
to dig among the roots of time misspent
or prepare for a future yet unknown;
without you…

CHAPTER SEVENTEEN

A LETTER FROM AMERICA

At the beginning of December Charlotte heard from John Bradley that there was to be a Christmas dinner party for Zurich Wolf employees and for those that had left before the company moved to Barnet. He said it would be a chance to meet up with her old friends who had made the move and enjoy a good meal at the same time. Charlotte was tempted and rang her old friend and working companion Mavis Hart, now head of the department, to find out if she could stay the night with her in Barnet after the event.

After a generous meal with plenty of wine laid on by the company, Charlotte heard news of Tom. Mavis had known of their relationship and had remained a loyal and trusted friend. She now told Charlotte that he was in a London hospital recovering from a triple bypass operation. Charlotte told Mavis that her relationship with him was over and then told her of Ian and their short time together. On the way home the following day she reflected on her decision not to go to Barnet with the move and was pleased that she had made the right one. Everything she saw was on a much larger scale and lacked the intimate surroundings and niceties of Whitworth. Her friends had seemed subdued and had little to talk about. The new social hall where they had dined appeared cavernous and empty of atmosphere. Zurich Wolf had amalgamated with another pharmaceutical company and become Zurich Holland.

The size of the new site was considerable. Charlotte was sad to see her friend Mavis looking tired and stressed.

Charlotte was also plagued with thoughts of Tom in hospital. She had resisted the urge to write or send a card. One day on an impulse she decided to visit him secretly.

December 18th

I am a stupid, stupid fool. Whatever possessed me to take it into my head to go up to London and open old wounds; and then have the knife well and truly shoved into my heart. I gained access to the ward and told the nurse I was a friend just passing through. She told me that his wife was with him at present if I cared to wait outside but I changed my mind and made to leave. It was at that moment that a woman came out of his room but the woman was not Lorna. Another woman. She didn't see me as I shrank against the wall. I stared incredulously as I took in her identity. It was Rosemary Bartlett, a scientist friend of Tom's. It seems he has wasted no time in extending it to a more meaningful friendship. I am demoralised and have nothing more to say.

Three days before Christmas an unwelcome fall of snow brought chaos to the south and west of England. Fortunately for Charlotte her students were back in Kent for the Christmas break, but Jay and Jemma were yet to arrive home for the holiday. Seb too had sent confirmation to say that he was looking forward to spending time with the Fieldings. Charlotte busied herself with housework and the reorganisation of extra sleeping accommodation

On the morning of Christmas Eve she trudged to the local shops through the snow and came back laden with last-minute groceries and treats. On the doorstep, she met the postman, who handed her a bulky package with an American stamp. At the same time, on entering the house, the phone rang. Both these separate items of news would propel her into uncharted waters during the following year.

Diary entry:
24th December
I was so pleased to hear Greg's voice on the phone. He had not kept in touch since he left for America. He asked after Seb and told me to tell him that he had bought the blues album and tee shirt he wanted in downtown San Francisco. I told him about the snow and the expected arrival of the family and Seb at any minute. He said that Simon had put up a memorial plaque to his friends who died at sea and that I would be welcome to come over any time and he would take me to see it. Goodness! America! I will have to save my pennies for that but what an amazing thought! I have not opened the package from the Priors as everything happened at once when they all arrived an hour later. Jemma will miss Ben who is stuck in Exeter with no train running, but Seb will be around to make up the foursome. Jay and Kelly looked happy together. It's good to see them all. I'm hoping to get to know Seb better. Let's all have a happy Christmas!

December 28th
They all went up to London today to some show or other and I had a chance to finally open the package from the States. I have been knocked over by the enormity of what it contained and don't know where to begin. I'm filled with joy and dread at the same time. I will have to make a decision whether to pursue my

dreams or hide forever from the truth of my existence. My search could lead me anywhere in the world. What will the new year bring? I have two invitations to California and the possibility of finding some real truth about my family but am I strong enough to cope with it all on my own?

The letter from America

1035 Arlington Boulevard
Santa Monica CA

Dear Charlotte

I'm sorry not to have brought this information to your attention before now. Jill and I intended to come to the UK last year and visit you when we attended the band contest but it was not to be. S.A. relief work here in the States is ongoing and we are constantly in demand; fire, flood or earthquake, we are here to do the Lord's work and help the victims of these disasters.

The enclosed papers belonged to Netta and were in a metal file in our loft. The main bulk of the contents of the file were photographs and memorabilia associated with the Prior clan and had been left untouched since they came into our possession after my father passed away in 1975.

The information concerning you and your mother was mixed up with these effects. We apologise again for not giving them to you sooner but with our important work and the two moves to new quarters over the last ten years, the file has been overlooked until now.

If we can be of any help to you in tracing your family we will be only too pleased to do so. Our organisation is excellent at tracing missing persons. We have the latest technology at our disposal.

Have you ever thought of visiting the States? Jill and I would be delighted to see you and show you some of our geographical treasures. We run a summer camp in the Malibu Hills. You would be most welcome to join us.

Yours affectionately

Graham Prior (Major)

Among the many enclosed letters and documents sent to Charlotte from Graham was a scrawled note on blue paper. Between the inkblots and tearstains was a sad and telling message.

Ward F
Eastcote Hospital
Finchley

Dear Miss Prior

Thank you for looking after my baby girl. I'm sorry that I'm so weak in body and in mind that I tried to hurt her, but I will get better soon and claim her back. My baby boy, born at the same time as Charlotte was taken away from me by Gertrude Macey.

She said he was dead but he cried. She said he would pay for my keep. Please look after Charlotte and tell her that her mummy will get well soon.

Yours truly

Vanessa Hammond

Netta had written across the bottom of the letter *'Another child unlikely. No trace of a Gertrude Macey. V is mentally deranged but has periods of lucidity.'* Other letters from the hospital to Miss Prior confirmed this theory, together with medical records and meetings with psychologists, claiming that Vanessa was held there for attempted infanticide and self-harming tendencies. A more sinister report mentioned brain seizures and fits. One letter recorded that Marcel came to see her on the day before he was due to be drafted into the army but they were never to be married, as he had hoped, as she would remain in hospital until his death four years later.

Another enlightening and crucial letter was written by Natalie Hammond and although not dated, was deemed to be written some months earlier than that of her sister.

<table>
<tr><td>The Matron</td><td>The Larches</td></tr>
<tr><td>Bourne Lodge 84</td><td>Highfields Road</td></tr>
<tr><td>Hackney</td><td>Hampstead</td></tr>
</table>

Dear Miss Prior

The Avalon Nursing Home in Bethnal Green has informed me that my sister Vanessa Hammond must leave their premises. She is an unmarried mother with a baby only five days' old. My sister and I were unaware of Vanessa's predicament and it has come as quite a shock to both of us.

Neither my sister nor I are in a position to take care of Vanessa and her baby. I am getting married after Christmas and moving away from London with my husband and new job prospects. Elsbeth is sailing for America in the new year where she will be on tour for some months. Our parents are frail and worried about bombs and blackouts.

We have word that your charitable and Christian

organisation is kind to women in this situation and trust that
you can help us?

Yours sincerely

Natalie Hammond

Charlotte did not know how or where to start with her search
as recorded;

December 30th
Everyone has gone and the house is like a morgue. I
tried not to think about these astonishing and
heartrending revelations and did not confide in Jay and
Jem while they were here. It will take time for me to
make sense of it all and hopefully make a plan. It was
lovely having the young people about and to see Seb
enjoying the company of Jemma. He has a lovely
nature and is so appreciative of everything. He gave me
some sketches he had made of me and Jem. They are
very good. Greg phoned before Seb left and is coming
back next week.

I've decided to make a start and will go up to
London next week, to the City Registry Office as
Natalie's letter states that I was born in Bethnal Green.
There is much to do and both the agency and the Kent
boys will soon be claiming my attention but before that,
Maggie's New Year's Eve party tomorrow will be a
welcome diversion.

In the months that followed, Charlotte was to undergo many
setbacks in her search. Both The Larches in Hampstead and
the Avalon Nursing Home in Bethnal Green were no longer

in existence, the building that housed the latter being demolished by the Blitz. At the City Registry Office, however, she was rewarded with a copy of her original birth certificate stating that her mother was Vanessa Esme Hammond, aged twenty-four with the address given as the Avalon Home. There was a blank space beside the name of the father as they were an unmarried couple. Before this Charlotte had been issued with the shortened version of her birth certificate with no other information save her name, Charlotte Patricia Hammond, and her date of birth. This was then later replaced with her adoption certificate, bearing the date of her adoption and the surname of her grandparents, Laurent.

The helpful clerk at the registry office told her that the local library held some records of nursing homes and clinics but Charlotte said that she would have to come back another day. There had been no record of a twin boy born at the same time.

February 6th

Today I went to London again as I'm finally over the flu. In the library, after much searching, I found a report about the Avalon Home. It was closed down in January 1942 due to malpractice and poor hygiene. The malpractice included illegal adoptions and on two occasions illegally performed abortions. Wards were closed due to puerperal fever and other infections. A Mrs Doris Collins was later held responsible and imprisoned for three years for crimes against vulnerable women, adoption for monetary gain and abortion. After reading this I was deeply shocked. What was my mother doing there? Why hadn't anyone taken better care of her? What sort of man was my father? No wonder she became mentally afflicted. I must talk to Rita and Myra. Surely they must know something about all those years ago from my father? I must find out if there was a Gertrude Macey at the clinic. Would the police hold records?

Her writings show that unfortunately for Charlotte, Rita was unable to fill in the gaps she so sorely sought. Her aunt told her that she had joined the WAAFS just before Charlotte was born and that her sister Myra had been in the Leeds Infirmary training to be a doctor. Myra and Marcel had not been privy to each other's mode of life and, had Myra known of her twin brothers' irresponsibility towards Vanessa, would have disapproved wholeheartedly. Rosamund, the eldest sister, was no longer around for consultation. Rita thought that their parents were equally ignorant of their son's indiscretion, or it could have been that he asked for their help and they were coldly unsympathetic. The news would certainly have shocked both Mrs Laurent and her husband, the latter a pillar of respectability at work and in the community.

What Rita was able to tell Charlotte was that, as the youngest sister and closest to her brother, he had confided to her that he was seeing a girl from Hampstead who was going to sit for him in his studio in the King's Road. His earnings as a portrait painter had been minimal and his parents had bailed him out of the pawnshop on many occasions but this was all she knew as she then signed up with the Air Force. She could only assume that their poverty had led them to the Avalon Nursing Home, where prices for beds and care was probably low with no questions asked.

February 20th
Decided to find out if there was anyone still living at the Larches who could give me some information. It was quite a trek over to Hampstead in spite of an early

start. The result was disappointing as the house in Highfields Road was now divided into three flats. Feeling despondent I went into the local library to look at the census for the 1930s and 40s, when the Hammonds would have been in residence, but they told me that these records were held in the office in London. After some lunch and a nostalgic walk around Whitestone Pond and memories of my childhood with my grandparents, I was driven to revisit their house on the suburb. I was lucky enough to meet the present owner as I rudely peered over the hedge. To my amazement she invited me in and I revisited rooms I had not been in for thirty years. The house had not altered much from what I remembered apart from the loggia being made part of the sitting room instead of a garden retreat. The biggest shock was the garden itself. One cherry tree was huge and the other had been chopped down. There were no beautiful flower borders or kitchen garden. There was an air of neglect that my grandparents would not have approved of but I wouldn't have missed today's visit for anything.

Charlotte was to discover that the Hammonds had lived in Hampstead until 1945. Certificates stated that as well as their three daughters they had a son, William, who died of tuberculosis at the age of sixteen. Charlotte had thought it strange that both of her families had three daughters and one son who had died at an early age.

The information she was gathering about her family now added a new dimension to her life and Charlotte took on a more focused attitude. She had resumed evening classes at the art college and was auditioning for a part in the Four Seasons' forthcoming production of Terence Rattigan's *Separate Tables*.

She was also looking forward to Easter and another family gathering including Sebastian who would join them for Easter Day. In March she received an unexpected invitation to visit Ireland.

March 1st   *2, Brayside Rise*
                                                 Newtonards
                                                    Belfast.

Dear Charlotte

I'm sorry to be so late in answering your newsy Christmas letter but have now finally moved as you can see by the address. I promised that you could come over and visit me when I was straight and have a taste of this beautiful island. I will be able to show you the sights! Sadly there are still troubles over here but you will be OK with me. Let me know if you can come some time in April? I will be going away in May and June is a busy month at work.

All for now as there is still much to do. I'm working on designs for the new wild life calendar. Glad you liked my Christmas card. I may adapt it for one of the designs.

Best regards

Alison

Charlotte decided that after Easter it would be a welcome change to go and visit her friend and talk of their happy days in Spetses and visit a new country at the same time. Alison had not known Ian but it would be good to talk about him to her. Perhaps she would meet Alison's mystery amour? There was another reason for visiting Ireland. Charlotte had discovered that her maternal grandmother was called Therese O'Connor and came from Dungannon in County Kildare. Maybe she would find some records of her family? Charlotte replied to her friend and made a date for the following month.

Before Easter she went again to London to find police records regarding the closure of the Avalon Nursing Home and more details of the aforementioned Mrs Doris Collins. She was also keen to know whether a Gertrude Macey had also worked there at the time of her birth.

It was not easy to find the records that she sought and it took two trips to East London to track them down but eventually she was successful. According to Charlotte's notes Doris Collins was in fact Gertrude Macey who had changed her name to Macey when she came over to England from Australia with faked references in 1935. She worked as a nurse at the home but was not registered there as a midwife but had practiced as one in Australia before being struck off for misconduct in her home town of Cairns two years before. Among her possessions at the time of her arrest was a pocket book that listed some names of adopted babies, and mothers whom she had "helped" illegally. Payments and non-payments for her services were also noted in her book together with the dates.

Charlotte was overwhelmed to find that a baby H, male, was the only birth entered on the same day as herself at the home. Another date, entered some three months later, reports that he was handed over to a Dr and Mrs Grant L Harper of Michigan USA for a considerable sum of money. It was speculated that Macey had faked the death of this child and smuggled him out to an accomplice before caring for him herself at her home in Mile End. Dr and Mrs Harper may not have been fully aware of the situation and were probably pleased to take the baby and return to the States as soon as possible without asking any further questions.

Charlotte had no further proof that baby H was her twin brother but with her mother's letter to Netta and a sudden memory of a visit to the clairvoyant some years earlier, she became convinced that he was her twin. There had been no trace of a death certificate but with the negligent management of the home this may not have been surprising, as it would probably have been overlooked. Charlotte would probably never know but it made her all the more keen to try and trace her lost brother.

Her next step was to look into the records of the hospital in Finchley, where her mother was a patient but that too would have to wait, as it was no longer in existence. She would have to travel to North London and she was committed now to full-time work until Easter.

Tuesday April 6th
The Easter weekend really lifted my spirits. It was helped by the weather, the sun lighting up the daffodils I had planted last year although there was still a cold wind. We pushed the boat out and all had turkey for Sunday lunch and Easter Simnel cake in the afternoon, this being a tradition inherited from Netta. Seb seemed quieter than usual and I put it down to Jemma's boyfriend, Ben, joining her for the Easter break. I have been a bit slow in realising that Seb has become quite fond of Jemma. Now what am I going to do? I don't want him to feel that he can't visit us anymore. Perhaps Jem could introduce him to some of her London friends. I must speak to her about it. Greg's taking him off to visit his sister in Cornwall next week.

I'm looking forward to going to Ireland on Sunday. Jay says he'll take me to the airport. Both he and Kelly went off after tea to a gig somewhere. It really was a lovely day.

Charlotte's notes were brief regarding her stay as recorded a week later.

Sunday 11th April
Arrived in Belfast and struck by the silence and inactivity. Maybe it was too early (11ish) as no one had stirred, or were they plotting behind closed doors? Felt a little nervous. Alison met me and we drove to her house in Newtownards. The house was bright and airy, raised up on an incline with a distant view of Strangford Loch from my bedroom window. After lunch we took a walk by the loch and then a drive to the coast and a walk along the beach at Bangor. It really is an emerald isle. Alison said it's due to all the rain that falls here.

Monday
A visit to the Ulster American Folk Park! Apart from the usual small historical dwellings and artefacts I was amazed to see written up on the wall of the reception place a long list of names of presidents of the United States of America, each one having been an Irish immigrant at some time or other. No wonder these countries share a common bond.

Tuesday
It was lovely sunny day, and a trip to Mount Stewart House and Garden. The garden was delightful, so beautifully laid out and fresh with spring flowers and shrubs. I loved the large terracotta pots and the sculptures of animals and "little people" that the Irish treasure. There was a lake, palm trees and tall thin conifers that made me think of Italy as well as other

species of tree and shrub from distant lands. We did not go into the house but enjoyed tea and cakes in the conservatory.

Wednesday
We set off early for County Antrim to explore the Carrick-a-Rede Bridge, Giant's Causeway and Portrush. I was bowled over by the Giant's Causeway. It was staggering. All those basaltic hexagon columns joined together and yet separate, and formed by volcanic action was amazing. We scrambled over the uneven plateau that formed the causeway and took to the cliffs made from the same basaltic columns. These columns rose like very tall, thin trees, packed together to form a cliff. On the way up to the ledge I took a photo of Alison in the "wishing chair" formed by the columns. The narrow ledge that formed a path hugged the side of the cliff. It was awe-inspiring and scary at the same time. You needed a good head for heights!

Further along the coastal path was the rope bridge at Carrick Fergus. This was another exciting and scary moment. The rope bridge is slung between two prominences of rock with the sea dashing far below.

It was a pleasure to finally arrive at Portrush for tea and cake and rest from such unforgettable experiences!

Other diary entries mentioned the Mourne Mountains and a very energetic and violent game of indoor hockey with Alison's circuit group. Charlotte remarked: 'I nearly lost a finger but the exercise and excitement was literally breathtaking!' Another 'scary' experience was the sight of a soldier with a huge Sten gun on patrol in some woods nearby. There had been little time for painting and sketching and Charlotte had been disappointed that the trip to Dungannon in County Kildare had to be cancelled due to heavy rain. She had hoped to find some records of her grandmother or her family but declared that she would return one day.

She arrived home refreshed at the weekend and set about preparing for her students' return on the Sunday evening. It had been good to talk to Alison about Ian, and although Alison was not one of her close friends, she had been a sympathetic listener. Alison spoke of her 'man' but gave little away. Charlotte supposed that he was busy with his wife and for once she was glad to be free of such complications.

Later in the week she took out the letters and documents sent by Graham Prior and re-scanned them. There had been photographs too, of Charlotte age three, with thick tumbling hair, pure white in the photo, a platinum blond. There were photos of a smiling Netta and Annie, both with her on the beach, others in the garden at Dovecot. The pictures brought a lump to her throat and a sudden longing to be that child that was so loved and treasured by these good people. But why had they not told her the truth? Why the secrecy? Was it because it was the law that an adopted child must wait until he is eighteen before he is allowed to know the full details about his real parents? Why have I waited so long?

Returning to the medical documents, Charlotte wrote down her mother's case note reference number and on the following day at work, made some discreet phone calls concerning the Eastcote Hospital in Finchley. This entailed two visits to the record office, and after payment was made, she was finally in possession of copies of further medical documents and was able to piece together what happened to her mother. One letter was particularly distressing.

Eastcote Hospital　　　　　　*Juniper House*
Finchley　　　　　　　　　　*London Road*
London　　　　　　　　　　　*Kingston*

Dear Dr Smallwood,　　　　　*Case Ref E4 1079*

I have been looking after my sister Vanessa Hammond since her discharge from hospital two months ago. Sadly I made a mistake in taking her to visit Marcel Laurent's grave in Dover. Since his death last year she has been keen to make this effort. She had seemed much better and I thought that she could cope but I was wrong. Unfortunately she became extremely agitated and made for the edge of the cliff at St Margaret's Bay where he had died in a climbing accident. I had the utmost difficulty in restraining her. It is in my opinion that she had every intention of committing suicide so as to be with him. She is now at our house under prescribed sedation and we will await your instructions on how to proceed. Our general practitioner is writing to you. It is so sad after she had made such progress.

Yours sincerely

Mrs Natalie Lytton

Another alarming fact came to light with a report from the hospital denying a charge of sexual misconduct brought about by one of their staff. Vanessa Hammond, a patient on F ward, had reported the details of the assault to her sister, Mrs Natalie Lytton in November 1944.

May 18ᵗʰ Friday
Today I made a further revelation about my poor mother. I took the train and tube to Finchley and found

the local library. By using their facilities I was able to find a more detailed report on the rape case at Eastcote in 1944. It was reported that V.H., a patient at the hospital, had made an accusation about one of the staff to her sister Natalie Lytton. In a clear and concise way she had described the offence that involved Dr Martin Sedge and a forty-two-year-old woman patient, Emily Parker, who was both a paraplegic and mentally disturbed. The act of rape had apparently taken place at 3am and there were no other witnesses. Vanessa had claimed that she had called out, but her cries had gone unheeded, as it was not unusual in the hospital environment, where she was held, for cries of disturbed patients to be ignored.

The magistrates' court ruled against the evidence of V.H. on the grounds of diminished responsibility and insufficient proof. Her sister Natalie Lytton who had brought the case on Hammond's behalf had testified that Vanessa had been in a lucid state of mind when she reported the incident and had been extremely upset by the whole business. Emily Parker was never examined as it had been too late to confirm the charge of rape and the case was dismissed.

Further information gained from the Eastcote records brought a premature end to Charlotte's search for the time being. It appeared that after the scandalous incident in November 1944, Vanessa was transferred to another hospital for several months before finally being sent to a medical research centre in Chicago for a new pioneer treatment that was being tested for brain malfunction.

Phenomena Point was attached to the University of Chicago Hospital in Chicago and it was unclear what procedures were adopted at the centre or why Vanessa was chosen to go there. Was it to keep her quiet? Had her parents signed a consent form or paid money? Charlotte would have to make plans to go to America to find out and, at the same time, search for her twin brother.

Natalie's letter concerning Marcel's grave prompted the idea that Charlotte herself would like to make another visit to St Margaret's Church, and, if agreeable, take her daughter with her. Neither Jemma nor Jay had been to Dover but Netta had taken Charlotte when she was fifteen. They set off one morning early in May as recorded, in emotive terms, by Charlotte.

After a week of mixed weather, Tuesday dawned bright and sunny. A good drive down to the Kent coast. The landscape lay green and undulating under the sun. We turn off to St Margaret's Bay and find the church. The church dwarfs the tiny village. It stands magnificently upon the cliffs, grey and rough with flint, washed and brushed by the weathering centuries. We find the grave. The white smooth headstone belies the years my father has lain there, his name and age cut deep into the stone. We kneel in silence, then rise and tend the grave. I leave a kiss and a glimpse of his granddaughter, as we tread the soft path back to the lich-gate.

We drive down the twisty narrow lane to the sea. The bay is held by giant cliffs. We feel warm sun as we plough through pebbles to the shelter of a breakwater. We eat our lunch and contemplate the view. We listen to the low roar and swish of the sea as it breaks upon the stony beach. The lacy edge of the water swirls restlessly. The smell of the sea mingles with our food and lingers on our lips. I gaze at the bleached breakwaters; here when he was here, planed smooth by wind and sun, watched over by seabirds. I look at the distant cliffs and wonder how they can be so deceptive. They claimed my father's life, but today they stand proud and unmoved.

CHAPTER EIGHTEEN

NEW HORIZONS

As the summer of 1986 approached, Charlotte made some important decisions. Her book sales had increased and over the months she had managed to add to her savings. Her students were in their last term at the college and would be leaving at the end of next month. It was time to take stock of her life and seek out new horizons. After her commitment to The Four Seasons in July, she would book her flight to L.A. as suggested by the Priors. They had offered her accommodation and any help that they could give her in her search. Charlotte was grateful for their promised support and armed with this certainty she knew she could attempt what, at one time, would have seemed almost impossible. She confirmed her intentions in a letter to the Priors and booked her flight for the first week in September.

Charlotte had felt certain ambivalence towards her part in *Separate Tables* and was not sorry when it was over. She had played the character of Ann Shanklin, the glamorous ex-wife of John Malcolm. The part had been both demanding and intense, leaving her 'wrung out'. Each of the two separate plays had entailed many items for the dining room scenes and this had been a headache for 'props'. 'Major Pollock' fell ill during the penultimate week of rehearsals and his part had been taken by another, much younger player, whose costume was ill-fitting and whose lines, not surprisingly, were shaky. Charlotte wrote of *Separate Tables*: 'It was not a lot of laughs and the only happy person at the end of it all appeared to be Sybil!'

One weekend, Seb came to tell her that he would be spending the summer with Greg in America. It had appeared that Greg had taken on the position of sailing instructor for disabled youngsters, a charity set up by his brother Simon. Seb would be Greg's assistant, getting boats ready and generally pitching in with whatever he could do to help. Charlotte had been surprised but pleased that Greg had taken up sailing again and for such a good cause. She was undecided whether to take the opportunity whilst there, of the brothers' invitation to visit them. They would take her to see the plaque that Simon had erected in memory of Ian, as suggested by Greg last Christmas. She was unsure of Greg. He was still an unknown quantity and shrouded in an aura of mystery. Her basic knowledge of him was only that he had served in the army as an education officer for some years but was now teaching part time in a boys' public school. She decided to confide in her friend Maggie.

August 7th
When Maggie said she thought Greg might be gay I was astounded. It had never crossed my mind! She had met him at my party a few years back and told me then that she thought him quite attractive. My knowledge of gays extended to great disappointment when my favourite actor, Bogarde, went from being a lovable heterosexual doctor, to a persecuted homosexual in the film *Victim*. Before I was married, I was totally unaware of these practices until Ralph enlightened me. Such a sheltered life I had lived! I suppose it's possible Greg might be gay, and when I think of him and Sebastian together, I shudder, but then I dismiss the thought altogether. Maggie thinks that I should go anyway. She asked if

Simon was married but I said I didn't know that either. She just laughed and said 'try living on the edge, it could be exciting!' I had not told her the details of my family search programme, only that I was staying with the Priors. I'm still conscious of the stigma that is attached to mental illness although I'm sure she would understand.

I think I'll go for it!!

Further news from the Priors gave Charlotte hope for her mission. In a recent letter Graham had told her that he had located a Dr Grant Lincoln Harper, retired paediatrician and living in Detroit. At this stage it was only a hunch that it was the same Dr Harper but it sounded plausible.

Charlotte's excitement grew as the weeks turned into days, and the days into hours before her long-awaited trip was to begin. Finally, on September 3rd she closed the door of 92 Fenton Road, picked up her case and climbed into the waiting taxi that would take her to the airport; she was on her way.

The plane touched down in L.A. International Airport at 5pm. Charlotte was greatly relieved to recognise the smiling faces of the Priors as she emerged from "arrivals". She had nurtured a deep fear that they would not be there and that she would be alone in a vast metropolis. She had never quite conquered this fear of ineptitude that had, at times, haunted her well into her adult life, and the long flight had left her fragile and apprehensive.

Friday September 6th
Have been here three days now but still jet lag hits me around 3pm. I'm really loving the relaxed atmosphere, as Graham and Jill are so kind and nothing seems too much trouble for them. They have a beautiful home,

immaculately furnished and very different to their S.A. counterparts in Britain if Ralph's parents were anything to go by. I spend most of my time in the large family room below the kitchen and dining room. Both Graham and Jill work and I'm left to my own devices. In a euphoric moment I decided to contact the Lawsons in San Francisco and received a most welcoming offer to go and stay with them in ten days' time. This has put me into another spin! How far is Santa Monica from San Francisco? Greg will be packing up the sailing school soon. Perhaps we could meet in Malibu? There may be a holiday let there and Seb and he could surf on the beach!

Tomorrow we are off to Chicago for three nights and staying with S.A. friends of the Priors. In return Graham will take the Sunday night meeting (service) at their hall. We hope to track down Phenomena Point and Grant L Harper. It seems P. Point has now become a research lab but there should still be records going back to the 1940s when it was first set up.

The roads here are amazing! I love the huge shiny trucks, the enormous gantries that span the Santa Monica Highway and Route 66! I'm back with Simon and Garfunkel. I have the use of a car but I don't dare to drive. Perhaps I'll catch a Greyhound! I'm so happy! Will something go wrong?

The Priors booked the flight to Chicago's O'Hare Airport and arranged a 'billet' with friends of theirs on the outskirts of town. Charlotte was amazed at the convenience of the Salvation Army network; it reminded her of her early days of marriage when doors had been opened to them by complete strangers. A Pontiac was put at their disposal and they were invited to come and go as they pleased. The Priors had spent time in the Windy City as officers some years ago and so knew Chicago fairly well.

Graham had put through a call to Dr Harper in Detroit the previous week and had been favoured with a surprised but intelligent and willing response. A venue had been agreed upon in Detroit and would take place the next day. Charlotte wrote of the meeting:

I was quaking with nerves. I felt that I was really going to get somewhere with my search. We pulled into the car park of the diner and made for a secluded cubicle. The diner was busy with the lunchtime crowd and a lively atmosphere prevailed. After a while, a grey-haired man, lean and tanned in appearance, stood searching in the aisle. Graham stood up and held out a hand. The man ambled over to our table and introduced himself. His first words went straight to my heart. 'I am Grant Lincoln Harper, widowed, seventy-eight years old with an adopted son Ryan Edgar Harper, now aged forty-six. How does this help you?' Before anyone could speak I blurted out 'does he have one blue eye and one eye brown?' I couldn't help myself. It came from nowhere. The Priors were staring at me and I immediately apologised. The doctor's eyes had widened but he made no comment. I had uttered the words of the clairvoyant that had until now been buried all those years ago. The question was ignored and we went on to talk about Phenomena Point.

Charlotte went on to say that Dr Harper agreed to help them arrange a meeting at the medical Research Centre in Chicago with a colleague he knew was working there. He regretted that he would be unable to accompany them but had imparted useful information about the centre. He confirmed that it had been an establishment at the forefront of advanced clinical research and that various trials and investigations had been carried out on patients, in most cases successfully, during the 1940s and 50s. He showed a reluctance to discuss his own personal involvement with Phenomena Point but inferred that it involved Ryan when he was seven years old. He had not commented on his son's adoption or the fact that he might be Charlotte's twin, but he had shaken hands with her and promised that he would make his own enquiries and then be in touch with her before she left America.

Diary entry: Sunday Sept 9th
Back in Chicago we arrived early at the centre and although it was a Sunday, we were expected, as friends of Dr Harper, and shown into an office on the ground floor. The centre is a large, airy building forming a horseshoe; white, sterile and futuristic, the main offices being at the middle of the U and the labs at either side, quite unlike Z.W. We were shown a register of the names of patients for the year of 1948 and there was my mother's signature; I recognised the same scrawl as I had seen in her letter to Netta. Other records showed that she had been a patient there for two years and that her treatment, whatever that was, had been successful. Next to her signature on the discharge sheet was an address in New York. I wrote it down. Graham asked to see if Ryan Harper had been admitted as a patient in 1947 but the clerk was not forthcoming. I asked who had financed my mother's stay at Phenomena Point but this was also met with the same inscrutability. I had to

be content with the proof of her stay by the signature and address given at the time that she left.

In the evening, although still traumatised by events and the constant wondering about my twin, I attended the S.A. meeting that Graham had agreed to take when he knew he was coming to the city. I found myself listening to the comforting sound of the army band and the trilling of the songsters and being transported to the Sundays of my youth. I joined in the rousing songs and found myself praying fervently that I would finally make peace in my heart with both my past and my future yet unknown.

Tomorrow we go back to L.A. but not before a sightseeing tour of this city of needles; I have been promised a view from one of the tallest, the Hancock building, over ninety floors high, and, if we time it right, a view of the setting sun from the visitors observatory floor, painting the whole town red as it sinks in solar splendour.

Although suffering from the usual bout of apprehension at the start of a new journey, Charlotte reassured Jill that she would be fine. Jill had driven her to the coach station and made sure that she found the right Greyhound bus for San Francisco. Both Graham and Jill had thought it a good idea that she should visit her friends there. As she journeyed she reflected on the previous two weeks of her stay with them. Charlotte had got to know Jill quite well, and was pleased to find that they had enjoyed each other's company. Jill took her to many shopping malls and places of interest when days off work allowed. Charlotte was amazed at the size of the malls and at her new friend's capacity for trawling through them. It was a revelation to her how many shops there were, their size and opulence. Never having had money to spare, it came as a culture shock and she realised that she had been living in the dark ages by these standards. She had bought herself some new clothes and looked good in them according to Jill, who was well dressed but more conventional in her taste. Charlotte had maintained both her looks and her figure and felt confident in the new trendy garb, a more casual look which was not difficult to achieve in this paradise of choice.

The long journey to San Francisco was uneventful and because it was made overnight she slept most of the way. Finally they pulled into the yard at the depot and Charlotte glimpsed Greg and Sebastian standing side by side, Greg's arm about Seb's shoulder. They came towards her as she alighted and smiled their greeting.

Charlotte wrote:

Monday.
I arrived feeling far from by best. I felt grimy after the long journey. I was introduced to Simon, his wife Jessica and dog Raffles. I was quite relieved to know that there would be another female in the house. I found Jess a kind, motherly person who fussed about me and made me feel at home. Simon is older than his brother by some years but has the same dark eyes and wide smile. They have a married son and daughter; Paul lives in New York and Maria in Denver.

The house is big, rambling and untidy. The backyard is littered with old bits of boat and two rotting canoes. Simon is a large friendly type rather like his dog; Raffles took to me right away! I have a good-size room with a big bed. There are various mechanical items dotted about, probably over from a previous age, together with a vintage wireless and something that looks like a fancy petrol pump, clean and polished. Perhaps Simon is an engineer or maybe this was Paul's room? Seb is feeling down as he has to fly back to London in two days' time but he is keen to take me to the sailing school in Half Moon Bay tomorrow. He looks terrific: fierce blue eyes burning out of a tanned face and hair bleached the colour of ripe corn. He is a catch for any girl. He asked after Jemma and I told him to give her a ring when he got back but I don't know whether he will.

The following day Charlotte accompanied Greg and Sebastian to Half Moon Bay where they finished locking up the boats and generally pottering about. They ate lunch in the Beach Café and then went for a swim. It was still warm in the Californian sunshine but for some reason Charlotte felt awkward in front of them both in her swimsuit, but it went unnoticed by both men as they romped and splashed like children let out of school. For a fleeting moment, she wondered about their relationship but put it aside.

Wednesday
Said 'Goodbye' to Seb as he went off to the airport with Greg. I reassured him that we would meet up as soon as I got home. Simon and Jess took me to see the plaque that Simon had erected in memory of his friends. It was fixed to a rough rock at the side of a viewing point, overlooking the sea on a lonely stretch of coast road. The wording was simple and four names were etched into the solid brass plate. We stood for several moments contemplating our loss and then climbed back into the Ranger and drove to a restaurant for lunch. I thought of Sebastian and his father. Ian

would never see him come of age and start a career but he had done his job; Seb was a credit to him.

When they returned, Greg was waiting for them and now that Sebastian had left for London, there was a buzz of excitement and talk of a visit to the Yosemite National Park. It appeared that bookings had been made earlier in the summer for the reservation of two cabins for three nights but an error with the date at the office meant that Sebastian would not be able to go as planned, as he was due back at the Polytechnic and changes at this later stage were not possible. Simon asked Charlotte if she would be happy to take Seb's place. Jessica reassured her that she and Charlotte could share one cabin whilst 'the boys' as she called them would share the other. Charlotte was delighted to be asked to go. She had remembered the description given by the Appleyards, of this vast track of scenic beauty set in the Sierra Nevada, when they had returned from Yosemite with their photographs some years ago. Never had she thought that she would see this marvel for herself. The plan was to set off early Friday morning.

Extracts of Charlotte's account of their visit.
After several hours of driving we came to this marvellous place set 2,000 feet above sea level. We entered the valley along a corridor of giant sequoias, towering fir trees and the largest of all living things but nothing could have prepared me for my first glimpse of the grandeur of the mountains: El Capitan and Half Dome. I gasped audibly at the sheer beauty of this glacier-carved canyon and the power of the mighty falls, plunging down to the sparkling lakes below. A natural breathtaking paradise! Simon and Jessica had been here before but Greg and I were left suitably

dumbfounded. We drove to a "village" campsite in the shadow of Glacier Point and Half Dome, and parked the car. In the office we were given the keys to our cabins, but it seemed another error had occurred; instead of being installed in heated log cabins, we were to be under canvas. After further enquiry Simon learnt that these more humble cabins were the only ones available. Inside they were indeed devoid of comfort, containing two iron bedsteads, reminiscent of my school dormitory, and one long table piled high with thin folded grey blankets. Fortunately the "tents" stood on a concrete floor and the door was made of wood. The toilets and washrooms were some yards away down a stony track and the hot showers even further away, situated in the main part of the "village". Jessica seemed perturbed by these arrangements but I was thrilled beyond measure. It didn't matter to me one bit. I was experiencing this amazing valley that was so spiritually uplifting so nothing could dampen my enthusiasm but what I was yet to find out was how cold it could be at night.

We found a restaurant and enjoyed a late lunch looking out on the panorama. Then we boarded an open-air shuttle bus that toured part of the valley, the guide highlighting places of interest plus Ranger stations, general stores and a gift shop. At one point we stopped in order to watch free rock climbers scaling the granite wall of El Capitan, but these pinpricks were too small for my eyes; I needed binoculars. I couldn't imagine anyone managing to do such a feat.

There was so much to take in. I felt like a prisoner who had been set free in French Market. Simon and Jess smiled at our appreciation and Greg's face was so changed it was almost beatific! I hardly recognised him. After a hearty evening meal and a stroll in the now dark and very cold air, we collected our things and made for the hot showers. As the temperature had fallen so low I was advised to wear my tracksuit in bed and to heap on the blankets. Jess grumbled that she would have liked a snack before tucking up but that all food, even toothpaste, was forbidden in the cabins as it could attract the brown bears. Outside, in the car park, were rows of metal lock-up bins especially for the purpose of storing provisions and keeping them safe from the bears should they come down at night. I could not sleep as image after image chased behind my closed eyes and the lines of a poem began to form in my brain, but the lighting had failed in the tent and I was too cold to write by torchlight. They will keep, I hope!

The following day was taken up with sightseeing and following the trails that led along the Merced Canyon. This river ran through the length of the valley and over time had carved its way through the rocky bed. After lunch they took the track that would lead them to the Yosemite Falls but on the way a small snake darted across their path. Jessica, who was climbing up on a rock, took fright and slipped. She fell heavily, her foot twisting between two boulders and her elbow hitting a large stone. This unfortunate accident was to change the nature of the rest of their stay. After seeking help at a nearby Ranger station, they were given a lift to the Ahwahnee Hotel. Simon took the decision to book the one remaining room available where he hoped Jess would be more comfortable. Jessica was full of apologies for the change in circumstances but suggested that they all meet the following morning in the hotel, where they served an excellent breakfast.

Simon joined Charlotte and Greg later with the news that Jess was 'OK and taking it easy' and that the three of them would stick to their plans for the rest of the day. As late evening approached, Simon departed for the hotel and Charlotte and Greg made for the hot showers.

Diary entry
I was tired after the events of the day but happy and determined to write my poem. I missed Jess but was too tired to worry about being on my own; or so I thought. I had just finished writing and had finally got off to sleep, blankets piled high and still no electric light, when I heard a forceful scratching and snuffling coming from the back of the cabin. I sat bolt upright with my heart thumping and the sudden memory of forbidden biscuits in my rucksack. I snapped on the torch and aimed it at the corner of the tent where the canvas appeared to move. I was frozen with terror. I was faced with a terrible dilemma. Should I wait and be attacked in my bed or should I go outside and be mauled? They say that a fox will make a hole in the wire and then wait patiently for the terrified animal to finally bolt through it. I was that terrified animal and I bolted out of the cabin and in to the one next door.

A sleepy Greg stood in the light of my torch, wearing a tracksuit, his hair tousled, and his feet bare on the concrete. I garbled out my fear and asked to sleep in the spare bed. As I stood there shivering, he put his arm round me and guided me to a bed, the torch now revealing that it was one of double size, originally designated for Simon and Jess. I hesitated, but not for long and drew the thin blankets around me. Greg found his gas lamp and struck a match. He took two plastic cups and poured a generous measure of bourbon into each. He grinned at me and apologised for the lack of another bed or even a spare chair. I sipped the unaccustomed drink and felt it engulf me. I managed a smile as my fear slipped away. I asked if it could have been a bear but he said 'probably not, but some lonely creature also wanting a bed for the night!' His chuckle was warm and reassuring. Eventually we tried to sleep, each keeping religiously to his own side of the bed. But sleep wouldn't come. In spite of the distance between us I felt the power of his presence as I lay beside him. It was tangible. I became aroused by a sudden longing, which rose unbidden. We lay together, each gripped by our own thoughts and desires but not voicing them. Then Greg spoke and the words tumbled out in an impassioned rush: 'Charlotte, I would never take advantage of you, I respect you too much.

'You are quite safe with me although the thought of you beside me is pure magic and I think you feel it too. I have never told you of my past but I will tell you now if you don't mind. I lost a young wife in childbirth. She suffered a heart attack and as they tried to save my son, mistakes were made. I swore then that I would never seriously date a girl of childbearing age and I have kept my word. It was fairly easy whilst I was in the army all those years, and later at the boys' school. I'm not saying that I didn't find a willing casual partner who understood the situation but it left an aftermath of loneliness. People have thought me a homosexual; you too perhaps, but my love for Sebastian is the love of a man who lost a son. I'm just a lonely widower.' When he had finished we lay in silence and in the darkness I could feel his pain and his unshed tears. My hand crept towards his, and in this manner, we fell asleep.

In the morning we looked at each other, shyly now in this new light. We had not consummated our strengthened friendship as some would have done but gave each other space to reflect. We both valued this new aspect of our lives but wanted to tread softly, and to take care of what we already had. Time will tell. We decided to hide our light when we arrived at the Ahwahnee and assume our normal roles. We did not want to complicate things or arouse undue interest from Simon and Jess, but all the same, I felt a warm glow inside that I'll find hard to hide.

At breakfast, Charlotte avoided Greg's eye and tried to give her attention to the Native American artwork that surrounded her in this beautiful dining hall. She loved the log-beamed ceilings and the huge stone hearth and was so engrossed that she barely heard Simon say that unfortunately they would have to cut their visit short. He apologised and explained that Jess needed further medical attention back home on Monday morning. They would leave after a late lunch but were to make the most of the morning. Charlotte and Greg hired bikes and went off in search of Mirror Lake, whilst Simon took Jess to a gift shop and filled the car with petrol for the journey home.

Finally they left for San Francisco but Charlotte was able to take back with her a new poem and a possible new and meaningful friendship.

CHAPTER NINETEEN

THE FINAL TRUTH

When Charlotte arrived back in Santa Monica she found that Graham Prior had once again been busy on her behalf. He had taken the address she had given him in connection with her mother's discharge from the clinic in 1950 and asked the Missing Persons department to make enquiries. The subsequent information was that the apartment mentioned in New York had been occupied for over thirty years by a Mr and Mrs Brent Dewar and that Mrs Dewar's maiden name was listed as Hammond and her Christian name, Elsbeth. There had been no mention of a Vanessa Hammond but this could have been because she was not an official resident. A further search revealed that the couple had been childless and that Brent Dewar had died aged seventy-four in 1981. The apartment was sold the following year and Graham surmised that Elsbeth had possibly returned to her sister Natalie in England. She would probably have taken Vanessa with her, as there was no evidence of either of them in New York.

In the meantime there was a letter addressed to Charlotte Hammond from Dr Harper, judging by the printed name and address on the back.

Dr Harper's Letter.

Detroit

My dear Charlotte,

I feel I have not been totally honest with you.

I was taken by surprise when Major Prior revealed to me the reason for his phone call and I wanted to make sure that I was in fact the person he was looking for on your behalf and needed to make enquiries re your claim that you and my adopted son are related but after meeting you, how could I have doubted it?

At the time of Ryan's adoption I was unaware that your mother, Vanessa Hammond, had given birth to twins in the Avalon Clinic as the midwife Macey (alias Collins) recorded only one baby born on that day in her personal file. I have since traced the discrepancy and know now that you are in fact related.

I sought medical information concerning your mother when Ryan was seven years old. He was suffering from unexplained brain seizures that I thought could be genetic and so I wanted to trace his natural mother for tests and family history. There was no mention of a daughter. My wife was working at Phenomena Point at the time, when new and exciting developments in brain scanning and surgery were on offer. My search for your mother led me to Dr Smallwood of the Eastcote Hospital in Finchley and whom I had met before on some previous occasion. He told me of Vanessa's mental history and arranged for her to come out to Chicago. I paid for her stay and treatment. Fortunately for her and Ryan, great advances both in mental and brain disorders had been made and both were to benefit 100%, although their problems proved to be unconnected. I contacted her sister Natalie Lytton as suggested by Smallwood to tell her of this good news and to ask if she would be willing to take care of her sister now that their parents were deceased. Natalie told me that her elder sister Elsbeth lived in New York and gave me her address. I had not told Mrs Dewar that my real connection with her sister concerned Ryan as I did not want to cause fresh problems for either her or my adopted son. That's how it was in those days.

Finally, now that you have made yourself known to me I think it only right that you and Ryan should meet. I have since told him of his true parentage so this has not come as a complete shock. He is in Malibu at the moment working on a shoot with his film crew and looking forward to meeting you there if possible. I will be staying with him. Please telephone me and let me know if this is convenient to you, as I know that you will be returning to England shortly. Ryan may be hard to track down so would appreciate an early reply to this letter.

Kind regards

Grant L Harper.

Diary entry: Friday September 28th
Spent a sleepless night wrestling with thoughts of both Ryan and Greg: two people who have now become important to me. With regard to Greg I feel that I am not ready for a more permanent relationship but nor do I want a brief affair that could end in even deeper loneliness for both of us. Whilst I bathed in the afterglow of our unexpected liaison, I have had time to cool off and collect my thoughts; maybe he has too, but I have his postcard that invites a reunion when we both get back. Perhaps things will change. I do find his shyness and self-effacing personality attractive and feel an underlying warmth and understanding – but could I love someone again who I would hate to lose?

Meanwhile, Ryan is on my mind and the anticipation of meeting him is overwhelming! I don't know whether he is feeling the same way about seeing me but we'll soon find out! Our poor mother may never know what has become of her children but there still may be time to tell her.

Jill Prior offered to drive Charlotte to Malibu as Graham was away for the week. Dr Harper had suggested the following Wednesday, three days before Charlotte was due to fly back to England. Jill said that she could benefit from a short break and that the two of them could stay with a friend of hers who lived on the edge of town by the sea.

Charlotte spent the next few days making trips to Los Angeles: shopping, attending musical events, and a baseball game, also preparing for her departure home as there would be little time on her return from Malibu. She tried to keep her nerves in check with regard to the forthcoming trip and hoped that she would come up to Ryan's expectations.

Diary: Wednesday 3rd October.

There are times when we don't need written corroboration: when we see and feel things for ourselves. This was one of those times for me. I saw it in his face, in the way he moved: his bone structure and mannerisms. They were familiar. They were also mine. We were not identical but the resemblance was apparent, apart from his eyes. One was blue like mine and the other hazel. He was tall with light brown hair that hung boyishly over his forehead. The tanned limbs below his shorts were strong and straight and his shoulders broad beneath his tee shirt that bore the slogan "On the Wild Side". I shook his hand and it was warm and strong. He looked quizzically at me, his head on one side, with a wide smile spreading across his face. 'Welcome Sis,' he had said, and I knew, in that moment, that he had meant it.

Grant took us to a restaurant down by the beach. I was hesitant to tell Ryan about my book (my only small success) or my unexciting life in Surrey but led him to tell me about his. He films wildlife for television documentaries. He is married to Mary and they have a nineteen-year-old daughter, Juliet, nicknamed Jo Jo; they live in Michigan.

Ryan regaled me with exciting escapades and brushes with bears when filming in Canada. He held up a hand that had lost a finger. 'Could have been worse!' he had laughed but I guessed that he was teasing me.

Grant sat and listened to our animated talk, smiling at our exuberance. Too soon, Ryan said that he must get back to his crew. Apparently some horse riders had seen mountain lions in the hills. One unfortunate person had fallen from their horse in the flight to safety. His crew were there to see what they could find.

We took our leave but not before an exchange of photos of each other and our families, addresses and promises to meet up in London next year. He has an assignment in the highlands of Scotland, chasing after red deer, but would come south when he had finished.

I noticed his feet when he removed his shoes to shake out the sand; they were long and thin, just like mine!

Four days later, on a golden October afternoon Charlotte boarded the plane to fly home. She could not find enough words to express her gratitude at the kindness of the Priors and comforted herself with the knowledge that they had agreed to stay with her next time they were in England. Ryan had said that he would try and bring Mary and Jo Jo with him when he came to London where they could do their own research into family history. Charlotte breathed a deep sigh of contentment and slept most of the way home; dreaming of the next and final phase of the search for her family.

Among the bills and junk mail that greeted her on her arrival home were several letters that commanded immediate attention, the first from Rita bearing sad news, two from Rowena's Recruitment Agency and a surprise letter that evoked a gasp of delight.

Charlotte rang Rita who told her that David was critically ill in the Norwich Hospital with emphysema. Charlotte expressed her dismay and offered to drive to Norfolk straight away but Rita assured her that she was coping well and would keep her informed.

Of the two letters from the Agency the first advised her that a suitable permanent job vacancy had arisen with a pharmaceutical company, starting in November subject to a successful interview and would she please report to the office as soon as possible. The second letter, dated a week later, was short and to the point. 'If we have not heard from you by Monday 8th October we will assume that you are no longer seeking employment from this office.' Realising that she had no time to lose, Charlotte had rung immediately and arranged to see Rowena the following day.

The 'surprise' letter had been from the 'Gala Gallery', enclosing a cheque for the sale of one of her sculptures. Wendy had recommended that she enter a piece for their exhibition that was being held when she was away in America. 'Gala' also mentioned that there were further commissions for her in the pipeline. Charlotte was thrilled as this was her first big breakthrough with this form of art.

After a sleepless night Charlotte arrived at the Agency pale and bleary-eyed at 9am. She was finding it hard to get back into a normal sleep routine and everything seemed alien after the five weeks away. The town seemed to have shrunk and the main roads mere country lanes by comparison with the American highways.

Rowena listened to the explanation of her absence from the Agency and then told her of the new company, Rowlands, based in East Grinstead. Charlotte hid her disappointment and wondered how she would journey to East Sussex each day but agreed to an interview. The job description appeared to suit her abilities and the pay was good but she was unsure as to whether the job would fit the pattern of life that she now sought. A date for the interview was set for the following week and in the meantime she would attempt to get back to normal as soon as possible.

On the day of the interview Charlotte received the news that David had died. She drove to East Grinstead with her mind on Rita and her sad loss and gave little thought to what lay ahead at Rowlands. Her inquisitors were kind and the meeting went well enough but Charlotte was left uncertain as to whether she wanted the job should it be offered to her. Creativity beckoned in the form of writing, and more adventurous sculpting and artwork; she wanted extra time (although she was astute enough to realise that one book to her name and the sale of a sculpture was hardly life-changing) and so was prepared to continue with part-time agency work and live frugally while she hopefully blossomed into an artist of repute. The death of her favourite uncle had marked a change in her. It was as though she were moving into an era of fresh values and unknown family members. She wanted to reach out and touch these new discoveries but first she must finish the task of finding her relatives. It had become the most important thing of all, before they too departed this life, taking with them their secrets and their triumphs.

After David's funeral a happier family event was to take place at the end of the month, when Jemma celebrated her twenty-first birthday.

Charlotte wrote:

> It was good to focus on the younger members of the family and their friends. Jemma had delighted me with the news that she and Ben were engaged and looking for a flat to share in London. Sadly Jay and Kelly have split up, but he is looking forward to a tour with the band next year in Germany and didn't seem too downcast. I asked if he had enough work for an art exhibition but he said maybe next year.
>
> Jemma had insisted on inviting Sebastian and Greg to the party and it was the first time I had seen either of them since returning from California. Greg cornered me in the kitchen and asked if we could meet up next month. I was taken off my guard with the euphoria of the party and agreed a bit too readily.
>
> After the young ones had gone off to a local disco the rest of us sat around talking. Maggie raised her eyebrows at me when she saw me with Greg but I refused to be drawn. I have not told her of our adventure in Yosemite as I don't want to make something out of nothing. Perhaps after I have seen him again. I'm still reluctant to embark on an affair that may leave us damaged. Greg did not stay the night but Seb came back late with the others, a bit worse for wear. He camped out on the settee surrounded by mole-like

mounds of sleeping-bagged bodies on the floor.
Got to bed around 3am.

Charlotte and Greg met outside the town for dinner at the old
Mill Wheel, an oak-beamed hotel with roaring fire and trusty
chef. It was two weeks before Christmas and the weather was
cold and damp. Charlotte had decided to tell Greg about her
family background and her ongoing search for them. He had
listened attentively and then offered to help her if he could. He
had been unaware of what she had discovered in America and
seemed amazed that she had found her twin brother Ryan.

In return he told her something of himself: a happy stable
background with older brother Simon and younger sister June;
grammar school, university and the army. His interests were
books, music, sailing and various sports. He had astonished her
with his beautiful baritone voice whilst singing along with a
tape recording of *The Pearl Fishers* on the way home in the car.

Charlotte wrote:

'I'm such a sucker for voices and Greg has such a deep
rich quality to his. Beware Charlie, it could lead you
into temptation!'

Charlotte spent Christmas in Norfolk with Rita. Jemma had
gone skiing with Ben, and Jay stayed with his friends in
London for the week. She had heard from Greg that both he
and Sebastian would be staying with his sister in Cornwall for
the break, together with husband Bill and their children.
During the days with her aunt, Charlotte was able to help with
the various minor problems that had arisen since Rita had been
on her own and returned home with a feeling of satisfaction
that she had been of some use. Learning to live without David
was hard for Rita as they had been together for a long time.

After the New Year celebrations, when the family were reunited and Jemma and Ben were full of their skiing exploits, Charlotte found time to resume her search for Natalie Lytton with the address given to her by Dr Harper, only to find that she was already in possession of it: Juniper House, Kingston. She wondered why she had neglected to chase this up last year. It did not take long to discover that the Lyttons were no longer in residence but it was thought, by the present owner, that Mrs Lytton had moved to Hampstead. Charlotte chided herself for being slow to pick up on this possibility as it was not unreasonable to suppose that her aunt may, for some reason or other, have moved back to the parental home. Had she missed a vital clue? She would return to The Larches and check more thoroughly when she had finished her sculpture.

For the last few months, every minute of her spare time had been taken up with this new project. Now that it was almost finished she could make plans to go to Hampstead although there had been no sign in the directory of a house called The Larches in Highfields Road. The large sculpture depicted the figurative form of a full-sized kneeling young man positioning a rugby ball ready to score a goal. It was cast in Ciment Fondue, a new medium for Charlotte. She had been working on it in her small cold annex for weeks and now wondered how she would transport it to Polesden Lacy next month where it would be on exhibition. Jay would be in Germany but could she ask Greg?

Diary entry:
April 10th
An exciting day! Greg arrived early with a borrowed estate car and with some difficulty we both managed to lift my heavy Boy into the car, sliding him onto his back, where he lay in an ungainly heap. We took off for

Polesden Lacy, the set-up being between 10am and 12. As we drove along it was wonderful to see that spring really had arrived; my hopes for the future rose with the song of the birds and the uplifting bursts of blossom that blazed along the way (or was this the first sign of new love and the rise of sap in the veins of a not so old biddy?!) Greg was in his shirtsleeves; his brown arms bare to the elbow; sunglasses on his aristocratic nose giving him an air of mystery and intrigue.

At Polesden Lacy we were allocated our space and trundled Boy to a good position on a grassy slope overlooking the terrace. Other sculptors were busy setting up their pieces and it was a revelation to see how many different forms of art would be on show in the grounds over the next few weeks.

On the way back we stopped at a pub for lunch. It was warm enough to sit outside and bask in the gentle sunshine and each other's company. Is this love? We are both so coy about it if it is!

Greg had offered to drive her to Hampstead the following week, opting to wait in a nearby pub should she be successful in locating her aunts. Charlotte was glad of his company as it would placate her nerves and cushion her against either euphoria or disappointment depending on the outcome. On closer inspection Charlotte found that 84 Highfields Road was now numbered as three flats but that the ground floor flat was named 'Larch Place'. She stood at the door and summoned up her strength whilst Greg waited in the street below. She wrote 'there was no answer to the bell and I was both disappointed and relieved at the same time. I didn't know what to expect, but I had come prepared. I posted a letter through the letterbox. I had enclosed a photograph of myself, together with detailed explanations, and telephone number. Now I must play the waiting game, but perhaps nobody will reply?

When Charlotte received a letter some days later postmarked North London her eyes flew immediately to the signature: Natalie Lytton. Her aunt advised her that she indeed lived in Larch Place, her parents' old converted home, together with her sister Elsbeth Dewar. They were both amazed to hear from her and would she telephone for a convenient date to visit? Charlotte sat down, holding the letter, tears suddenly springing to her eyes. Was this the end of her search? Would knowledge of these unknown people fill the gaps that had widened over the years? They would be able to give her news of her mother. She would have been the youngest. Perhaps she had married and there were more siblings? Charlotte couldn't wait to find out:

I decided to go on my own to Larch Place. It would be a very personal journey. I went by train, as it was less stressful, and arrived at 11am. Over a previous telephone conversation I had learnt that Natalie was 'no longer with her husband' and Elsbeth, as I already knew, a widow. They hadn't mentioned Vanessa.

The large three-story parental house had been sold for conversion into flats but the sisters had kept the ground floor and garden for themselves. The rooms were large with deep Georgian windows. Natalie was a retired art teacher but at seventy-three she was still teaching in the local community. A tall easel dominated the rusting Victorian conservatory and stacks of canvasses stood around. She had been married to a marine biologist who had spent too much time away. Elsbeth, now seventy-seven, no longer taught dance lessons but gave occasional private piano tuition. A grand piano stood in the sitting room, together with a music stand and a clarinet. I was amazed at the obvious talent of both of these sisters. Elsbeth was tall and thin with greying hair, a triangular face with high cheekbones and blue eyes. She had been a professional dancer and married Brent soon after she arrived in America. Natalie, the kindly humanist, was shorter and more rounded, with hazel eyes and brownish hair and not at all as I remembered her on that day she came to Ilford. She was the more confident of the two and told me of her futile search for me, and the snub she had received from my paternal grandfather when she offered to adopt me, and the silence maintained by Netta. Elsbeth reminded me of Ryan in looks, or perhaps she was a mirror of myself? Was this where my love of dance and rhythm came from? I could have learnt so much from them. Another life, but still they hadn't mentioned my mother.

Eventually I was shown photographs, which told of the family fortunes and misadventures, together with their own lives: Elsbeth in various shows, and with husband Brent, Natalie's children; my cousins, and at last, pictures of my mother. Because they had not spoken much about her, my intuition told me that she was no longer around and when I finally asked, they confirmed my suspicions. Elsbeth told me she had died many years ago in America of some viral disease, caught from one of her pupils at the primary school where she worked. The child had lived, but Vanessa had not been so lucky. Elsbeth said that Vanessa had been happy at the school and the children had loved her. They had both looked sadly at me, as though devising both anticipation and disappointment in my face; that they were unable to supply the good news I was hoping to hear; that she was alive and well. At this point I was not prepared to mention Ryan. Did they know of him? It would have to wait another day. I suddenly felt drained and wanted to go home. I gratefully accepted the photographs they gave me of Vanessa and promised to return. Was I afraid all along that I would never find her? It had all been too much.

CHAPTER TWENTY

FULFILMENT

As the months went by Charlotte rearranged the gathered fragments of her past into a pattern of her own. The greyness of uncertainty took on shape and colour and she was able to identify with the many strands of DNA that were woven into her nature, some darker than she cared to admit. Her love of music and dancing had not belonged to the Laurents, or her love of fast cars and machines. As a child she longed for boys' toys and declared that she would one day become an engineer, but the time for such advanced thinking had not been appreciated.

Visits to the aunts had revealed that her mother, a gentle, shy person, who had not shared her daughter's ambition, had been a pianist and singer who had lacked the drive to realise her own potential. She had been flattered by the attentions of Marcel unaware that she had been his second choice. He had been in love with the unattainable Elsbeth.

Charlotte was proud of her pedigree but not of her maternal grandparents' indifference to her. They had both been clever and had brought status and wealth to the Hammond family. Arthur Hammond had been a test pilot during the First World War and Kathleen a VAD. She tried not to feel bitter towards them because she had not been allowed to be part of it. She had not asked her aunts if their parents had known of

Vanessa's pregnancy. Had they wanted the news of their daughter and her unborn babes swept under the carpet? Netta had shown her a better way to live, by her example of unconditional love and compassion for the wayward and unwanted. Charlotte would never know how things might have turned out. It was too late now, but her new sense of belonging meant that she no longer felt trapped and inferior but could rise like the phoenix in her book.

In the last quarter, sales of *The Fire and the Phoenix* had risen dramatically and the writing of her new book was going well. Her *Rugby Boy* was one of many sculptures she would sell in the next decade together with paintings, poems and scripts, but before this other memorable occasions were to take place later in the year.

Charlotte had kept in touch with Ryan and had noted the date for his assignment in Scotland where he would be filming with his crew for most of August. Two weeks after his arrival at the estate in Perthshire she received a hurried scrawl from him:

Stalking red deer is a great way to discover Scotland! I have seen some marvellous landscapes, mountains, glens, and forests. Even the weather has been on our side. The animals are magnificent and it's a shame they must be culled but it's about land management and keeping the population down. I've got some memorable footage. More when I see you. Glad you have met up again with Mary and Jo Jo. Mary will miss her when she starts at Guy's.

Hope the wedding goes well next week.
Ryan

Charlotte had met Mary and Juliet when they first arrived in England. They were staying with Mary's cousin, Sue, in

Greenwich and had all arrived for lunch one day before Ryan's departure for Perthshire. Charlotte had been carried away by the occasion and had found herself inviting them to Jemma's wedding, although Ryan would be unable to attend.

The wedding was a modest affair and took place in the Town Hall Registry Office with a buffet meal in the hotel nearby. Neither Jemma nor Ben were in favour of 'pomp and ceremony' and had opted for a smaller family group and the couple's close friends. Ben's parents arrived from Wiltshire and Jay came with a new girlfriend. Both Sebastian and Greg were among the guests who joined the party at the hotel.

Charlotte noted:

'Jemma looked slim and elegant in a tailored suit and fetching hat. I was so proud of her. Ben wore a jazzy waistcoat under his jacket and had managed to tame his unruly mop of hair. (I noticed that his father had the same unruly mop.) Jay, as best man in absence of Ben's brother who was in the Navy, made a very good speech and, as usual, made us all laugh including Donna, who seems quite smitten by him. After the meal and the traditional "cake ceremony" the music started up and dancing began. I was pleased to see that Seb and Juliet were hitting it off as they took to the floor. Earlier they had talked earnestly about America and her forthcoming training. Greg had been giving me the eye, across the room, and before long, we too joined the dancers. Was it the alcohol or his magnetism? I felt rather hot and bothered as he drew me closer during the slower numbers. Oh, it would be so easy…

When the new Mr and Mrs Davies left for Paris, the rest of us drifted away in a haze of warmth and delight that comes at the end of a perfect day.'

Two weeks later Ryan and Mary left for New Jersey, leaving Juliet behind with Sue in Greenwich to start her medical training at Guy's Hospital. She would be following in Grant Harper's footsteps as he had trained there in the 1930s. Was Jo Jo in fact following in Myra's footsteps, their father's sister who also became a doctor? Before his return to America, Charlotte had got to know her brother better as they had talked about both sides of the family and pored over the newly acquired photographs given to her by the aunts in Hampstead.

After the excitement of the preceding month Charlotte began a new sculpture for an exhibition in November, but was distracted by Greg's proposal to take her away to a surprise destination in October. It was not a decision to be taken lightly and Charlotte strove between her natural desire to accept, and prudence. Her love of travel and new places to explore usually won but she knew that if she agreed to go with him things would not be the same again between them.

Greg had been artful in choosing Monte Carlo as the appointed place, knowing that Charlotte nurtured a love of the South of France and would probably jump at the chance to go there with him. He was rewarded. Charlotte agreed with certain alacrity. She wrote:

'How could I not go to Monte Carlo? I still have sharp memories of the Cote D'Azure. I love the light and the scenery; the little sienna-coloured, hill-topped towns, the Alps Maritime. I associate Monte Carlo with excitement and glamour: the famous car rally (Sheila van Damm was an inspiration!), the Monaco Grand Prix (David would favour Nigel Mansell but I loved watching Ayrton Senna), the giant casino that beckons, 'the devil's playground' according to Netta, and truly forbidden fruit, where lives are made and lost by the reckless spin of the wheel; but the excitement, just for once? By contrast we could visit the Prince's Palace and see the changing of the guard and take in the harbour where the yachts are lined up in palatial rows and walk in the coolness of the Jardin Exotique.

How can I not go to Monte Carlo?

The date for the flight was the 16th of October. Greg arranged to drive Charlotte to Reigate where they would spend the night in a hotel before going on to Gatwick early the next morning. It would be an "aperitif" before the "gourmet" dish that awaited them in France. As Charlotte came out of the bathroom she remarked that the wind was 'getting up' and the rain 'lashing down'. Greg confided that the forecast had not been good but that they would be 'ok' and to come to bed. Hardly had they settled themselves when the sound of loud crashes had them both back on their feet. Peering through the curtains they observed tiles sliding off the roof and hitting the concrete yard below. Lightning flashed and thunder rolled as the wind strengthened with what seemed like each passing minute. 'Back in bed we lay together and listened to the sound of "Armageddon" as it rained an avalanche of slate tiles from the roof above. There was nothing we could do but cuddle up. I was truly scared and trembled like a leaf in spite of Greg's warm protection.'

With the dawn came comparative calm but the damage had been done. In the car park a tree lay across three cars and outside in the road another was buried under a wealth of foliage. Fortunately for Greg his car was untouched but their journey to Gatwick was one neither of them would forget. Charlotte wrote:

'Everywhere we looked, there was devastation. Power lines were down and great trees lay with roots reaching for the sky in tangled agony. We navigated around scattered bits of shed and coop, corrugated iron roofing and all manner of smaller debris. Nearing the airport in a field we saw several light aircraft lying haphazardly against one another like thrown down discarded toys.'

Despite the problems on the ground the plane was only marginally delayed and took off into a clear sky. From the air, the aftermath of the hurricane could be clearly seen. Charlotte had tried to telephone Jemma but had not been successful. She had prayed fervently that all their family were safe and well if not a little shaken. Whilst Northern France had also suffered from the hurricane, it was calmer in the south. At Nice airport they hired a car and drove along the A8 in the direction of Monaco.

There was no record of their time together in France but Charlotte had been right: things were never the same again, but it was to be the beginning of a relationship that would stand the test of time. When they returned, they were in no hurry to cohabit, both having lived very independent lives previously, but by spending time together over the next two years, at weekends and on holidays, they learnt to trust one another.

Finally, on her fifty-third birthday, having both sold their respective properties, Charlotte and Greg moved into Tayberry House. They had bought the property between them and started to set up home, both bringing favourite items from their past and buying new for the future. Charlotte wrote:

'Tayberry House is Victorian and stands on the edge of Godalming. It is set back from the road, has a wild garden and much to do inside. Greg says he is not much use at DIY but will be a willing labourer! I must summon up my design skills and set to work. I'm so excited by the whole idea of starting from scratch. There is a wonderful period fireplace and other attractive features, but the kitchen is in need of a complete overhaul and the plumbing hisses and bangs. There is an "out-house" for my studio and Greg has a large den for his books and piano where he can follow his interests and musical pursuits.

It will be a lovely place for Jemma and Ben to bring the children when they are older and can play in the jungally garden. I can't believe that I'm actually enjoying being a grandmother! I thought only old people were grandmas! I shall enjoy revisiting my childish pleasures with them in a few years' time.

Since the discovery of her past Charlotte was able to let go of the fears that had haunted her and get on with the present. She revelled in the new house and used both her personality and practicality to bring it to life. Greg was happy to go along with her ideas and helped her to bring them about. Charlotte was moved to see how tenderly he held the twins and knew that he would come to love them as his own. They had both been delighted that Sebastian and Juliet had become close, and looked forward to visits from them. Jay was still following his dream and recording when he could with the band. He supplemented his income with his glorious illustrations and lived with Donna, a fashion designer, in London.

The diary entries fizzled out as Charlotte relaxed into comfortable middle age. She no longer felt the need to keep a daily record of events but continued to write up her high days and holidays: bereavements and additions. She also noted successes with both sculpture and writing.

One pleasing event recorded was when they were invited to Sebastian and Juliet's flat warming. 'Both Greg and I had been so pleased when we first knew they were an item. Now Jo Jo has finished her training she can spend more time with Seb in Dulwich. Greg has bought them a bed and I stumped up with a chest of drawers, small table and chairs. It's amazing how things have turned out; I wonder what Ian would have made of it. Wherever he is, I'm sure he's smiling!'

Charlotte Laurent died in July 2001 after a tragic accident in the Scottish Highlands. She and Ryan had been walking to raise money for their favourite charity "Mission for the Missing". Her last diary entry reads:

Am getting used to my new boots, bought yesterday in the Lake District on the way up to Skye. Ryan hopes that I won't get blisters! Arrived here in Torrin this evening as the sun was setting over this heathery wilderness! Tomorrow we will start to walk to Loch Slapin and then towards Blaven. Torrin is a crofting and fishing village on the eastern shore of Loch Slapin and there is a view of Blaven from our window in the old schoolhouse where we are camped. Ryan wants to climb to the summit of Blaven with Jack but I might opt to keep to the lower slopes with the others. They are a good group and will keep their eye on me! (I'm one of the oldest and least fit!)

I'm so happy to be here in this beautiful place and wish Greg was here too. Must get some sleep. It's going to be a lovely day tomorrow!